The Men We Never Knew

Books by Dapne Rose Kingma

COMING APART
Why Relationships End
and How to Live through
the Ending of Yours

A GARLAND OF LOVE
Daily Reflections
on the Magic and Meaning
of Love

TRUE LOVE
How to Make Your
Relationship Sweeter, Deeper
and More Passionate

WEDDINGS FROM THE HEART
Ceremonies for an
Unforgettable Wedding

The Men We Never Knew

Women's Role in the Evolution of a Gender

Daphne Rose Kingma

Conari Press
Berkeley, CA

"Hay for the Horses" from RIPRAP and COLD MOUNTAIN
POEMS by Gary Snyder. Copyright © 1958, 1959, 1965 by Gary
Snyder. Reprinted by permission of North Point Press, a division of
Farrar, Straus and Giroux, Inc.

Printed in the United States of America on recycled paper.
Cover: Pawlak Design; photo: Yvan Poirier
ISBN: 0-943233-46-1

For
William Edward Glennon, Jr.
brother, protector, mirror, accomplice
who made the remarkable journey

My special thanks

To F.X. Feeney
my epiphanizer *par excellance*
for always believing in me

To Les
the sacrificial lamb
for embodying the need

To W
the sweetest man in the whole wide world
for enacting the possibility

To Sunta and Michael
for living the pain
and telling the stories

To Victor
for holding the light

To Yvan
whose steadfast love
made all the difference

My deep thanks also

To Mary Jane Ryan
my editor of genius
for clarity, strength and patience
and for having the courage to live
whereof she edits

Foreword

Most women today have experienced a man mysteriously closing up and withdrawing. One minute he seems available and the next he is emotionally gone. At such time a woman wonders, did she say something wrong or does he just not care about getting closer. When she doesn't understand his behavior she either takes it personally or begins to mistrust and doubt his love. Either way confusion and disappointment follow.

Without a doubt, it seems women generally are more interested in relationships than men, but it is really true. Go into any bookstore and you will find more women buying books about relationships, communication, and love. Publishers know that women buy 90% of the relationship books. Listen in on almost any therapy session with a woman and she will feel her partner is giving less to their relationship. This is not only frustrating but depressing to many women who love their partner and want to improve their relationships.

Does it mean these men are cold, mechanical, heartless, and uncaring? Could it be that men don't have feelings or need love? Certainly at times they do seem that way, but nothing could be further from the truth.

Men need love just as much as women do. The major difference, however, is that women are generally more aware and expressive of their need for love. In addition, men sometimes need love and support in different ways. For example, if you ask a woman probing questions in a sympathetic and attentive way, she will generally feel cared for and supported. Yet if you treat a man in this way he may feel quite annoyed and want to be left alone. At such times, without a clear understanding of what he needs or what he is going through, it is hard for a woman to be supportive. He generally doesn't communicate what he needs and she can't know unless he talks about it.

A women can, however, discern a lot about the special men in her life through learning about men in general. For a host of reasons, men are restricted in their ability to express their need for love and intimacy. These reasons are vital for a woman to understand if she is to see through the walls surrounding a man's heart and know the real man wanting to love and be loved.

There is no better or more loving invitation for a man to gradually open and share himself than a woman who understands him enough to accept him just as he is. Not only does the man benefit, but the woman does too. Imagine her not taking it personally or feeling left out in the dark when a man closes up but actually knowing what is going on inside of him and why. What a relief.

In *The Men We Never Knew*, Daphne Kingma assists readers in understanding men in such a way that the walls of mistrust between the sexes begin tumbling down. In many ways she knows more about men than most men. It is refreshing to listen to a woman who truly loves, understands, and accepts men just as they are.

For too long, authors have placed women in a powerless victim role in relationship to men. Very skillfully, without invalidating the legitimate pain that women have endured at the effect of men and without minimizing their need to express that pain, Daphne reveals how women also share in the responsibility for the proverbial war between the sexes. Through glimpsing the secret life of men, a woman can not only nurture the men in her life better, but also receive the support she needs as well. This book offers hope and shines out as a gift of love to both men and women.

John Gray, Ph.D.,
author of *Men Are From Mars, Women Are From Venus*

Introduction

This is a book for women about men, the men we love, the men who love us, the men who drive us crazy, the men we drive crazy. It is a map of where men are, what keeps them there, and how and why women must help in the process of male transformation. It is a plea—and a plan—for women to assist men, so that in the end we may all be the beneficiaries of their transformation. It contains a potion for opening the eyes of women about men, so that in time men can open their eyes about women. It also contains an elixir for opening the eyes of men to the feminine dimension, toward which we all now desperately need to be turning.

This book makes certain psychological assumptions, namely that in general, men tend to be more cut off from their emotions and women tend to be more in possession of theirs. While there are thousands of exceptions and variations to this generalization, it is the degree to which it is true in society as a whole that has created the problems addressed here, and which we must acknowledge if we are to make any further progress.

In the midst of all the wars we are living in—the war for economic survival within our own country, the wars for the preservation of nations, the war for the survival of the planet— the most intimate and insidious war is the war between the sexes, the fact that we cannot make peace in our kitchens and basements and bedrooms, the fact that we cannot make peace in our hearts with the persons—male and female—whom we supposedly love.

Although intuitively we know it is only love that can bridge the abysses within and outside of our own wounded psyches, very few of us have been taught how to practice the true medicine of love. Even more than that, however, because of the evolution of our society, women have a very incomplete picture of men, and men have almost no way of understanding their inner sensitive selves, nor, as a consequence, of understanding women.

In a way, our culture has pitted the sexes against one another, as if it were a given that men and women should be endlessly at odds, that whatever in each of us might nourish, uplift, or heal the other be ignored, and that, instead, our differences and difficulties should be endlessly underlined. We assume that "boys will be boys, and girls will be girls,"and that we will never understand one another. We will make and be the subject of funny, bad, and downright devastating jokes about our respective attributes and attitudes, and we will go on—as we have always gone on—accepting this as "the way things are."

When this drama between the sexes comes down to intimate relationships between men and women, we are all in a sense perpetuating the tragedy we fear is inevitable. We live our lives being endlessly at odds with one another, accepting our marriages or romances as the private battlegrounds in which these frustrating inevitabilities will be repeatedly played out. The deeper tragedy in this is not only that we have remained embroiled in the drama between the sexes, but even worse, that human intimate relationships have become not an image of what is possible in the world at large, but a despairing symbol that harmony at any level between any two disparate factions will be difficult, if not impossible, to achieve.

The good news is that there is a way out. By facing the sorrow women feel about men, and the deep and often unidentifiable sorrow men feel about women, we can let go of the myths that have separated men and women from one another, and create a new beginning.

To come to this new place together is not to create a case for the self-indulgence of either sex, so that one can beat down the other with impunity. Rather, it is a meditation on the possible future of relationships between men and women. The spirit in which it is offered is one of reflection, one that presumes to offer neither bandages for all the wounds nor redress for all the grievances of either sex. Rather, my purpose here is to talk gently and quietly about the difficulties men are having so that we can restore balance and community between men and women by discovering true compassion and its consequence, real healing.

This book is a guide to that purpose. It will move you through a process of seeing men differently, a process that will change how you feel and, as a consequence, enable you to have the depth of relationships with men that you desire.

Part One takes you on a very specific visit to the male condition. Some of what you will be invited to contemplate about men will frustrate or anger you; other revelations may seem self evident; still others will surprise you, open new doors to your perception. The point is to take what you already know about men and marry it to what you discover here in order to bring you to the place where you see men as human beings, who, when perceived with compassion, do have the capacity to relate to us as we always wished they could.

Part Two is the journey of healing, a handbook for the emotional resurrection of men and a blueprint for women's role in that process. Here you will be instructed in the art of emotional initiation, in how specifically to help men learn the language of feelings, the skills of emotional intimacy.

* * *

This is a book about men by a woman, and I write it from several perspectives. My first study of men came as a girl observing two men, my father—sensitive, expressive, emotionally communicative and daring, with a gift for relationship that brought him and those with whom he shared that gift a lifetime of joy—and my brother—the handsome, target shooting, tree-felling, fence-building prankster, boot camp Marine, later management executive. I saw the distance between these two men--for they were never at peace with one another nor in receipt of the balance a dose of each of them could have brought to the other—as emblematic of the distance between every man and himself.

I watched as my father, so able to express, was unable to act, and my brother, able to act, was unable to express. Together they would have made one great man—the man who could do *and* express—but each of them lived out the overdeveloped aspects of his particular identity without ever being able to receive the fulfillment of being wholly balanced in himself. These two men, the tent-pins of the little community that was my family, were the first examples of what is both possible and ever elusive for most men to achieve.

Second, for more than twenty years, long after I left the schoolhouse of my family, it has been my privilege to work with men in the sacrosanct ceremony of the psychotherapeutic encounter. There, when they lost their jobs, when their wives and sweethearts left them, when they went to war or anguished about not going to war, when their parents or children died, they gradually unveiled themselves not only to me but also, and more importantly, to themselves. They were happy, angry, sad, overwhelmed and overjoyed by their discoveries. They came "to solve a problem;" they ended up taking possession of themselves. They came, hoping "it wouldn't take too long;" they left being glad for every moment they had spent.

These men opened themselves. They came upon and claimed the intricate, powerful feeling dimension of themselves that got hazed out in kindergarten, at football camp, and in the corporate boardroom. They taught me many things. They taught me that men do want to feel, that men are willing to go through their fears, the restrictions, constrictions, and demands of their role, as well as criticism and judgment from without and within, in order to feel.

In a sense this book is a gift to me that I am passing on to you. What I share with you here was given to me by the many seeking men who revealed the deepest reaches of their consciousness to me. Through it I can only thank and praise the men who trusted me with their intimate selves in order that I might bear witness to the depth of men's desire for emotional lives. Their individual testament to the beauty, complexity, and sensitivity of men stands as the example—and the plea—for all men who are begging to be invited more deeply into living.

For, although we have all heard a great deal about unconscious unfeeling brutes of men (men who can't love, men who can't grow up, men who can't commit, men who hate women) and although the things being said about such men are not mere fiction but a tragic commentary on what can become of the male sex, these aren't the only men in the world. Men run the entire gamut from heartless brutes to men who are sensitive, capable, tender-hearted, eager to nurture women toward their own fulfillment, and hungry for the privilege of living from the full breadth of their own rich sensitivity.

There are many good, feeling men in the world, men whom we can celebrate, honor and enjoy, men who are seeking to come into harmony with themselves, with women, and with the world they are creating through their power and expertise. It is these men who need to be applauded, and to the degree that such men don't exist among us, it is these men whom we must invite into being. For all of us, this is the next step. In the progress of our psychosocial evolution, this is the undertaking which is now, collectively, ours to do.

The Great Divide

"The peculiar and perhaps fatal American violence is the refusal to connect."

-*John Edgar Wideman*

To say that in 1993 the sexes are in a crisis is an appalling understatement. Never before have men and women been farther from one another's emotional consolation. Indeed, as we stand at the threshold of the twenty-first century, it would seem that relations between the sexes have never been worse. Insofar as an individual relationship is a microcosm of society, the frustration, bitterness, and discontent that currently characterize individual male/female relationships are a measure of the gigantic discontent that exists between the sexes as a whole. Men and women are no longer helpmates, companions, and supporters to one another; instead our relationships are characterized at best by confusion and frustration, and at worst by hostility, violence, and hatred.

Women are most vocal in their discontent—in book after book they tell us how terrible men are, what fools we are for loving them, and how useless and disappointing our relationships will be unless we learn to put up with male behavior. That large numbers of women feel this way is evidenced by the sales of such books and the mythologies that have grown up around them.

In the past it was men who complained about women—their moods and attitudes, their emotional volatility, instability, and insatiability, in short their wearisome wiles and ways. But now the tables have turned. Focusing on their own oppression, the many injustices and inequities to which they have been subjected, women have now adopted an opposite and equally unrealistic position, seeming to presume that men suffer nothing, while they themselves are crawling and clawing their way toward the paradise that men have inhabited forever.

If men were unreasonable in the past—and they were—it is now women who have become unrealistic. For, in seeking to solve the conundrum of our own long suffering, we have become almost blind to the sufferings of men. We seem to have lost—or never to have arrived at—a sense of the intricacy and complexity of the individual man in terms of his circumstances and his history. Instead we seem to be dealing with him as a sort of generic member of a frequently despicable—and dismissable—species.

In the same way we used to feel men addressed women as a generic—and inferior—class of being, so now, without consciously acknowledging it, we tend to think of men as emotionally monolithic and insensitive beings who will never be able to speak to, nourish, console, or feel with us. Although we don't come out and say so, we have virtually given up on men.

Men: Lost in the Woods of Post Liberation

"In the past, we protected women and dominated men. Now the warrior image is obsolete but we still don't have a new image to replace it."

-Corporation Executive, 48

More than we imagine or suspect, the current cold war between men and women can be seen as the unavoidable efflux of the women's movement. In the socio-evolutional process we have come to know as women's liberation, women fought to make a place for themselves in "the man's world," and over the last thirty years the long gruelling push toward gender equality has brought women to a place in which we have incorporated certain aspects of what we might call masculine power.

Even if it's still true that women don't hold equal positions in the highest echelons of society, from corporation executives on down, what is also true is that as a society our social attitudes about women have changed to a significant degree. We do now live in the presence of the belief that women deserve to have their place as equals, whether or not we are always willing to grant equality to them. At every level of the social structure—from the Supreme Court to the construction site—women have infiltrated the traditionally male-dominated world, and in so doing have incorporated much of the masculine identity into their personas.

Yet so far as women are concerned, this work is still incomplete; for many of the rights, opportunities, and possibilities toward which we have long been laboring still have not been brought into being to the extent we desire or intend.

Unfortunately, in the process, neither men nor women have done the job of resolving how men can or should live in relation to this profoundly new alignment. So far as men are concerned, they are desperately scrambling to find their way in the Post Women's Liberation world, seeking haltingly and uncomfortably to define themselves in relation to the radically altered circumstances of the 90s: What does it mean to have a woman as your boss? What does it mean to have your wife make more money than you do? What does it mean to be a "sensitive" man?

Part of what makes the present circumstances so difficult for men is that in women's evolution, women weren't satisfied simply to incorporate the masculine into their personalities. They also hoped and expected, albeit perhaps unconsciously, that men would immediately make the counterpart changes of incorporating the feminine into theirs and then life would be blissful. Women didn't know exactly what this would mean, but in some vague way they knew they wanted it. We didn't necessarily say to ourselves: "Now that I bring home a paycheck, he'll learn how to cry," but at least at an unconscious level we expected men would change simply because of our changing.

But women are only half the equation and the changes they make will not and have not in and of themselves changed the whole. Indeed, rather than instinctively responding to the opening for change which women created through their own transformation, men are running scared, feeling a frightening sense of uncertainty about the revised social structure and their male identities.

In effect, men are lost in the woods of a post-liberation society, suspended in a reactive state, awkwardly trying to keep their balance in the whirlwind of women's changes. In relation to what women have effected, men are no longer in charge. Now, rather than being the architects of the structures in which they function—their traditional position—they find themselves in the role of mere respondents to women's changes, scrambling to keep up with what seem like the ever-changing rules, demands and altering vicissitudes of women's search for themselves. Beneath this struggle to keep up with women lies a seething cauldron of confusion, panic, and anger; for men have been separated from everything by which, in their salad days, they had defined themselves.

In the past, men had an identity that both men and women acknowledged and valued. But now even that has been thoroughly eroded. The male position has become more and more difficult to identify and has thus become virtually untenable. Far more than women can imagine, since they generated these changes and therefore stand outside the circle of their implications for men, men have undergone a profound identity loss.

Whether it's an older man who grew up in one male reality and then found all the rules suddenly changed, or a younger man who grew up in the heyday of women's transitions, men have been suffering the consequences of a major social upheaval. At the level of how we conduct our daily lives we all seem to be adjusting to these changes, but at a deeper level we've hardly begun the process of psychological integration that is the absolute and only condition in which men and women can reestablish a harmonious meeting ground.

Thus is it that right now, men are alternately treading water and sinking into the quicksand of the multitude of changes initiated by women. It isn't acceptable any more for men to be the kind of "real men" they used to be, but at the same time they haven't yet had a chance to feel their way into being the kind of men they might want to become. And whether women can appreciate this or not, to be identitiless in this sense and to this degree is to experience a disorientation so intense as to be virtually immobilizing. As one man summed it up, "I'm a man, but I don't know how to be a man anymore."

A Longing for Change

"There is nothing I've wanted more than to be able to express my feelings to a woman. But, frankly, I haven't been able to find such a woman."

-*Publicist, 42*

Rather than imagining that male transformation would be a process that would take time, women, somewhat unconsciously, seem to have become more and more demanding of immediate changes from men. We want them to be more emotionally open, to feel, talk, and listen, to console, to want the kinds of relationships we want. We want them to become like us—and *immediately*—simply because we want them to, and just because we've asked.

But for their own reasons, as we shall see, men have been unable or unwilling to change, and, as a result, women are furious. Despite a fervent desire to have good relationships with men, we are constantly dissatisfied with the men we do have. We're mad that they still won't pick up their socks, we're mad they won't make an emotional commitment, we're mad they won't talk about their feelings. In short, we're angry men haven't changed as much as we want—or in the ways we would have liked. We reinvented ourselves, and now we're enraged that they haven't too—and afraid that they can't or they won't.

Ironically and unfortunately it is often the very demanding ways in which women have asked men to become sensitive and intuitive that makes it virtually impossible for men to respond to women's desires. All too often women's requests include implied or stated insults of male inadequacy which are so hurtful to men that they can't possibly respond in any way that might be satisfying to women. Female criticism, complaining, and impatience do more than almost anything else to thwart the male transformation we all so desperately need. It's as if we're holding a gun to their collective heads and proclaiming, "Be sensitive right now or I'm going to blow your brains out." Not a particularly conducive atmosphere for the soft, emotionally-open responses we desire.

In the past, when women were first fighting for their rights and privileges, breaking new sex role frontiers, they *did* have to be fierce in their approach, to marshall their anger at men as the catalyst for forward movement. In order to act, it was necessary for us to focus on men's inadequacies, betrayals, and failures partly in order to fuel the flame of inspiration for change. Anger inspires action and in the very process of being enraged at men, we became able to value ourselves more highly—highly enough to traject ourselves into an orbit of change that resulted in the dramatic expansion of our identities as women. In this sense, anger at men was precisely the emotional condition necessary to secure women's liberation.

Unfortunately, this habit of women's rage has remained as a kind of emotional hangover long after the rite of passage has been completed. By now we have focused on men's inept and insensitive ways so intensely and for so long that we're in danger of completely destroying the possibility of a reconciliation between the sexes.

In addition, something we conveniently overlooked in our anger is that the changes we made were neither initiated, requested, nor (much to our distress) supported or encouraged by men. They were changes we initiated because of our own discontent. In making them we were looking out for ourselves. We weren't doing men any particular favor. We wanted the glory and benefits of being our powerful, effective selves, in addition to the softer joys of being our emotional, nurturing selves. We wanted to liberate the male in us and we did. Rising up together we suffered and battered our way to achieve our goals without realizing that the consequences for men—and for men and women in relation to one another—would be both multiple and complex.

In noting this, I'm not saying that we shouldn't have forged ahead in our reach for power, nor that the demands implicit in our changes should be deplored. This evolution was a necessity and it stands, now, as an invitation to further change by men. But women's changes have generated enormous consequences for us all, and women, especially, have not acknowledged this sufficiently. We've upset the apple cart and are now ignoring the apples rolling down the street. We've pretended that men would just catch up and carry on, without a counterpart upheaval of their own. We've behaved as if we could transform century-old sex roles overnight without any negative consequences and imagined that we could step immediately into the land of relationship enchantment where all our dreams would be fulfilled.

Unfortunately no major transformational process is that simple. Any epoch of change has both positive and negative aspects; any change in the definition of our psychosexual identities strikes at the very core of our being, and in a psychosocial upheaval of the magnitude of what we have called the women's liberation movement, there are myriad profound and subtle emotional consequences for both men and women. Among these is a restructuring of our notions of what it means to be masculine and feminine—a gigantic revision indeed. And the far-reaching implications of this are something that we have just barely begun to sense.

What is terribly important to remember here is that in any great wave of social change, the corresponding psychological evolution is always very slow to come about. When we see the social impact of change—new jobs, revised work schedules, maternity leave, new division of labor in the household—we tend to think that the change is complete. What I can't emphasize enough, however, is that what we see is just the tiniest sliver of what we are actually getting. Externally things may look very different, but internally we're still struggling to keep the lid on, trying to get things to still feel the way they used to, even though, moment by moment, they are transforming in our midst. Thus while we're all, on the outside, doing different things, on the inside we are still in a certain sense longing to feel the way we did before everything changed. Our psyches are decades behind the legal and economic changes; emotionally we're still occupying a regressive position.

While women may now be theoretically equal to men in social opportunity, in their hearts they still want all the things they've always wanted from men. While intellectually we may be satisfied or even overjoyed about what we've accomplished, emotionally we are still functioning from an outdated set of notions and emotions vis à vis men. We have changed our behavior to a certain extent, but like a child with a pull-along toy, we're still dragging our old emotions along behind. We want men the way we want them to be now, *and also* the way they were then.

The situation is even worse for men because for the most part they haven't even identified the changes they need to make. Emotionally they're standing with one foot in the past and the other on a banana peel. They can't be who they were, they're not sure who they're supposed to become, and even if they did, they don't have the foggiest idea of how to initiate their seemingly inevitable transformation.

Because of this, one of the essential undertakings of the 90s must be to deepen the dialogue about the emotional consequences of this social change. More specifically, it's time for women to take an honest look at how profoundly men have been affected, to see men from men's own perspective. And along the way, we must also take a look at how we have colluded in making men disappoint us.

Not Quite a New Leaf

"It's a tragedy, but men and women are still doing their psychological healing alone."

-*Inventor, 46*

Despite women's ongoing frustations with men, there are a number of indications that men *are* beginning to participate in their own corresponding evolution. Men themselves are finally starting to complain about their own untenable situation. Amid the chorus of female frustrations are the small, desperate, heart-broken voices of men who are raising their own cries of despair about their condition. Not only in regard to the women in their lives, but also about their lost identities, their sacrificed bodies, their separation from their children, and their sense of disconnection from what they are coming to understand as their own deep selves.

Some men on the frontier of what can by now legitimately be called a men's movement are becoming aware of their pain and are quietly (and sometimes not so quietly) beginning to disclose their wounds. A growing number of men are having conversations and ceremonies, sharing privately and in community the gestures, embraces, tears, and words that would, until recently, have been not only suspect, but impossible. Thanks to groups led by Robert Bly, Sam Keen, John Lee and others, men are reclaiming the wild male within, healing their separation from their fathers, embracing their tribal and ritualistic roots, coming home to their maleness in ways that long have been denied, set aside or roundly criticized. Although these men are still in quite the minority, their actions reveal that men are beginning to reclaim the lost dimensions of their manhood.

While these changes represent a permission for men to contact and reintegrate their deep maleness and encourage a celebration of maleness in its quintessential forms and contents, they haven't necessarily served the purpose of bringing men and women together in relationships of greater harmony. It's great that men bang drums and bond in the woods, that they're getting together to redefine their sense of male identity, but in order to be whole, in order to be loved and loving, in order to have relationships *with women*, men also need to gain possession of their feminine identity, and this cannot be accomplished in isolation from women. For while drumming and bonding define a man as a man—in terms of his strength, his tribe, his father and his father wound—being in possession of his female essence gives him community, brings his heart home. And coming home to the feminine is what we all need to do now.

To come to this place asks for even more changes from men, for to be a man is still, by very definition, to be separate from your own emotions. To be male is to have, in a sense, given up on relationship—except as a structure in which, having set your own feelings aside, you must serve. It is this state of affairs, in which men are isolated unemotional functionaries, that both men and women are screaming about, though women are doing most of the screaming, for men have had to suppress the very feelings that would allow them to know how pained they are in their isolation and how much they need to scream.

Indeed, if there is one single premise in this book it is this: Men don't know what they are missing and women have to show them. Not knowing what they are missing is what has always made men men. To be male in our culture has been to be required not to feel and in that unfeeling state it is utterly impossible to feel the loss of being able to feel. If women want men to have, be, give, partake of, and deliver what they are now missing without help from women, it will be an endless, hopeless, wailing cry in hell for us all; for men can only give women what women need when women *show* men what it is they don't have. Men still can't give women what they want because the very thing women want from men men can only get from women in the first place. In order to unearth the feeling part of men, women must stand beside men, rowing the boat like Charon to the emotional underworld where, in the dark swirling waters, the feminine resides.

As a therapist and teacher of relationships to multitudes of men and women, I have come to believe that most men are still emotionally disenfranchised and that they experience their inaccessibility to their emotions as an unbearable void. It is the hidden pain men feel about this void that women must finally address—not with criticism or anger, but with acts of kindness, discovery, and understanding.

Such a notion stands in direct opposition to the critical mood in which we all have been submerged, and it intends to. For if women go on denigrating and separating men from the fold of the emotionally conscious, we will all be starved for emotional communion.

To meet this challenge will mean many things for women. It will mean embodying, modeling, and encouraging the behaviors we desire from men. It will mean giving up criticism, whining, complaining, and judging. It will mean service, patience, and compassion. In a sense, this is bad news all around: more work for women and startling, uncomfortable, emotional excursions for men.

Will it be worth it? Yes, if we really want to have deeply felt relationships. For we come into relationship to be mirrored, to have company on the journey that is life, to pursue our own development, to fulfill our spiritual purposes. Indeed, whether consciously or unconsciously, we come into relationship for the purpose of accomplishing our individual evolution.

Thus it is in relationships conducted at the highest level: two free beings reflect and commune with one another, seeing who each of them is, becoming whom each of them is meant to be. Viewed in this light, a relationship is a spiritual enterprise, an opportunity to develop oneself to the highest degree, while simultaneously evoking the uniqueness, the elegance, and the perfection of another human being.

Such a bonding, a relationship of freedom-in-union, represents the greatest potential of male-female intimate relationships, yet it is a configuration we rarely see. Instead we see the half-alive relationships that women so often complain about—stagnant unions in which neither men nor women's emotional or spiritual needs are being fulfilled.

It is precisely because a relationship is essentially an emotional bonding and because men have been denied access to their own emotional essence that women are disappointed, men are wary, and relationships between men and women are in the sorry state we find them in. This is because, in a sense, simply by virtue of being male, men lack "relationship capacity." What I mean by this is that men can't reveal themselves emotionally, don't have the words for disclosing their souls, and therefore have a limited capacity for intimacy with women.

This is why no matter how many books we have on how to improve our relationships, or how to supposedly avoid the pitfalls which in fact are potential in any relationship, male-female relationships in general have still not improved to the point where men and women wholeheartedly agree that we can all optimistically undertake them. These books have acquainted women with men, told women why men are the way they are, taught us how to live with them if they are difficult, advised us about the sort of men that we should at all costs avoid, and advised us not to lose ourselves by loving them too much; but they have not talked about the possibility of change.

In effect, these books have said that women must work with men the way they are, accommodate to them as it were, be thankful we can have satisfying emotional encounters with women and be grateful that, after all, men can chop wood, pay the electric bill, fix the garbage disposal, make love to us, and provide for the children.

This is no longer enough. We need to imagine the possibility of an awakening in men and we need to discover how to help them develop their relationship capacity. The acceptance of men as they are, a worthy enough position for an intermediate stage in our conjoint process of psychospiritual evolution, is no longer sufficient for either men or women. We all not only long for but absolutely require the experience of compassionate intimacy that binds us together not only in the elegant *pas de deux* of our romantic relationships, but also in life in general.

I believe—I know—that men are ready for this transformation. They have shown us this by stepping back into the primeval forest where their own lost images of manhood wink back at them in the twilight. But the feeling, bonding, emotion-sharing, spirit-revealing, solace-giving-and-receiving dimension of them has still not been evoked, and both women and men have yet to receive the inestimable benefits that will accrue from the liberation of men.

This is the next step in human psychospiritual evolution and it is a huge undertaking. It represents a revision not only in outlook—the way we think and what we believe—but also deep changes in our behavior.

Men are ready for this. But they cannot undertake—and they certainly cannot accomplish—this metamorphosis without women, for only women know the path to the place men need to go.

He Is What He Does: The Tragedy of Work as Male Identity

2

Hay for the Horses

He had driven half the night
> From far down San Joaquin
> Through Mariposa, up the
> Dangerous mountain roads,
> And pulled in at eight a.m.
> With his big truckload of hay
>> behind the barn.
> With winch and ropes and hooks
> We stacked the bales up clean
> To splintery redwood rafters
> High in the dark, flecks of alfalfa
> Whirling through shingle-cracks of light,
> Itch of haydust in the
>> sweaty shirt and shoes.
> At lunch time under Black oak
> Out in the hot corral,
> —The old mare nosing lunchpails,

Grasshoppers crackling in the weeds—
"I'm sixty-eight" he said,
"I first bucked hay when I was seventeen.
I thought, that day I started,
I sure would hate to do this all my life.
And dammit, that's just what
I've gone and done."

-Gary Snyder

In order to be willing to share with men the map to the land of emotions, women must first view them with new eyes, to accept the fact that men need our compassion for what they have undergone in living out the traditional male role. Instead of simply dismissing men as the emotionally-retarded gender, relegating them to the rag and bone pile of human emotional experience, we need to embrace them with empathy for what it has meant to be a man. For empathy is the necessary condition of change.

Empathy, the capacity to feel with another in his suffering, is born first of awareness, then of sympathetic connection. It requires first of all that you yourself have felt the pain, limitation or frustration that will subsequently allow you to feel with another, and secondly, that you can identify another's suffering and perceive him, therefore, to be worthy of your compassion.

For women to empathize with men means not only that we continue to hold an awareness of what we ourselves have suffered at men's hands, but also that we educate ourselves about men's sufferings. To do this is to take the crucial first step toward finding our way back to one another. Because it is only when women truly understand what it has always meant to be a man that we can come from the place of loving connection, the only place from which transformation is possible.

This is difficult, however, because since men don't know how to admit they need women's empathy, we're still not aware of how badly they need it, and anyway we're so fed up with men that we're often blind to their suffering. In our quickness to focus on our own deprivation, what we have overlooked is that men are as oppressed by the male role as we have always been by women's. Men aren't being the way they are simply to frustrate or negate us. They, too, are behaving according to the expectations of society, which, since time immemorial, has divided up social obligations along lines predicated by the dictates of gender and the inexorable demands of the forward movement of human civilization.

Just like women, men have *had* to be the way they are. Nobody has ever particularly asked men if they like the way things are, but willy-nilly, it has been their lot to bring home the bacon, pay the bills, climb the corporate ladder, keep the wolves from the door, do the sexual initiating, give up their places in lifeboats, and willingly die in war.

Rather than empathizing with the burdens men have had to carry, women tend to think that men lead charmed lives: that work always gives them a sense of meaning and fulfillment, that it's easy for them to fall in love, that they don't go through the kind of emotional anguish women do—in short that their lives are a bed of roses. Even when women conjecture that life may have left some nasty scars on men, they generally end up believing that the power and sense of identity men get through their work more than makes up for anything else they might suffer or feel deprived of.

For generations women have watched men performing the functions of the male role and assumed that they take to it like a duck to water. We tend to think that men's lives are the cat's meow, that they have all the power and all the freedom, that they love to be heroes, protectors, providers, power-wielding world-shakers, grantors of our security, and the court of the last resort for broken plumbing, out-of-hand children, overbearing mothers-in-law, and financial disasters. Of course it's true that men do have and always have had very obvious power in the world, and that they enjoy the sense of identity they derive from it, but in projecting so much value and satisfaction onto the male role, women have managed not to see that there is also a distinctly down side to the male experience.

The Male Role is No Bed of Roses

"I'll tell you something, and maybe you won't believe it: it's hard to be a man."

-Nurseryman, 36

In reality, for both men and women, it is through work *and* love—our adult romantic relationships, the loving relationships we have with our children and our friends—that we most deeply encounter ourselves, that we gain the greatest sense of who we are and a sense of the meaning of our lives. This is why women have been so passionate in fighting for the chance to express themselves through work, why we make such extravagant emotional investments in our love relationships, and why most of us choose to have children. Yet it is in precisely these three areas—work, love, and parenthood—that men are suffering because of the incarcerating demands of the male role, which has prevented them from having deeply rewarding emotional lives.

Men are in pain about work because, without quite knowing it, they've allowed work to become virtually the entire definition of what it is to be a man; and men are in pain about their relationships with women and their children because in allowing work to define them, they've either lost or never had an opportunity to develop the qualities that could open or deepen their capacity for intimacy. Far more than they can ever articulate, men sense the betrayal and violation inherent in spending so much of their lives at work. Although a sense of what else life may contain remains obscured for many men, they nevertheless sense in some primitive way that they have sold their birthright for a mess of pottage.

Men and Work: What He Does Is Who He Is

"Who has time to feel? I gotta pay the rent."
                                    -Truck driver, 34

Since time immemorial men have identified themselves by, through, and in terms of their work. Much more than is true for women, a man *is* a carpenter or a gardener, an attorney, or a rock star. In a very real way, a man *is* what he does. It's the business he runs, the company that hires or fires him, the career he pursues, the mark he makes in the world through his work that grants him his whole sense of identity.

More than many women realize, a man is his work. One 64-year-old man recognized the truth of this when he contemplated stopping work: "I'm terrified of retirement. The problem is simple: If I'm not working, who am I? It'll be as if I've ceased to exist."

This definition-by-work has been a boon to men. It tells a man and everyone else, without the burden of much elaboration, how he spends his time, where his interests lie, what's important to him: in short, who he is and what we can reasonably expect of him. There are many benefits to having a work-defined identity. It's a great relief to have a clearly demarcated set of things that you can say about yourself. ("Who are you?"

"I'm a corporate V.P." "What do you do?" "I sell insurance.") Without much effort, work gives others a clue as to who you are. It allows you to interact with you as a certain identifiable quantity, while at the same time granting a measure of protection from any emotional vulnerability. Through work you can have an identity without emotional risk and, as both men and women know, there are certainly some benefits to being emotionally protected.

Nevertheless, there are also a hoard of nightmares lurking within the handy container of work as the full measure of male identity. To be identified so strongly with work means that work becomes the sole source of meaning in men's lives, that they must compete with one another in order to gain and retain their identity, and that work becomes the substitute for authentic self-expression.

Man's Search for Meaning

"What do I want? The courage to follow my heart."
                                                    -Physician, 42

As society is presently constructed, work is the only arena in which a man can see his value, power, and uniqueness. Thus a man's job must not only sustain him (and his family) in day-to-day life, it must also comfort him about the meaning of his entire life. If the value of a man's life equals what he has done in terms of work, then if after he has died what he has done is recognized to be significant, he is thought of as having been a good man; but if what he has done is bad or insignificant, or has created no lasting ripples in the human stream, then he is thought of not only as a man who failed at work, but as a man who failed at life. Because of this existential charge around work, a man is endlessly propelled toward work since he believes that it is only through his achievements that his true stature will ultimately be revealed. As one 49-year-old business-man said, only half jokingly, "If I don't succeed now, I'll be a nobody when I'm dead."

This creates a tremendous pressure on men. In order to get a sense of his own value, a man must constantly ask himself as he weaves his way forward and sideways through life, "Am I succeeding? Am I doing enough to leave my mark?" This somewhat grinding and deeply internalized need for achieve-ment so that their lives will have meaning forces men to ask too much from their work and, in turn, allows their work to ask too much of them. This is why so many men are caught up in the trap of overwork. In an endless, hopeless endeavor to believe they have accomplished enough for their lives to have value, men willingly stay in the rat race and unwittingly sacrifice their lives to work.

The male focus on achievement has deep psychospiritual roots, for it is intrinsic to human nature to need to believe that our lives have meaning, that our existence is not, in the words of Ernest Hemingway "a dirty joke." All human beings carry this deep longing for a sense of the purposefulness of life, but men and women have always expressed it differently, with men gaining fulfillment through work and women through the bearing and rearing of children.

Although most women now also work, work will never be quite the quintessential source of identity it is for most men precisely because of women's emotional capacity for meaning-ful relationships with children and friends. I'm not saying that the work women do isn't powerful or significant, but no matter how distinguished a woman's work may be, she will always find a significant measure of her identity in her capacity for emo-tional connection.

The same isn't true for men. Although of course men

take pride in their children and enjoy their interactions with their friends, raising children and developing deep friendships have never been the primary sources of identity for men that they are for women.

Since work remains the most obvious and important way a man defines himself and is the medium through which a man must leave his mark, it is inevitable that it is also through work that the drama of male competition will inevitably be played out. For, not only must a man *be* what he *does*; he must also do it better than anyone else in order to have a sense of himself as valuable and unique. A man is supposed to be successful and, as a result of how he stacks up in relation to his competitors, to get a sense of who he is. In being bigger, better, stronger, or wiser than his peers, he gains a certain measure of definition of himself. The measure of the good man, our society presumes, is the magnitude of his success as compared to other men. The successful man has the expensive car, the beautiful wife, the six-figure salary. Then, supposedly, he has arrived; then he knows who he is.

The Rat Race is Over and the Rats Won

"Relax? How can I? There's always some other guy jockeying for my place. If I lose my spot, I'm a nobody. You can't be a man and go backwards. Or even sideways. It's always up, up, up. Otherwise, how can you live with yourself?"
                                      -Middle management executive, 48

Paradoxically, even success doesn't necessarily confer a true sense of identity on many men, for rather than being able to relax into a sense of who they are because of what they have accomplished, they become caught up in the rat race of competition to further distinguish themselves—if they're on top, to stay there; if they're still struggling, to try to make it up to the next rung on the ladder.

In this ever-competitive pursuit of identity through work, men's efforts are often catalyzed by the fear of failure, not by the love of the labor itself. Although there are those men who genuinely love their work, too often work offers not the comfort of an increasingly secure identity, but rather a series of emotion-suppressing and spirit-crunching efforts. Thus, instead of being enhanced by his work, a man's life is all too often ruined by it. Any hope he might have had about the joy of his vocation or that even more elusive satisfaction, an experience of self-expression, is squashed by the pure necessity of work as an economic pursuit and a requirement for the bolstering of male identity. The man who dreamed he would love his work or come to know himself through it becomes the man whose work does him; the man who believed success would grace his efforts becomes the man who looks anxiously over his shoulder to see who is gaining on him or ahead down the long winding road to see whom he must best next in order to keep his place in line.

It is this competitive race to success that drives so many men to early deaths. Since men have virtually no identity except their work, they *have to* succeed—and better than anyone else—or else feel as if they have ceased to exist. It is this never-ending quest for success—and for the identity that inheres in it—that makes men so driven about their work and unconsciously invites them into the self-destruction that work directly (15-hour work days) and indirectly (the 3-martini lunch) requires.

Father/Son Wounds: The Harsh Paternal Legacy

"My father was a professional tennis player. When I was a kid he always used to beat me at tennis. The first time I beat him, he quit playing with me."

-Builder, 26

The psychological base of male competitiveness which is endlessly played out in the world of work often has its origins in a man's relationship with his father. For in seeking to establish his own male identity, a son looks to his father for the blueprint of what it is to be a man. Since sons see their fathers functioning in a world where competition is the medium of success, young men almost invariably adopt this as the model for their own behavior. In words, but even more through behavior, fathers teach sons that it's a dog-eat-dog world, that the best man wins, that the winner takes all, that you don't get mad, you get even. A boy learns that in the world of work there is no such thing as camaraderie or relaxation vis à vis other men; instead the life of work is a constant struggle for a man to define himself against other men.

Boys must not only follow their fathers' example of competition, they must often also defend themselves from unspoken but powerful competition with their fathers. Without knowing it, and therefore often without taking any conscious emotional responsibility for it, many men challenge their sons in life-long invisible competitions. Subtly or directly they insist that their sons be bigger, better, and stronger than they are, but then often resent it when their sons threaten to surpass them. In dealing with their own insecurity about whether or not they have succeeded as men, they pass on the mixed message that their sons must equal or surpass them, and at the same time, they make sure they aren't surpassed and thus discredited as fathers.

One classics professor, for example, overjoyed that his firstborn was a son, began reading Greek tragedies to him before the boy could even talk. Years later when the benefit of all this early education had the effect of greatly accelerating his son's academic career and the boy was admitted, at age 16, to a prestigious university, the father suddenly had a "financial crisis" which made it impossible for him to underwrite the boy's education. At his father's insistence, the son was required to work for several years, until at age 18, when his father "had recovered financially," he matriculated at the local university at the same time as his former high school classmates. The father who had encouraged his son's precocity couldn't handle it when his son's potential academic achievements held the possibility of upstaging his own and so unconsciously he made sure it wouldn't happen.

Much more destructively, in tableaus of verbal brutality that are sometimes plainly shocking, many fathers intentionally or unintentionally cut down their sons to boost their own egos: "You'll never be half the man I am"; "You'll never be taller than I am"; "You'll never make as much money as I do"; "You'll never be the athlete I was"; "You don't have as much smarts in your whole head as I have in my little finger."

Paternal abuse can also be indirect, when fathers shut down their sons' expression by interrupting, changing the subject or finding themselves suddenly unable to listen. As a 30-year-old contractor says, "My father's willing to have a conversation so long as he's talking about himself, but when I have something to say, he suddenly has an appointment he's late for and leaves."

Needing the blessing of their fathers in order to feel they've arrived, or one day will arrive as men, sons push themselves beyond their reasonable limits in a hopeless, heart-wrenching effort to win their father's approval. In an all-too-typical encounter, I once witnessed the following: "All I ever wanted was for you to be proud of me, Dad," cried the 35-year-old successful screenwriter son of a multi-millionaire real estate magnate. "I could have been," said his father, "if only you'd stayed in real estate."

I hear stories like this all the time. A successful young stockbroker, trying to finally impress his father by taking him and his mother to an expensive dinner at the town's most elegant hotel, was told by his father, "I've told you ever since you were a kid not to waste your money. Why are you bringing us to a place like this?" Still another father, an editor, "insulted," as he said, by his son's poor academic work, insisted that his son give up competing in track when the year before he had won a varsity letter. The boy became so despondent because of being deprived of the one thing at which he excelled that he dropped out of school entirely and eventually committed suicide.

The magnitude of this tragic competition between fathers and sons remains virtually unacknowledged in our society, especially by women, whose perspective on men rarely allows them to see or comprehend it. Men are overwhelmed to discover the breach of faith that exists between themselves and their fathers, amazed and horrified to discover that their fathers, rather than being allies, champions or supporters, are, often as not, like Darth Vader of the Star Wars saga, an intimate and insidious version of the enemy.

Men's pain over this wound of competition with their fathers is the secret male sorrow that is revealed again and again in psychotherapy. As one massive and seemingly indestructible construction worker told me, "When I was little, my father—who is 260 pounds—always used to tell me that I'd never be as strong as he was. Then, when I grew up and started to work for him, he could never acknowledge that I had surpassed him in strength, that, in fact, he depended on me to do all the heavy work. I was his son and his employee but he always treated me worse than everyone else. In fact, he never said one nice thing to me in all the years I worked for him, and when I finally left to start my own business, he told me I'd never succeed. Whatever I did he tore me down; he always made me feel inadequate."

This man speaks for the vast number of men who, because of the legacy of competition with their fathers, live in despair about the value of their own achievements. To them are added the legion of men who are never able to accomplish even half of what their fathers did. These men gave up competing before they even began because they got the message that they would be punished for even trying, or because the discrepancy between their power and their father's when they were children did make it seem impossible for them to ever attain their father's level of achievement.

"My father made millions of dollars in real estate and here I am at 34, still trying to figure out what to do when I grow up," noted one man. "He sends me money every month—an allowance, just like when I was a kid. No matter what I could think of doing, I could never earn as much as he sends me just out of his back pocket. I'm defeated before I begin. Besides, we'd have nothing to talk about if it weren't for the money he's sending."

These myriad deep imprintings of fatherly competition are something that, knowingly or unknowingly, every man carries with him to work every day. For no matter what his occupation or status, he will invariably encounter other men who bring up his issues about his father. In relation to these men, he will very likely either act like his own father and compete with them, or, continuing to occupy the role of the son still desperately seeking approval, will feel defeated and discouraged, unable to gain a sense of his full stature as a man. In the world of work, which provides innumerable opportunities for replaying the drama of father-son competition, men are rarely able to see one another in the kinder supporting roles of brother or colleague, and are more frequently haunted by the specter of the filial relationship which defeated them in the past. Thus for men, work is often an endless reenactment of the painful childhood relationship which, for most men, has never been resolved.

Common Tales of Buried Dreams

> *"Do I like my job? I don't allow myself to think about it. It's work. I do it. Period."*
>
> *-Book salesman, 54*

Definition by work is so intrinsic to the male identity that we all unconsciously assume that the doing of work will give a man a sense of wholeness and fulfill his creative impulses. Of course a man will gain satisfaction from selling insurance, working in the coal mines, or running a corporation. Of course he will thrive on work because work is what men do. Women tend to be unaware that men's careers don't necessarily represent the fulfillment of their dreams. Because we've felt so defeated by the dailiness, ordinariness, and economically-insulting aspects of what has been traditionally termed women's work, we've tended to assume that men's careers have been the apotheosis of their desires. But in reality, for many men, work has been not only a life-long disappointment of their hopes, but also a violation of their spirits.

Women have believed that this particular negation of identity—the negation of talents and setting aside of life dreams—was an exclusively female province, that only for us did the curtain ring down prematurely on undeveloped talents.

While it's true that women have lived for what may feel like eons in a state of enforced denial of all that aches to be brought forth from us, what is also true is that, in ways we haven't imagined, the same has always been true for men.

In fact, the innumerable unfulfilled dreams of men is a classic American tragedy—from Willy Loman in *Death of A Salesman* to the taxi driver in Cleveland who told me he'd been a champion figure skater in high school, but had to give it up when his sweetheart got pregnant. He married her his senior year and subsequently became the father of twins. To provide an income for his instant family, he became a cabby—which he still was when he picked me up at the airport twenty years later.

There's also the used car salesman who gave up a crack at professional baseball because his second child was born with a congenital heart defect that required repeated astronomically expensive surgeries; the hotel manager who dropped out of medical school because his four daughters arrived: "We had a child a year, one by each major method of birth control," he joked. And the articulate attorney who is a closet novelist. The same facility with language that led him into law is closeted against the day when he himself can write the stories that ignite his imagination. But he despairs of that day ever arriving. "There's no way I can ever afford to become a writer," he says. "I have to support my wife and children. It's too late for me to have a creative life." Such common tales of buried dreams are typical of the many men who, because they had to become providers, lost the chance to explore the full range of their possibilities.

Although we don't like to think so and because so many men's successes render their tragedies invisible, the burdens of family have squashed as many men's dreams as women's. Multitudes of men aren't doing what, as young men, they hoped, imagined, dreamed, or expected they would do. In fact, rarely have I spoken to a man over fifty who didn't express some sense of regret about his work: "What I really wanted to be was. . . ." "What I wish I could have done was. . . ." "But I got married, the children came along. . . and somehow everything changed."

Whether it's the college administrator who wishes he'd been a cartoonist, the CEO of an electronics firm who dreamed of becoming a physicist, or the real estate developer who wanted to be a musician, hoards of men haven't had a chance to follow the work they desired, and instead have had to take up the work that was there to be done. Even the man with the seemingly enviable career can be grieving the loss of his own most passionately felt intentions. A movie executive told me recently that he'd always wanted to be a surgeon, that whenever he makes a film about a doctor he finds himself in tears off the set. "I can't believe my life's half over and it's too late to become a doctor; I'll never have that chance." Indeed, for a great many men, the disappointment of unfulfilled dreams is the heartache which, along with their paychecks, they carry home.

That's because in relationship to his family a man always sees himself first of all as a provider. It is not only his definition of himself, but his family's internal expectation of him. Whether or not he is assisted in that undertaking (as he now often is, by his wife), internally, on an unconscious level he views himself as inescapably cast in this role.

As a provider, a man is a wallet, the money which, as a result of his work, he brings home to his family. While for many men providing does bring satisfaction, for a great many others it doesn't. In either case it represents the living out of a deeply ingrained expectation that a man will shape his life around the demands that being a provider creates. Should he choose, by virtue of creative impulse, to try to have a more free-form life, he risks not only financial incertitude, but also the onus of losing that part of male identity that is defined by playing this role in his family.

Not The Real Picture

> *"Work is what you do for others, Liebchen, art is what you do for yourself."*

> -Stephen Sondheim,
> Sunday in the Park with George

Even if work weren't contaminated by all these problems for men, in reality the definition of identity through work provides only a portion of that sense of self which is the inescapable psychological necessity of every human being. We forget at times that work is work—and that a sense of identity, that delicate aggregate of perceptions that confirms for each of us who we are, is made up of far more than simply what we do. We *all* need a definition of ourselves which, while it may include our work or profession, reaches far beyond what we do to provide financial support for our lives. Yet so many men are so caught up in their self-definition by work that they can't possibly gain this larger sense of themselves. In general, male identity has by now become so bound up with what is external—with incomes, achievements, and possessions—that men's identities can't possibly reflect the deeper essence of their personalities. In the same way a man's work creates an identity for him, to that precise degree it can also rob him of discovering his deeper, more complex and beautiful identity.

For, in reality, a man is not just his work and neither it, nor the money he gains from it, nor the sense of power he feels as a consequence of it, can give him a portrait of his full identity. Only the deeper relationship he has with himself can show him who he truly is: his questions and answers; his joys and curiosities; his heart-felt affiliations; his longings and sorrows; his fears; the acts of his imagination, his spiritual depth. All these spring from the deeper ground in any man, whether he is plowing the fields, painting signs, cooking hamburgers at McDonald's or running for President of the United States. Work can never deliver a man to his whole identity, and to the extent that men continue to be caught up in the notion that it can, they are depriving themselves of the opportunity to discover the full richness of who they are.

Interestingly enough, it is only as women take on their own work identities, assuming a portion of the economic burden and leaving men waiting at home for wives who themselves are entertaining clients, studying for the bar, or working the graveyard shift, that men can finally have an opportunity to explore the selves, pale and embryonic, that have been long buried under the rocks of their professional identities. In isolation perception deepens, and in the space that women's more frequent absences have created, men's perceptions of themselves are starting to include an exploration of the farther reaches of who they might be. Like the trapped housewives of the past they are finally in a position to contemplate their true condition.

As they do, they begin to see that there is a self behind the man who performs, a self that has never had a chance to blossom. Just as many women are shocked and angry to discover some of the negative aspects of work, men are angry as they uncover the awareness of their lost identities. While their discoveries have the happy potential of opening the way to change, for the time being most men are still stranded, their spirits still prevented from full flowering by the limiting definitions imposed by the inexorable necessity of work.

In Search of Love: Men's Sorrow in Intimate Relationships

3

"Men just don't connect the way women do and on some level we're sad that we can't."

-Father of three, 28

We all know that one of the difficulties for men in living out the male role is that men have trouble expressing their feelings, that, as a result, male-female relationships tend to be primarily functional in character, and that, as a consequence, most women in relationships feel as if they're living in an emotional desert. What we haven't realized, however, is that men also feel emotionally deprived and also suffer because of the emotional aridity of their relationships.

Since men aren't defined primarily through their personal relationships, we tend to overlook the complexity of feeling and hence the potential for tragedy inherent in a man's relationship with the women and children in his life. Herein lies the potential for an endless array of emotionally wounding experiences for men. For, in failing to comprehend the depth and scope of their true emotional attachments—so often acted out, rather than directly spoken—women tend to further short-change men in how we see them. Men themselves may not comprehend, and women, missing men's rudimentary attempts to communicate, may very likely overlook the magnitude of the pain men are in.

What we discover, if we view men through the translu-cent window of truth instead of the dark glass of our prejudice, is that when it comes to relationships, men too are suffering. The man on the white horse, who may look like a hero, wonderfully happy, splendidly fit, unwoundably invincible, is, in fact, struggling to keep from exposing the wounds that his struggle for love have inescapably inflicted. In faithfully enact-ing what it is to be a man, men bleed without knowing they are hurt, and while we may mistake their silence for contentment, the evidence of their suffering surrounds us.

For men also seek relationships that provide them with emotional sanctuary, peace, diversion, and consolation. Like women, men need to be nurtured and cherished, to feel secure so they can function in the world. Men, too, need the emotional connection that ameliorates the experience of human isolation. Like women, men need to be loved and to see themselves as loving, as capable of delivering from their own goodness, strength, and ingenuity the gifts, responses, and gestures that create the intimacy they want so badly to share in.

This is sometimes impossible for women to believe. We tend to think that in the love marketplace, men have unlimited choices. Since there is such a preponderance of single, available women and since women all seem to be so eager to be in relationships, we tend to assume that men won't have a problem in finding the perfect relationship, that they can just turn around on a dime and find the mate of their dreams. But there's far more to a happy pairing than just the availability of a member of the opposite sex. Just because there are more single women than men doesn't mean that any of the available multitude is going to be the right woman for any particular man. You can't generate the perfect relationship out of statistical probabilities. For a true relationship defies the banal truth of mere statistics. It's a gift, an unsolicited miracle of attraction, interaction, and deep subterranean purpose, and it's as rare for men as it is for women.

Indeed, the thing I hear men grieve about most is that they can't seem to find a woman who really touches and delights them. More men than you can imagine are as lonesome as single women–it's just that they usually suffer in silence so we don't know what they're going through. But when they do open up and start talking, their anguish is heartbreaking.

"I live continually with the longing of sharing my life with a woman," lamented a male friend of mine. "I want a woman to want to know me as I truly am, but even now after years of looking I haven't been able to find one."

"The women I've met are desperate to get married," says a sensitive young man I know. "They want security, someone to pay the electric bill. They don't care about you as a person."

Another, a dental student, said: "I never would have believed how hard it was going to be to find women to date after college. The bar scene; the single's life. AIDS. It's a jungle out there. Women have no idea. They think it's a party for a man. Sometimes I feel as if my chance to get married has already passed me by. It's devastating thinking that."

An attractive man in his mid-fifties, decimated by the

ending of a two-year courtship, said: "Everyone thinks I'm doing great. In fact, one of my best friends, a widow, said to me, 'What's your problem? You're handsome; you're solvent; you're available: you're a great catch. What have you got to complain about?' People just don't understand. I'm not—and women aren't—just a commodity. As ridiculous as it may sound, I want a woman I can really love, and that's not just anyone. I couldn't tell my friend of course, but I've literally spent most of the last four weekends alone, just staring at the wall."

Too often men, like women, discover that the real experience of love eludes them. Women know how awful it feels to be deprived of emotional intimacy, the interpersonal magic which we believe, if only we could get it, would endlessly delight us and spin a beautiful web of meaning around our lives—that's what we're often complaining about. But the truth is that men feel this too, although they're rarely able to identify or articulate these feelings.

As a consequence of living out the male role which in itself inhibits feeling, men tend to be incapable of making that deep connection and unaware that they are suffering because they can't. Instead, they continue to be brave, to act as if everything's all right, to ignore the little gnawing sensations that might inform them that they're hurt or discouraged, that something's wrong, that they're hungry for love. Instead, they experience their specific disappointments as a generalized vague discontent, the grayish sense that their relationships should bring them more joy than they do.

While men can rarely pinpoint—as women usually can—the exact nature of their romantic discontents, they express them by not believing in the possibility of love, by focusing all their attention on work, by being scared of making commitments, and by avoiding emotional intimacy when they are in romantic relationships. "Why did I marry *her*?" a divorced attorney confided to me. "I didn't think I'd ever fall in love. She wanted children and so did I, so I married her. She was as good as anyone else."

Furthermore, men's frequent unwillingness to commit themselves to marriage isn't just a ruse to spite women as we might suppose. It stems from men's unconscious awareness that once they have settled into it, a relationship won't necessarily meet their emotional needs. Instead of being loved, they'll have to provide security. Instead of being emotionally supported, they watch while their wives over-nurture their children. Fearful that their needs won't be fulfilled, many men avoid getting into the marriages they instinctively believe will disappoint them.

This fear isn't because women are, in fact, incapable of meeting men's needs or of being loving to them. It's because the male role has required men to be separated from their emotions for so long that once inside a relationship, men are slammed up against the wall of their limited relationship capacity. Wanting love they discover—whether they consciously face this or not (and most of them don't)—that they lack the ability to evoke the emotional responses they need from women as well as the capability of providing the emotional responses women need from them.

This poignant gap always reminds me of *The Gift of the Magi*, the tragic O. Henry story in which such marital miscommunication takes on a heartbreakingly ironic twist at the end. In the story it's Christmas and the two main characters, a man and his wife, financially destitute but wanting to give each other a beautiful gift, decide, without talking it over with one another, to ransom a particularly valuable possession of their own in order to buy their beloved the perfect Christmas gift. The wife cuts her long hair and sells it to the wigmaker so she can buy a fob for her husband's gold watch; and her husband pawns his gold watch to buy a comb for her marvelous long hair. When, at the end of the story, they exchange their gifts, they discover that neither one of them still owns the one possession that would allow the other's gift to be the magnificent present it was intended to be.

As this emotion-wrenching story shows, love and good will aren't enough to create an experience of fulfillment in relationships. No one meets anyone's needs when those needs aren't identified and revealed, and, just as in the story, men's pain in love will continue so long as the male role makes it virtually impossible for men to connect with the emotional truth in themselves that can engender the responses they need and want from women.

To Have and Have Not

"Boys hurt, cry and feel empty after breaking up with someone close, just like girls. But we hide our pain behind closed doors because–unlike girls–we've been brought up not to express our feelings in public."

-High school boy, age 16

When it comes to love, men are in pain not only about the relationships they're in, they're also in pain when their relationships crash to an end. Half of all marriages presently end in divorce, and in response to this rather shocking statistic, we all tend to be primarily focused on what happens to women when relationships dead-end. We readily commiserate with the woman who has to raise the children alone, who isn't fairly recompensed for all her years of being a wife, who's afraid she's too old to fall in love again, who has to go back to work or belatedly invent her own vocation.

But, again, because of the male mystique, the notion that

men go through things without feeling, what tends to be overlooked in all this is that men, too, are suffering through the endings of these one-out-of-two marriages. The stunning consequences of ended relationships are also overwhelming for men—in terms of financial and geographic revisions, parenting crises, emotional traumas, and the assumption of a range of domestic responsibilities for which a great many men are completely unprepared. In divorce men, too, are struggling with major life adjustments: having to give up half of their net worth, leaving homes they helped create, going through feelings that rock them to their normally well-defended cores.

I don't mean here to negate or minimize the desperate emotional and economic straits that divorce puts women in, and it's true that because of the still rampant economic inequality in this society, women do suffer more financially in divorce. But our albeit legitimate anger about this inequality often makes us incapable of seeing that men are also suffering financially, that men too are undergoing an immense emotional crisis when divorce occurs.

In truth, the emotional pain I've observed in men whose relationships have ended is staggering in its capacity to virtually derail them. Men find themselves having taken a quantum leap, being forced into an emotional condition for which they are absolutely, totally unprepared. While these emotions are no less intense for women, they generally represent movement on the continuum with which we are already somewhat familiar, rather than movement to the extreme of an entirely new continuum.

Men, however, find themselves stranded in a morass of feelings for which the usual male methods of coping—planning, reasoning, problem-solving, analysis—in short, taking charge—are all completely useless. Since emotions are, in general, off the map for men, emotions of the titanic magnitude that accompany the end of a relationship can seem purely overwhelming. The whole experience can make a man feel as if his expertise in any area is under fire, as if he is suddenly capable of nothing. Overwhelmed by this deluge of emotions, men, with surprisingly more frequency than women, contemplate or actually commit suicide. As one man poignantly confessed, "When she left, it was all I could do to keep myself from driving into a tree. We're supposed to be so strong, men. Who are we kidding?"

The rending apart of a marriage is also extremely difficult for men because in general, the only emotional relationship men are permitted to have is with the woman they are married to or live with. In general, men can't talk about their troubles with each other so when they lose the woman they've loved, they are suddenly stripped of all emotional connection. In contrast, since women are permitted a variety of emotional attachments throughout their life, they usually have a well-developed emotional safety net, friends and family to turn to in time of need. Not so for a man. When divorce hits, it's as if he's been dropped off in some foreign country and the only person who might possibly speak the language is the woman who dumped him off there in the first place—except she doesn't want to talk to him anymore; she's just taken the last boat out.

As a 40-year-old writer reflected, "After ruining my marriage through a relentless addiction to work, I finally broke down and got in touch with my regrets about my work obsession. My wife was the only person I felt I could talk to, the only person who knew me well enough. But she had divorced me, she was fed up, and of course, she refused."

Or as another man said, "I felt as if I was dying, as if I would literally die if I didn't go home to someone, but the only woman I could go home to had gone home to someone else."

Contrary to our assumptions, men don't recover easily

in divorce. They simply don't have the emotional resources women do to facilitate their own healing—nor do they have the emotional resilience. While they may be able, despite resentments, to restructure their decimated finances, it may be years, or a lifetime, before they can restructure their capacity to love. As another male survivor of divorce said, "It's one thing to lose your empire in divorce; it's another to have your heart smashed to bits. Frankly I don't know if I'll ever be able to trust a woman again."

If in his inability to bear up in the grief of parting, a man should seek help in psychological counseling, this is frequently seen as a weakness. Although therapy in itself is no longer viewed as a sign of galloping mental illness, the notion of seeking help is in itself antithetical to the precepts of the male mode of behavior, so men suffer a loss in self-esteem for even contemplating their need for assistance. This too is a burden that women don't have to bear—for it has always been acceptable for women to ask for help, to seek emotional solace, and to receive it.

A Man and His Heirs

"I've learned the hard way that it is one grand illusion if you start believing you can be totally dedicated to the demands of your job without shortchanging your pressing responsibilities to your family."
-Brandon Tartikoff, former head of
Paramount Pictures, when he resigned that
position to care for his critically-ill daughter

Not only are men shortchanged in their romantic love relationships, but living out the male role also has an inhibiting and depriving effect on what can occur between men and their children. Since men define themselves through work, they often structure their lives so they're endlessly racing up the ladder to success and scarcely have time to spend with their families. The truth of this was sadly expressed by a 39-year-old designer, who, when he went back to his childhood home after an absence of twenty-five years, was asked what the most important feeling his visit evoked was. "That my father was never there," he said simply. "He built the house and moved us in. Then he became a successful developer, and, basically we never saw him again."

The sorrow a male child feels about his absent father is the counterpart sorrow a man feels about his own absence from his children. For even if fathers should one day discover what an enriching experience it might be to develop a relationship with their children, most of them wouldn't have a chance to explore what this might mean. They simply don't have the time. There are too many clients to see, too many hang-ups on the freeway, too many late night meetings, too many stranded airplanes.

Although to some degree this is changing, families are generally structured in such a way that fathers are often mere figureheads, filling out the adult male silhouette in the nuclear family cut-out portrait. They may sit at the head of the table on Thanksgiving, mete out punishments at the end of the day, attend high school graduations, the school Christmas play, or soccer games and baseball practice; they may be the indulgent daddies of their darling daughters, and may have the "facts of life" talk with their sons, but their role is all too often only functional, having to do with the structure and maintenance of family life, and not with a true emotional exchange.

Interestingly enough, the male role does allow men to have emotionally expressive relationships with their very young children. A man can cuddle his babies, toss them up in the air and talk goo-goo talk with them, but at a certain point he's supposed to get over all that nonsense, become a father in the distant, acceptable way, and essentially cut himself off from his offspring. Although this too is changing to some degree, there is still an internal bedrock prohibition against men's physical or emotional over-involvement with their children. This is in general because of social taboos designed to prohibit incest which, although we don't openly discuss them, we consistently do act out. Since the taboo is generally stronger than even the most creative efforts to work around it, most men don't have a close physical relationship with their sons and daughters much past infancy; and as time goes on they find themselves having drawn farther and farther away from them.

Since men have such a difficult time expressing their feelings anyway, this amputation of physical contact only serves to exaggerate their distance from their children. Thus in time fathers become vague, shadowy or weirdly one-dimensional figures in their sons' and daughters' lives, seeming only to embody rules, principles, demands, and expectations, none of which are softened by the humanizing presence of authentic emotional exchange.

One young man tells his version of this sad tale. "When I was four, my father went through a terrible crisis at work, after which he suddenly changed. He became very hard on all of us, a five-star general, a walking rule book. Everything had to be done a certain way, at a certain time, and he never touched us again. I secretly called him 'The Monument' because from then on everything he said was set in stone. Later, looking at him in therapy, I learned that his father had been the same way, all hard, all demands, that my father, too, had been abandoned."

In a sense, men *can't* love their children, for not only are they progressively deprived of physical contact with them, but they are permitted to have only a small range of feelings about them. They can feel pride, rage, worry, or admiration, but not too much longing for closeness; and they certainly shouldn't show their own fear or sorrow, particularly if it's their children who have made them sad or afraid. Thus a man can be overjoyed when his son hits a home run or be worried sick when he takes up mountain climbing; he can admire his daughter in her prom dress or be distraught if she gets pregnant. But the warmer or more complex feelings he has about his children will likely remain unexpressed and the emotional connection he could share with them will mostly likely never develop in depth.

The cultural assumption that a man's parenting role is less important than a woman's also separates men from their children. We view mothers as the psychological parent, that is to say, the parent who is responsible for the child's emotional well-being and for developing the emotional component of the child's personality, while a man is generally relegated to the fall-back positions of structure-giver and financial provider.

Indeed, fathers are rarely viewed as the parent whose emotional input will shape the child, although paradoxically, it is often a man's interactions, or lack thereof, which most profoundly do. It's the few powerful words, the single exquisite gift, the one time he did show up at the school play, that become the life-shaping memories of father. With Dad, it's the exceptions that register. It's as if through his absence a father becomes indelibly present.

Recently men have shown some interest in challenging the underlying myth that children "belong" to their mothers by participating in the process of childbirth, acknowledging their role in creating this new life, and, at the outset, setting a precedent for the expanded role they intend to play throughout their child's life. Although this is only one of many encouraging signs that men are seeking deeper relationships with their children, we all still have a long way to go in revising our unconscious myths in this regard. As a society, we still uphold the position that a child is his mother's possession and a father just comes along for the ride.

This attitude—that men are second class citizens regarding children–also prevails regarding abortion. Men often have virtually no say in the matter of whether a woman will have his child or whether she will, as one man said to me, "just go out and kill it." To a degree that most women don't realize, men are in an incredible anguish about abortion, a matter about which in many men's eyes, women seem to have all the power.

I have sat innumerable times with men in unstoppable grief about this, men who said, "She never asked me if I wanted the child. She didn't let me go through the mourning process with her. She had the abortion on her own, then told me I had to pay for it."

Men also feel powerless when women decide to have a man's child without their consent. I've heard a number of men say sadly, "I have a son or daughter . . . somewhere." Men feel haunted about these children they will never know, and manipulated and angry at the women who hold them financially responsible whether or not they agreed to parenthood.

Here again men are in a virtually untenable situation, for when it's time to make a decision—to have a child or not—women's behavior all too often proclaims that it's their right alone to decide, that men will just have to go along no matter what their decision. This is so tragic because, of course, women have been moving across their own unique spectrum of anguish about abortion and the at times seemingly unbearable burdens of single parenting in the face of absent, uninvolved, and economically irresponsible fathers.

To turn a sympathetic eye toward the men who suffer over these issues is not to excuse men who refuse to take financial responsibility or abandon their children. Rather, it is to note that because of our own very difficult experience, women have tended to overlook that men carry their own grieving wreath when it comes to their children. My point is not to denigrate the real and often blatantly unfair hardships of the woman's position, which are awesome to be sure, but to ask that we have courage enough to view the situation also from the man's perspective.

Without Their Children

> *"The thing that kills me is the thought of my son waking up night after night and knowing I'm not there."*
> *-Divorced father, 29*

Nowhere is the male separation from their children more poignantly visible than in divorce. For when families are shattered it is most often men who must embrace the pain of losing their children. Men are expected to get lost, to want to return to bachelor status, and women, conversely, are expected to want to carry on with family life. Again, while there are many gruelling implications here for women, this is a pattern so universally enacted that its implications for men are constantly ignored.

Men are often accused of not caring about their children, of abandoning them after divorce, of not being involved in their lives. Yet the women making these complaints rarely consider what a man loses in being deprived of daily access to his children. One woman, criticizing her ex-husband for his non-involvement and seeming downright neglect of their young daughter was overwhelmed when he broke down sobbing at the front door. "You don't understand," he said, "I just can't bear to see her. All I see is how I'm not her father anymore."

Men experience a haunting and terrible sadness when

they realize that they are going to be mere shadows in their children's lives, that they will never be truly effective, never be able to create an arena of normalcy for their sons and daughters. So many of the ordinary avenues through which men discover and act out their feelings for their children are suddenly amputated in divorce—all the routine daily encounters, little offbeat moments, happy interludes at family outings in which a man is normally able to develop a relationship with his children—are suddenly ripped away. Without notice, a man is separated from the ritual of tossing his baby up in his arms, throwing a few baskets with his son every night when he comes home from work, fighting over the cereal box with his children every morning, kissing them good night. The divorced father may well not be present for his son's first shave, his daughter's junior prom, and if he is, it may be only as an uncomfortable, last minute witness.

When the continuity of a man's relationship with his children is interrupted like this, his ability to be perceived as loving is also severely scarred. All too easily he can be identified as the villain, the abandoner, the rejecting parent, no matter how mutual the decision to divorce may, in fact, have been. Because of distance, separation, and his absence from the dailiness of life, a father's image with his children is often much more easily damaged than that of his ex-wife's. Children feel loved by the parent who is there. To experience love through the occasional encounter, no matter how special or extravagant it may be, is a leap of faith that is difficult for most children.

While fathers can—and many do—find a way to bridge the abyss created by physical separation, to do so requires a willingness to walk through the pain and guilt of that separation. As one close male friend wrote me, "I always feel so utterly depressed and guilty when I bring the kids back to their mother, although I've seen them every week since the divorce. I really know so little of what's going on in their hearts and minds."

Because of divorce, men must struggle with changing perceptions of themselves as fathers and in this stripped-down condition they often have a hard time seeing themselves as good fathers. As the same friend wrote me later, "I do feel as if my staying near them throughout their lives will make a difference in the long run. It's my one hope, really."

In order to avoid the psychological conflict of these major post-divorce crises in self-esteem, men often bail out completely and have nothing at all to do with their children. Again, my intent is certainly not to excuse absentee fathers, but to provide a view of the sometimes excruciating context in which fathers must try to maintain a relationship with what are in effect their ex-children. We need to understand that theirs are not necessarily acts born of insensitivity, but of heartbreak, of total emotional overload.

Men's pain over their lost children is obscured from most women. For although growing numbers of men have begun to fight for custody and/or visitation rights to their children, we are still operating as a society according to the principle that men don't really have emotional relationships with their children. So what if their children are taken away? It's really no big deal. So what if fathers aren't around for the simple events of daily life? That's not a big deal either—so long as they're paying the bills and showing up for special occasions. Not only must men give up their children in divorce; they must also bear the pain of that loss and the burden of guilt over giving up or being separated from their children without any solace from society at large. As women loving men, we must surely begin to be cognizant of that fact.

Cut Off from Their Hearts

"The name of my sorrow? That there has been no one to know me and hold me and show me who I am."

-Lighting designer, 37

As women know, there are many loves—the sweet love of friendship, the abiding love of family, the great love of life-shaping romance. Love feeds us and saves us. It is both the staff of our lives and our lives' most happy diversion. Women love love.

And men love love too, or they want to—with their children, among their friends, with their fathers and brothers, with women in passionate, life-encompassing partnerships and unions.

But it is at exactly the point where love, the feeling, intersects relationship, the reality, that men have so many problems. Indeed, it is in the very relationships that have made women despair of ever having a real experience of intimacy with men that the true dimension of men's suffering is ultimately revealed. For it is in relationship, the very essence of which is to be a sanctuary for the nurturing and exchange of feelings, that men, by virtue precisely of what it is to be a man, are most deprived. In the province of feeling, men are called upon to serve and not to feel, to perform and not to reveal, to behave like heroes and not mere human beings.

Sadly, paradoxically, this is just what women complain about. We are angry precisely because men are strong instead of vulnerable, that they do their duty instead of open their hearts, that they talk about business instead of telling us their secrets, and yet these are the very requirements that we and they, through the dutiful living out of what are now rapidly becoming outdated sex roles, have always imposed upon men.

That our relationships with men are so often less than we wish they would be, that they so often cruelly disappoint us is the parallel measure of what men also miss out on in relationship. To be deprived of the solace of true emotional intimacy, of union, for whatever reason, is a loss at the center of life, and this is the ugly price men have had no choice but to pay simply for being a man in this society.

In looking at what men go through in their relationships with women and children, we stumble upon the reality that in many respects love hasn't been a happy enterprise for men. It has been the mixed bag of pleasure and abuse, deliverance and bondage, delight and aching disappointment it has also been for women.

When it comes to love, men are truly our suffering partners, and we must remember that the frustration we feel in the loves we have with them is precisely the measure of their disappointment in the loves they have with us. Until men can be liberated from the spirit-suppressing requirements of the male role, they—and we—will be consigned to relationships that deny us the joy of true intimacy, those that would allow us to discover each other in all our depth, power, and exquisite vulnerability.

Miles Away From Feelings: Surprising Secrets of Male Psychology

4

"When I was little, my pain towered over me. Now I tower over it. That's what it is to be a man."

-Toy salesman, 38

For the past several decades, women have been asking, crying and pleading for men to become more emotionally conscious. Indeed, the single apparently unequivocal message men are getting from women is that they should learn to express their feelings. Women have asked this so much, in so many ways that if men haven't gotten the message, women could easily conclude that they're deaf, blind, and dumb.

The fact is that in some sense men have gotten the message and have been trying to respond, but a variety of factors have converged to make this exceedingly difficult. Male socialization, men's psychological defenses and women's collusion have conspired to keep men in the emotional deep freeze. In order for them to thaw out, we first have to discover what's kept them in emotional cryonic suspension for so long.

The Burden of Biceps

> *"This culture is a giant arrogant John Wayne robot bully.*
> *It destroys the sensitivity in men. It annihilates the male*
> *emotionally, sexually, spiritually and creatively."*
> *-Graphic artist, 45*

In a sense, men have always been separated from their emotional lives by virtue of their, in general, superior physical strength. We know men are physically stronger. With their larger physical frames and superior biceps, men are the oxen of the human species, designed to pull the plow, hold the fort, and carry the burdens. In fact, it is physical strength, *per se*, which has traditionally distinguished "men's work" from "women's work."

But as a culture, we have also treated men's physical strength symbolically, extrapolating from it the notion that men would be willing and able to carry *all* kinds of burdens. Thus men have been the carriers not only of the physical burdens that their more developed biceps can shoulder, but also economic, social, environmental, political, and even a great many psychological responsibilities.

Since being strong is the antithesis of being vulnerable, it has been virtually impossible for men to get in touch with their own vulnerabilities, and in carrying out their vast array of duties, men have by necessity been separated from the tender fabric of their emotional lives, cut off from ways of being that are much more reflective and which might give them pause about a way of being that, unquestioningly, they have acted out.

The undertakings of men have left them very little room to discover what they feel, to consciously know what they intuitively perceive or to disclose to themselves—let alone to women--what occurs in the hidden chambers of their emotional selves.

Throughout history, men have been called upon to do the very things which, in order to do them, required the suppression of feeling. Men have had to kill the wild beasts, fell the forests, sail the seas, wage the wars and build the skyscrapers in order to secure the progress of civilization. To do this required, precisely, that they set aside their feelings.

A classic tale along these lines is the Greek fable of the warrior and the fox. As the story goes, in order to feed his starving troops, a Greek warrior stole a fox from behind enemy lines and tucked it under his cloak. As the warrior walked back to his camp, the fox started to suffocate under his coat, and, wanting to escape, attempted to chew his way out, eventually biting a hole in the soldier's heart. Found bleeding to death by his comrades, the dead warrior was lauded first of all for daring to go behind enemy lines and steal the fox, but above all for never having shown his pain.

This tale was recounted specifically to celebrate his true manliness: he was so brave that in order to save his countrymen he suffered and died in silence. The suffering soldier was the epitome of a hero because in his hour of anguish he neither cried out for help nor embarrassed anyone with his suffering. His reward was that he went with honor into his early grave.

If we wonder whether men are still living by this code of honor, and if we wonder if—or how—men still obscure their pain, we need only to look at the pain they carry in their bodies, in their faces, in their self-destructive habits—men between the ages of 18 and 29 suffer alcohol dependency at three times the rate of women in the same age group; more than two thirds of all alcoholics are men, and 50 percent more men are regular users of illegal drugs than women—in their heart attacks and early deaths.

Men have been taught that in order to hold the world together, to make political, economic, or social decisions, they have to ignore their emotions because the intervention of feelings could make mincemeat of their choices. Thus they have been encouraged not only *not* to have feelings, but have also been specifically instructed to shove down whatever random tendrils of feelings should, from time to time, manage to crop up.

A story from *The Odyssey* makes this clear. As you may remember, on one part of his journey Ulysses' boat was to pass by an island inhabited by beautiful Sirens—half-birds, half-women who let out a most enticing song. Because of the intoxicating quality of their music (a feeling, feminine experience) which might draw the sailors off course and entice them into emotional and sensual encounters with these beings, the gods instructed Ulysses and his men to plug their ears with wax and tie themselves to the mast of the ship, so they wouldn't be tempted to seek out the Sirens. The point, of course, was that should they become distracted by their emotions, they would never find their way home.

Like Ulysses, a man's call is always to duty, never to what might be emotionally fulfilling for him. This need for men to not feel is so universal that it has become, basically, our definition of what it is to be a man. It is, in fact, this very suppression of emotional vulnerability we are celebrating when we use the term "a man's man." We mean that such a man, by virtue of the fact that he shows no feeling, is to be highly admired. When we give men medals of honor for war, for example, we're saying in effect: this man was able to go into hell, feel nothing, and come out alive. Being dead to emotion is what we honor men for.

Indeed, we all carry in our deepest unconscious myths about the sexes the belief that men, by nature, are willing to carry and inflict the pain that is required for civilization to advance. Whether that's in the form of laying the railroad tracks or fighting a war, we have always assumed that men have a special capacity for bearing pain in silence. The forward movement of a culture is always accomplished by sacrifice and we have all counted on men to make this sacrifice without indulging in the luxury of also feeling about it as women are able to do. Indeed, we *assume* that men will not be affected by what the male role requires of them, that they will not be driven insane by packing their buddies in body bags, losing their children in divorce, enduring the irreversible insults of aging, suffering the violating words of parents, bosses, or spouses. In short, in our society, men are expected to be like the Greek warrior, the silent wearers and bearers of pain.

In spite of some tentative attempts to revise the male image, it is still the strong, silent type, the man who doesn't say what he feels, that is our most lauded emblem of the male hero— Clint Eastwood, John Wayne, Arnold Schwarzenegger. In their roles, these men all portray the male model of doing without feeling, of getting the job done without the unnerving distraction of emotions.

How They Got To Be that Way

"The fact is I have never had time to feel things. I have had to do them, *to make myself felt."*
　　　　　　　　　　-Henry James, The American

The man who can do all these things, who exemplifies this obdurate male essence and enacts its myriad forms of expression, doesn't spring whole from the womb. When men are infants, toddlers, and little boys, they *do* feel and they *can* cry. Their tiny hands are intaglioed with the same intricate imprints as any baby girl's. They have the same knowing sad eyes; the little insults of infancy, the troubling disappointments and brutal betrayals of childhood affect them just as deeply as they do their sisters.

In meeting young boys who are still somewhat conscious of their own feelings, I've found their degree of emotional vulnerability to be purely stunning. They may, in typical male fashion, act it out rather than express it directly by withdrawing, refusing to speak, or hurting themselves or others, but clearly they do have intense and complicated feelings.

One five-year-old boy, after an obviously contrived accident on his bicycle, finally managed to say that he was heartbroken because he loved his sister so much that it was unbearable for him when she went off with her friends at school and left him alone on the playground. A three-year-old destroyed the walls of his bedroom with "art," because, since the birth of his baby brother, no one held him anymore; and a seventeen-year-old arrested for petty theft finally confessed that he missed his workaholic father so much that he resorted to stealing in hopes of finally getting his father's attention.

Obviously male children feel and feel deeply, but eventually socialization takes care of all that: "little boys are brave; little boys don't cry" they are told, and the feeling boy is gradually molded into the unemotional man. If, indeed, a boy does manage to stay in touch with his feelings for a time, he quickly gets the message that being emotional isn't appropriate. As a man in his thirties told me, "When I was little I was so afraid of school I remember wondering how I'd ever be able to do the work in the third grade. I tried to talk to my father about it and he just said, 'You can't be scared. You're a boy. You'll do fine.'"

Another young man, struggling with overwhelming feelings of heartbreak when his sweetheart left him because of his seemingly uncrackable depression, said: "No wonder I'm depressed; My mother died when I was seven, but I could never get to my grief about it. Instead my dad always said, 'Keep busy, use your mind, use your hands. Never mind your sadness. It'll pass.'"

While most men aren't aware of it, many of them suffered greatly from being subjected to the rigid stereotypes of male development, the expectation that boys are tough, they don't feel, and nothing's going on inside. "Nobody ever listened to me," a six foot, two inch, 220-pound heavy machinery operator wrote to me recently. "I had so much I wanted to say—about flowers, about my feelings, about what I realize now were my psychic perceptions of things. But the things I had to say I couldn't talk about because they were so sensitive, so, if you will, feminine. No one ever seemed to be on my wavelength. I was very tender inside. But no one ever understood because I was so big outside."

Another man, a biology professor, said, "My parents were always giving me baseballs, hockey sticks and tennis rackets, and wondering why I never succeeded in sports. I had a whole secret life in the marsh behind the school. Everything I saw there fascinated me—the grass, the dragonflies, the algae on the pond. I'd go there when I was upset, lie in the marsh grass and look up at the clouds, wordless and sad, until I felt better. That marsh was my mother; no wonder I'm a biologist."

Stranded in the Stereotype

"Everything you look at, everything you read, puts men subliminally in this unfeeling role. I just want to stand up and scream: 'I'm human too; I'm just like you.'"
                                        -Business consultant, 41

While most women know men have been cut off from their feelings through socialization, we don't often realize the effect of this on the individual man. Although as a society we've announced that it's finally all right for men to have feelings, what we still aren't taking into account is the extent to which virtually every man grows up under the yoke of these stereotypical notions of what it is to be male. Real change comes very slowly and men are still living out the spirit-quenching consequences of classic male training even though we're starting to believe that both men and women suffer when men are denied their feelings.

However, even these vague glimmers of recognition that there's a problem still haven't had a significant effect at the core of our internalized myths about men. That is, even though on the outside we're beginning to think a little differently about men, inside, in the collective social unconscious, nothing has really changed.

As a society, we have a tendency to think that just because we've articulated a problem, we have enacted its solution. We're impatient. We thrive on the Open Sesame School of Life: say the magic word and you'll get immediate results. But unfortunately this isn't the case with either social or psychological change. The journey from diagnosis to transformation is always painstakingly slow, and when it comes to the legitimacy of a feeling life for men, the process may be even slower because the wound runs so deep.

Furthermore, although we've started to acknowledge the need for change, men's disconnection from their feelings is still being passed along from father to son. Even in families where stereotypes aren't strongly reinforced, boys still don't necessarily get the encouragement they need to explore their feelings. This is partly because most parents don't have the foggiest idea how to evoke the expression of feelings in their sons, and also because deep down we're still afraid that if they feel, our sons might turn out to be sissies.

It's also because, in general, boys still have nothing but the model of an emotionally suppressed man to follow. Rarely do boys see their fathers express any emotion besides anger. Hardly ever do they see their fathers cry, and almost never do they see their fathers express the subtler array of emotions of tender affection, fear, delight, sadness, longing, discouragement or heartbreak. As one twenty-four-year-old noted, "My father had one emotion—anger. Everything he felt he put into beating us up."

"I only saw my father cry two times," said a middle-aged college professor. "Once when I was seven and his mother died; and once when I was twenty-seven and he was dying. I learned that if you're a man you cry once every twenty years, and only if somebody's dying."

Not only do boys witness their father's emotional limitations, but in addition, in the interactions between their parents, they often get the message that it's bad to have feelings. Many male children see their mothers, with whom they associate the capacity to feel, being dismissed, ridiculed or ignored by their seeming unfeeling fathers. Rather than being offered the example of a father who takes his wife's emotions seriously by responding to her with compassion, attention or sensitivity, many boys watch as their fathers are frustrated and powerless in the face of their wives' emotional productions, often quietly ignoring or blatantly ridiculing their mothers: "She's out of control; I'm going for a walk." "You know women; they carry on about everything." "Don't pay any attention to your mother. She's just having a bad day."

In observing these transactions, boys get the distinct impression that there isn't a positive payoff for having a life of emotion. Instead, the message they get is that to have feelings and express them is to lay yourself open to being abused, dismissed, or ridiculed, particularly by men. Indeed, in an unconscious collusion that supports the suppression of their feelings, both men and boys often make fun of feelings wherever they see them occurring.

Because in general they deny that anything beneficial could be happening at the emotional level, men tend to treat women's emotional transactions like adolescent self-indulgences—as if women were aging high school girls who never learned how to get off the phone. In their somewhat simplistic reactions to women, men are oblivious to the fact that interactions on an emotional level also have impact on every other level of existence, including achievement, success, physical health, and spiritual well-being.

Unlike women, men don't tend to acknowledge that how we feel about what we do, or how we feel *when* we do it, greatly affects what we can undertake or the success of our efforts. For example, women assume that a woman who's worried about her ailing child may have difficulty concentrating at work. But men rarely make similar assumptions about themselves. They don't, for example, presume that a man who's had a fight with his girlfriend, a midnight conversation with his possessive mother, or an argument about politics on the golf course with his father also will be functionally impaired.

This point of view is ridiculous. Whether we consciously acknowledge it or not, we are all continually affected by emotional events. (This, of course, is why, without consciously defining it, men fear their feelings. Instinctively they know that their emotional state *will* affect their performance and, rather than having their functioning affected, they have evolved in such a way that, through the suppression of their feelings, they have protected their capacity to function.)

Even in families where parents do encourage boys to express their emotions, the larger cultural expectations of maleness may well prevent a boy from really being in touch with his feelings. I'm reminded, for example, of a family in which the thirteen-year-old son's unsettled feelings about entering high school were all but obscured in spite of his parents' genuine concern. Even when his father specifically asked him how he felt about making the change from a small private day school to the gigantic inner city high school he was about to attend, all he could say was "fine." Yet that same week in a school writing assignment he wrote about a character who was "so nervous about starting high school, because he was afraid he wouldn't be able to do the work, that he was dreaming up fantastic ways to run away and avoid it."

Even in his family's encouraging environment, this boy was unable to identify his fear, let alone express it. As is so often the case with males, his emotional truth came out indirectly. Although he was able to relieve his anxiety to a certain extent by giving fictionalized expression to it, he wasn't able to experience his feelings consciously, nor, as a result, to receive any solace about them from his family. He had learned—from TV, movies, and other kids—how as a male he should behave.

Whether young or old, men are victims of their own P.R. It's almost as if they believe that if you don't talk about how awful you feel, the feelings will just dry up and blow away. This belief enables men to maintain the emotional status quo so they don't have to venture out into the discomfort of exploring their feelings. But it has the unfortunate concomitant effect of making men even more separate from the emotional interactions which could actually bring them some relief.

It is because of being exposed to such a limited male emotional repertoire that even if they desire to express themselves, most men will struggle to gain access to the full range of their emotions for virtually the rest of their lives regardless of the "permission" granted by women or society at large. The example of eons is far more psychologically powerful than any last-minute invitation to change, no matter how warmly women may extend it.

The Mother Hangover

"My mother couldn't stand any display of emotion from me. When I was sixteen, my family's cat had to be put to sleep because we couldn't afford the operation to save its life. I was sobbing my eyes out on the way home from the vet and all my mother could say to me was, `Oh for God's sakes stop crying, it's only a cat.'"

-Photographer, 36

Men also have a difficult time believing women when we say that we really do want them to get in touch with their feelings because they unconsciously recall that their mothers were among those who, early in childhood, cooperated or, more than likely, even instigated the suppression of their feelings. Thus, rather than being able to think of his mother as the single continuous sanctuary in which he was permitted the unpermissable—feeling—he remembers that after the emotionally indulgent early days of childhood, his mother, too, joined the ranks of those who wanted him to be "a brave boy" or a "real man."

Thus any man who entertains the notion of revealing his feelings to the woman in his life is up against the memory that in the past the woman in his life, his mother, didn't really want him to have feelings. As a result, his unconscious contemporary expectation is that the woman who loves him now will also prefer him to remain unfeeling. As one man stated point blank, "Why am I afraid to cry? Because my mother didn't like it when I cried. She sent me to my room and shut the door, and left me alone there for hours."

Or, as another man told me, "My mother always spanked me when I cried, so I'd learn to take it 'like a man.' Don't be a sissy," she'd say, "or I'll spank you some more." In the course of growing up, men are moved abruptly from "feeling it all" in infancy to the enforced suppression of emotion when suddenly they're supposed to be "brave little boys," to the directive from women when they're adults to "let it all hang out." In the background of all these chapters, an out of focus photo of Mom still looms, and men, unconsciously recalling the emotional roller coaster ride they've been on, don't know how to proceed.

If You don't Feel It, You Don't Have to Deal with It

"The challenge is, how do we bring our woundedness into the world and still remain functional?"

-Businessman, 48

Men are cut off from their feelings not only because they have been socialized to be that way, but also because there are some significant payoffs for staying in emotional Antarctica. Simply, what you don't feel, you don't have to deal with, emotionally or any other way. Because they've suppressed their feelings for so long, men are unconsciously terrified of what might occur if they did experience their feelings. So, without being consciously aware of it, they're afraid that if they do become emotional, they'll totally crumble, collapse, and shred into smithereens. Or they'd be overwhelmed and disappear. As one woman's ex-boyfriend said, in a moment of emotional honesty, "I'm afraid if I talk about it, I'll explode. I'll lose control."

Most men don't own up to this of course, but generally speaking they arrange their lives and behaviors in such a way that they avoid stumbling into feelings they're not prepared to have. "I worked the graveyard shift for six years so I didn't have to deal with my wife," admitted a client of mine. "Three months after I changed to days, we had broken up." Intuitively they know they're not equipped to handle strong feelings and so, one way or another, they avoid the situations for which they're not prepared.

In particular, men fear they won't be able to move from the feeling state back into the rational state; that having tiptoed into the oozy quagmire of emotion, they will be lost there forever like gibbering idiots, unable to find their way back to solid ground where things are reasonable and sane. As one man in therapy said to me, almost defiantly, "O.K., now I can feel. But don't make me feel any more or I'll never be able to go back to running my hotel."

In general, men seem to have great difficulty in bringing their rational minds to bear on their emotional experience, and in letting their emotional experience affect the logical decisions they make. In other words, they don't know how to trust their feelings because they're usually unable to engage in an internal dialogue between what they're feeling and the conclusions they're able to arrive at through their logical, rational mode of thinking. They don't trust that they can cross back and forth between their emotional and rational minds. (Physiologically there is evidence that this crossing over is more difficult for men than women, but no one has yet suggested that it is impossible.)

Still, because of this lack of practice, men fear the sense of powerlessness that the feeling state creates in them and rarely allow their feelings to impinge on their logic in a way that changes their behavior. Conversely, their logic hardly ever impinges on their feelings in a way that allows them to become more comfortable with their emotions.

The Sacred Cow of the Rational

"What do feelings get you? A lot of tears and wasted time."
-Mechanic, 37

In order to keep themselves away from the feeling experience, men engage in a number of psychological defenses. The first is a glorification of the rational. Instead of attempting to welcome and integrate the emotional, men tend to glorify the rational because they so seldom have a chance to see that the emotional process leads to resolution. They know that logic, negotiation, bargaining, and mediation work. Civilization was built on these male functions. In business, politics, and war men come together, lay out the facts, analyze them, and arrive at decisions that bring results. But their experience with emotional process is still extremely limited, their sense of its efficacy almost nonexistent.

I'm reminded of a very successful real estate developer who went bankrupt because he didn't trust his "gut feelings" about a particular contractor whose credentials met, point by point, his logical requirements. He had "an instinct" about the contractor, "a hunch" that he should pull out of the deal, but he never acted on his intuition. As a result, his project turned out to be a financial disaster and eventually he had to file for bankruptcy.

As this example demonstrates, men tend not to understand that when an emotion is honored, new insight can be arrived at, and, as a result, new consequences can occur. Could men acknowledge their feelings and allow them to affect their rational minds, they might come up with solutions that are even more successful than the conclusions they achieve through rationality alone. But without being able to initiate this internal dialogue, men tend to use their rationality to try to keep their emotions at bay: "I shouldn't be feeling abandoned, I think I'll go out and have dinner." "I shouldn't be so upset because my girlfriend is leaving, I'll go work out at the gym." "I shouldn't be panicked because my business is failing. I'll schedule a new round of meetings."

Because men so infrequently experience the benefits of engaging in the emotional process, they tend to discount emotions altogether, to say (or at least feel) that expressing emotions is silly or useless. "It happened twenty years ago; what's the point of talking about it?" "She's gone; why cry about it now? She won't come back." "Talking doesn't do any good; it won't change anything." "Going through all these feelings just gets me all riled up, what's the point?"

Reaction Formation:
The Great Psychological Shell Game

"I like being a man—everything is so clean. You don't have to get all balled up with feelings the way women do."
                                                                    -Bachelor, 56

Along with glorifying the sacred cow of the rational, men hide from their true feelings through a reaction formation about their emotions. A reaction formation is a psychological defense in which a person discovers a frightening or unacceptable aspect of himself and then, in reaction, acts out its opposite. Thus, in reaction to what they might actually discover to be true (namely, that they have many and very intense feelings), many men tell themselves they're lucky not to feel, that they're fortunate not to be distracted the way women are by their wildcat emotions. Because they're afraid that a full-on experience of their feelings would be like letting a monster out of a cage, would turn their lives totally unmanageable, they talk themselves out of their feelings. In fact, they reinforce their reaction formation by glorifying the suppression of feelings. A classic in this genre was Ernest Hemingway, who, when asked what he was afraid of, said, "'Fraid a nothing."

This male penchant to deny and rearrange feelings still operates constantly and often in the most subtle of ways. For example, one of my male client's most poignant memories of his father has to do precisely with his father's suppression of emotion. As he tells it: "My father had nine children—and worked 365 days a year checking brakes on the railroad. He'd get up for 5 a.m. Mass, then go to work. He did this every day for 50 years—and never once complained. He was a saint. I wish I could be more like him."

While this memory is in one respect a beautiful honoring of his father's steadfastness, it is also a reaction formation, a celebration of the suppression of feelings: his father suffered, but refused to feel. It obviously hadn't occurred to my client to view as tragic the fact that his father was unable to express his sadness and anger about the magnitude of his burden. In fact, it was his very inability to do so which made him heroic in his son's mind.

Conversion: Trading in on a Safer Model

"I'm proud of you, son, you're doing great on those crutches."
"But who's going to love me, Dad?"
                    -Father and Vietnam vet amputee son

Another thing that keeps men from coming into the full range of their feelings is that they've been taught to convert their unacceptable feelings into acceptable ones. Starting in boyhood, men are encouraged to express certain feelings—pride and anger primarily—and then suppress all the rest. Thus, when unacceptable feelings such as sorrow, anxiety, fear, pity or tenderheartedness do arise, they're quickly, unconsciously converted into acceptable ones. This translation is accomplished so quickly, like a card trick, that a boy never comes to realize that he is actually sad or afraid. Instead, his sorrow becomes anger, for example, while disappointment may masquerade as misplaced pride. It is through these subtle and sometimes not so subtle conversions of any emotion whatsoever into either pride or anger that the scared and sorrowful boy of childhood becomes the angry young man, the ego strutting adult male.

When a man converts his fear to courage, his anxiety to bravado, his rage to condescension and his sorrow to self-pity, he is having a quasi-emotional experience even though he isn't expressing the appropriate emotion. This gives him a measure of emotional release, enough to create the illusion that he does, indeed, have emotions, without delivering him to the uncomfortable emotions that occur at the vulnerable end of the spectrum.

Many men convert the entire array of their repressed emotions into humor, literally making a joke out of everything. Rather than expressing any differentiated feelings, they develop a jocular, sarcastic, Good Time Charlie, or self-deprecating personality that is in itself the embodiment of the conversion.

But when it comes to conversion, pride is the ultimate substitute emotion. Since pride and vulnerable feelings are antithetical, in lieu of experiencing the whole range of negative or vulnerable feelings, men choose to feel pride. Instead of crying his heart out about all his buddies who died beside him in the trench, the soldier comes home from war and wears the Purple Heart with pride. Or the star athlete has pride about not giving in to unbearable pain when he breaks his leg on the 20 yard line. And the businessman father has pride about his son's achievements instead of loving him.

In essence, male pride requires that a man eliminate his real feelings in order to "act like a man" in the eyes of his peers—no matter what his sufferings may be. While pride as we have known it holds a certain elegance for men and provides an emotional container for their joys and sufferings, it is also, we must acknowledge, the medium through which men have cheated themselves—and women—from the rich experience of seeing the full tapestry of their multicolored emotions.

But pride isn't the only substitute emotion for men. The other male catch-all emotion is anger. In the emotional conversion game, when men are afraid, they will most likely convert their fear into anger. Saddled with responsibilities which at times overwhelm them, ashamed of their feelings of inadequacy, facing challenges which frequently baffle them and bearing the vast array of burdens that women both consciously and unconsciously deliver to them, men *are* often afraid. But they're not allowed to admit it. Trapped in the bind of feeling a feeling—fear—which they are forbidden by the male role to express, men often become physical or mental bullies, kicking the dog, yelling at the kids, shoving their fists through the wall.

Thus aggression, rage, bullying, manipulating, and controlling all are alternate faces of the fears which men are unable to express.

Displacement of Feelings

"I'm not angry at you. I'm upset because I can't find my swim goggles."

-Businessman, 29, after his girlfriend moved out of their home

Along with converting their more complex feelings to acceptable ones, men also simply displace a great many feelings. That is, rather than expressing fear, sorrow, tenderness, disappointment in the arenas in which they actually apply, men divert these emotions and experience them somewhere else. The male obsession with organized sports, for example, epitomizes this kind of emotional displacement.

Stated simply, men use sports in order to have an emotional experience. Whether playing or watching, their involvement in sports becomes a way of vicariously expressing a wide range of feelings: loyalty, passion, power, camaraderie, disappointment, and exhilaration to name but a few. Whether running down the field, sitting it out on the bench in a numbered jersey, cheering from the bleachers, or poised on the edge of the couch or the bar stool, beer in hand and glued to the TV, men get to feel anxiety, excitement, frustration, and fear without having to experience any of these emotions as they might apply directly and more uncomfortably in the circumstances of their personal lives. It's easier to be angry because the Dodgers are losing than it is to be mad because your wife has a headache for the 14th night in a row, to yell your head off at a boxing match than to have a confrontation with your teenage son about the ungodly hours he's been keeping. Without being consciously aware, men have agreed that sports will be the arena in which many of their feelings will be surreptitiously transacted, and although, in general, women hate it that men are so caught up with sports, they tolerate it because unconsciously they recognize that here men can have an experience that at least vaguely represents an emotional life.

But it isn't only through the great diversion of sports that men displace their feelings. Men also pump out displaced emotions by overreacting to little, ridiculous, and insignificant things. Since men frequently can't get a handle on their real emotions, they'll harp about almost anything else: that Johnny didn't take out the trash, that the kids left their skates on the driveway, that their favorite shirt got shrunk in the wash. What they're saying, without saying it, is that they're in pain about something but they can't identify the feeling and they certainly can't put it into words.

Without realizing the deeper implications of what they're doing, both men and women put up with this frustrating and sometimes even downright silly behavior. It's as if we all know it refers to something important, although we're not sure what—and so we all just go along with it.

While emotional displacement serves a valuable function for men, it often reaches the level of the ridiculous and always precludes the possibility of real emotional development. For example, a middle-aged executive, timidly courting a woman he had long admired, blew up at her because her mailbox, in which he had put a letter to her, had that very morning been stolen by vandals. He gave her a royal chewing out about how careless and irresponsible she was for having her mailbox stolen, instead of telling her how disappointed he was that she hadn't received his letter. As he confessed to me later in a softer, more vulnerable moment: "It was the first time in twenty years

I'd done such a vulnerable thing, and I just couldn't handle it when she didn't get my letter."

Another man, an orthodontist, became furious because, while he was working 90 hours a week, his wife couldn't seem to find time to go to the hardware store and pick up "one lousy bathroom fixture" for the dream house they were building. In fact, she'd been running all over town doing dozens of errands for the house—she just hadn't gotten to that one. What her husband was really upset about wasn't the light fixture, but that she'd never acknowledged that he'd been working so hard for so many years that they could finally build their dream house. But that isn't what he expressed—he hadn't the foggiest idea what he was really feeling, and so, instead of asking for appreciation for his long years of effort, he exploded because his wife didn't make it to the hardware store.

This was clearly a substitute communication, a trivial complaint that took the place of a real, more sensitive grievance. As is so frequently the case, men carry on about piddly little things because the vulnerability of complaining about—and hence discovering—the real things they're troubled about is far too frightening.

Loss of Identity: Men's True Fear

"Feeling, it's scary. It's being so exposed . . . on all fronts."
                                                    -Screenwriter, 36

Ultimately, men engage in these psychological defenses because they are terrified that in being encompassed by their feelings they will in a sense be robbed of their very identity as men. Since men see their identity in some incontrovertible way as consisting of the suppression of feeling, they see themselves participating in the male enclave by virtue of maintaining a non-feeling stance. As they unconsciously conceptualize it, to be in a state of emotional suppression is to have an identity, to belong, while to be in a state of emotional expression is to be identitiless, an outcast.

But men's terror of emotional expressiveness goes much farther than the simple fear that if they become expressive they will no longer be "one of the boys." Since the expression of feelings has always been identified as a female trait, men unconsciously fear that to reveal their feelings will turn them, in a sense, into women. The expression of feelings and emotional vulnerability are, in fact, the direct antithesis of what men expect themselves to be: forceful, direct, aggressive, impact-creating. In a word: male. As one man said in therapy, "I'm going through so many feelings, I'm afraid I'll turn into a girl."

This fear is actively reinforced by other men who ridicule men who have feelings because they're terrified of their own feelings. Such men hold to the male emotion-suppressing identity because they don't want the solid wall of male denial to come tumbling down and also because they desperately need to believe that choosing a life without feelings is the proper thing to do. Because men have cut themselves off from their feelings, they need and want the validation of other men, a confirmation that they have done the right thing because their value as men rests in that choice and its consequences. In the male world of power, it is the heartless, ruthless controlling men who are willing to step on and over everyone who tend to rise to the top. Their sense of self-worth is specifically and narrowly defined by this climb to power because they have no emotional life that could provide them with an alternate view of their worth.

Therefore the possibility that a man could have an emotional life and still be a real man is the ultimate threat to male identity; and a man who seeks to find his way into the world of emotions not only faces the internal difficulties I've been discussing, but must do so in the face of real, often vicious ridicule by other men who don't want their entrenched position threatened. Men have agreed, colluded, and confirmed that aggression, power, assertion, success, and the suppression of emotions are the true components of authentic male identity to be acted out at every level of experience.

Nowhere is the aggressiveness of the male identity more perfectly symbolized than in the erect penis, the physical emblem of male power which is oriented toward assertion and embodies male capacity to function. In keeping with this biological metaphor, a man's internal emotional code has also been designed to reflect this assertive position—to get before he is gotten, defend before he is decimated, destroy before he is attacked. In such a psychological set-up, men must categorically eschew their emotions, for the disclosing of feelings, rather than consolidating a man into the power position of being prepared to attack, delivers him to the frighteningly vulnerable position of being open to attack.

Therefore, for a man to express his emotions is very threatening indeed. To reveal the whole range of the contents of his psyche would rob him of his identity, make him feel flimsy and unprotected, vulnerable—too much like a woman. In a sense the male position is: If I express my feelings then I'll be open to attack, (i.e., female) whereas if I don't say how I feel, even if I'm in pain, I won't open myself to possible breakdown or assault, so I can still remain a man.

In dealing with such frightful alternatives, a young client said that shortly after he started living with his girlfriend, he came across some photographs of her former lover. "I got terribly upset, became completely dysfunctional. I felt like a jerk for loving her, as if I was a nobody, as if there wasn't anything special about me or us. I was so embarrassed about my feelings that it was impossible to tell her. Women are allowed to get upset about things like that, but men aren't suppose to. That's why I'm here. I can tell you, a stranger, but I certainly couldn't tell her."

As this story demonstrates, for a man, the revelation of feelings represents not only unfamiliar behavior, but also a threat to the very essence of his male identity—who he sees, remembers, and expects himself to be. And since a sense of identity is at once both such a potent and a fragile thing, men are terrified at the thought of taking on attributes that would further dilute a male identity that has already been encroached upon by women to such a frightening degree that men are already feeling queasy and off balance. For men, the male identity has been so subjected to redefinition of late that, in a sense, suppression of feelings is the only thing that still differentiates men from women.

That's one of the reasons why, even though male identity has been roundly assaulted recently, men who are more sensitive than the norm, who do have access to their feelings, who can have conversations about emotions, who enjoy so-called feminine things, (music, architecture, art, arranging flowers) and who could, therefore, become the healing role models for the future, are still shunned. These men are still seen as weird, somehow out of the norm, social misfits, or, in one of society's ugliest epithets, "faggots."

Indeed, the evolution of male identity is seriously stymied by a generalized, deeply-internalized homophobia. Men have been taught that to have feelings, to be tender, to live from, by, or through their emotions, to function to any significant degree from their feminine side, is to put themselves in jeopardy of being declared to be feminine to excess. To be soft, feeling, or sensitive has meant, *ipso facto*, that you are a sissy, a homosexual, a fate that in many quarters of our culture is deemed worse than death.

Thus the man who seeks to expand his identity as a man along the very lines being pleaded for by women is defeated before he begins. He's not supposed to be hard; he's definitely not supposed to be soft. Who and how is he supposed to be?

The Female Conspiracy: How Women Collude in Keeping Men from Their Feelings

5

"You wonder what I'm feeling? You want me to express my feelings? My emotional existence is so tentative that if anyone else starts taking up the emotional room it's all over for me. I don't have a rat's chance in hell of expressing my feelings."

-Attorney, 44

In spite of proclaiming that we want men to feel, women themselves play a role in keeping men cut off from their feelings. We do this by complaining and by emotionally colluding with men in a variety of ways to keep men unexpressive.

As we know, women have been asking for male transformation for a long, long time. This, in a way, is the gift of our complaining. Through our discontent, we have implicitly, if not always politely, been inviting men to discover their own feelings and to express them in such a way that we can have emotionally satisfying relationships with them.

But while complaining has its place, rather than encouraging men to dare the unfamiliar, it has affected men in a manner something akin to assault with a cattle prod. Instead of allowing men to explore their vulnerability, it has caused them to dig their heels even deeper into the mudbanks of resistance.

Complaining is an interesting psychological phenomenon. Like many of men's psychological tricks, complaining is a form of conversion. Women complain instead of asking for what they want because asking is a high level and high risk emotional undertaking—you need to know what you really want and you need to chance being rejected. Through complaining, women protect themselves. They get to announce that something's wrong and therefore get the relief of articulation, and they get to protect themselves by not taking the risk of asking.

Complaining isn't *de facto* bad for we always feel close to whoever we feel safe enough to complain to. Disclosure, sharing vulnerabilities, is a major path to intimacy. In fact, one of the primary forms of women's intimacy with each other has been complaining. Talking about our pains, hurts, betrayals, and deprivations, discussing the emotional inaccessibility of the men in our lives, carrying on about how men don't come through—these are but a few from the vast repertoire of complaints that women dish out with each other. Through complaining, women bond. Complaining glues us together. We take comfort in knowing that our best girlfriends, sisters, mothers, and office co-workers are also being ignored, frustrated, and emotionally deprived, that nobody else is out there having the wonderful relationship that we ourselves don't have. So when women complain to each other, they're building a bond with each other.

When women complain to the men in their lives they're also attempting to build some kind of connection. Since men have such a hard time having an emotional encounter, women often resort to complaining about that. Women focus, in their complaints, on what men haven't done, said, or felt, and in the very process of talking about their discontents, generate at least a limited kind of emotional exchange. In a very familiar male-female scenario, women complain about men's lack of emotions, men react defensively, and some degree of emotional intensity occurs.

Thus the woman who nags her husband for never calling to let her know where he is and, by complaining, finally gets him to scream at her, has generated an experience that shows he really does have feelings. She feels better not just because she's complained, but because when he reacts, she's finally managed to see some of his real feelings, even if they're negative. A passionate encounter of whatever kind is better in most women's eyes than no encounter at all. A woman would rather that a man blow up than be left out in the cold of his silent male detachment. Since women's complaining gets men riled up, it's one of the only kinds of emotional encounters women can lure men into. No wonder women indulge in it so often.

Unfortunately, in an unconscious effort to get even the smallest degree of emotional satisfaction, women rely on these second-rate emotional manipulations all too often. Instead of learning how to express the praise, delight, admiration, and appreciation that could deepen their encounters with one another, both men and women resort to the lowest common denominator level of emotional exchange that complaining and reacting to complaining are. Because men and women still don't know how to create the touching emotional interchange, women complain, and, like trained dogs, men bark back at women's complaining.

The Barrage of Language

"How do we want you to help us? Not by criticizing and complaining. Our fathers did enough of that."
-Marketing executive, 46

Additionally, rafts of complaints of any sort, but about men's verbal ineptitude in particular, serve only to exacerbate the problem, because when women launch into their barrages of complaining, language itself becomes an instrument of attack instead of the road to union that women insist it could be. "Everything would be better if only you'd talk," we keep saying, and then verbally bash him for the feeble attempts he makes.

So it is that instead of being a medium a man feels comfortable in exploring, words become the very weapons with which women keep men closed off and defensive. As a male friend said to his wife in my presence, "If you want my opinions or feelings about something, don't ridicule me or shut me down when I give it."

When women attack men for their inability to use language it does nothing to facilitate men's ability to develop the use of language for feelings. That's why at this point in history, far from being interested in learning the language of women in order to communicate better, many men are alienated and even enraged by language. That's what they're really expressing with all their negative comments about women's predilection for talking, for verbal exchange. "She talks my ear off. She's a motor mouth. She's a nag." These epithets all refer to women's assault on men with language. In much of men's experience, words haven't had a healing effect. Instead they've been used to point out the issues, failures and distance that separate men from women, and to divide men from the love of women whose words, used well, could be a balm to their spirits.

This attack-by-language has a tragic history for men, since for so many men language was the weapon of assault in childhood. Although in their romantic relationships, many men recreate an experience of verbal abuse they endured with their mothers, it is far more often in their relationships with verbally abusive fathers that this pattern originates. Because of the competition inherent in the father-son relationship, many fathers beat up and put down their sons with words. Comments from "You don't know how to mow the lawn right" to "You don't know what you're talking about. You're worthless" are so devastating to a boy's personality that he must defend his ego against them in the only way he knows how, which is by turning them off and not taking them in.

It's because words were so painful to so many men in childhood that in adulthood they feel so alienated from them and why "communication" is the most volatile issue in adult intimate relationships. Without remembering the source or magnitude of their pain, men try in love relationships to both live through and avoid the verbal encounters in which they feel belittled and powerless. In a sense, this closing off to words is the best thing a man can do for himself, the only way he can defend himself against emotional assault. This walling-off is a prime male psychological defense, one so ingrained that it's now described as "the way men are."

Unfortunately, the fact that in general men have found it so difficult to take words in has had the tragic side effect of closing them off to even the words that could heal their phobia of language. Their very defense keeps them from hearing the words of praise and encouragement that could change their ideas not only of themselves, but also of language itself. But since so many men are unable to take words in deeply, they continue to be deprived of the transformational experience that could bring them into a closer, more comfortable emotional proximity to women.

The All-American Mating: Passive Aggressive Men and Hysterical Women

> "*Whenever we tried to talk, I would end up in tears and he would leave.*"
>
> *-Editor, 39*

Another way women facilitate the problem is by forgetting that, when it comes to an emotional encounter of any kind, men and women are generally approaching it from opposite ends of the spectrum. Women desire it and feel comfortable with it, whereas men find it difficult, dangerous, and mysterious. Because of the verbally-oriented position women occupy on the continuum of emotional expression, they generally assume that an emotional encounter isn't nearly as hard for men as it actually is. While instinctively women do know that the emotional experience is more difficult for men, they can never quite believe it's as hard as it actually is. And since women love the verbal emotional exchange, they also don't believe that men won't too, if only they'd give it a chance. Thus both intentionally and surreptitiously women constantly force men into the uncomfortable position of engaging with them emotionally without realizing that they first have to make it safe for men to join them in the engagement.

Part of the difficulty here is that women lose or have never gained sight of the fact that emotional safety is the absolute *sine qua non* of emotional disclosure. Through their practice of emotional exchange, women have created a matrix of emotional safety among themselves in which they can operate freely with their emotional disclosures. This safety consists of the unconscious acknowledgment that emotions are fragile and have to be respected. Within this context women can talk and listen, weep and celebrate with one another; but even among themselves, if respect and safety are withdrawn, women can shut down.

This principle of safety has never really been applied to women's relationships with men. Because of their unconscious notions that men are either invincible or endlessly resilient, women tend to be less careful in conducting their emotional encounters with men.

In addition, women's insistence on drawing men forcibly into the emotional fray puts men off even further. Here's a typical example: She: "Talk to me. You never talk to me." He: "Yes I do. But right now I need to go to the store." She: "How can you do that when we need to talk?" He: "So what do you want to talk about?" She: "Anything. Just talk to me." He: "You drive me crazy. I'm going to the store."

The woman opens the drama by making an emotional statement; in response, the man withdraws. The man's withdrawal elicits an even more demanding invitation from the woman. This further threatens the man, and causes him to shut down even more. His shutting down accelerates the woman's emotional output to the point of exasperation or hysteria.

Thus develops the vicious cycle in which so many couples go round and round, year after year. Women insist, men resist and in the attempted emotional encounter the man and woman have missed one another once again.

This particular emotional spiral is a classic among American matings which, because of traditional socialization, are typically pairings between overly emotional females and emotionally suppressed males. Since, as we have seen, boys are directed to repress their feelings and girls are encouraged to express theirs, by the time we all get to the altar, the blueprint for male-female interaction has already been deeply engraved. Men and women have virtually no choice but to enact what has already been drummed into them. In adult relationships, this has the consequence of artificially polarizing men and women, with men maintaining their emotional repression and women behaving in an emotionally expressive and emotionally demanding way. While women do have the capacity to be more than emotional freak-out queens and men the ability to be more than feelingless automatons, when the sexes get together, they will most likely act out their socialized predilections.

Unfortunately this dynamic of polarization occurs in virtually all male-female intimate relationships. Thus even a woman who may be seen by her female friends to be extremely unemotional, will tend in relationship to her husband or male romantic partner to occupy the emotionally expressive position. Because of sexual stereotyping, men are generally forced into enacting the cool role and women the hot. This is still the basic emotional dynamic in male-female relationships, and when it is further exacerbated by too many trips on the passive-aggressive-hysterical merry-go-round, both men and women can become incredibly discouraged.

Because of the effects of this deeply engrained polarity, instead of viewing the other sex with sympathy or admiration, men tend to view women–and women, men–as the enemy. Men think women should be more like them, cooler, able to resist every passing emotional drama, and women are convinced that men should be more like women, moved to the core by almost everything. In order to find a way out of this disheartening morass, we will have to admit that maintaining this configuration restricts men to occupying the non-feeling position, and women to the role of hysterical, dissatisfied complainers. Unless we address this tragic stalemate of affairs, it will continue indefinitely.

Tell Me, Don't Tell Me

"Most women don't know how to deal with a man's sensitivity, let alone how to bring it out."
                              -Real estate entrepreneur, 37

Despite the language barrier and although this is perhaps the farthest thing from their instinctual reaction, men *are* trying to express their feelings. This comes through in their efforts to "figure out" what women want and in their attempts to say, albeit haltingly and awkwardly, the things women keep asking them to say. Men have tried but their efforts often haven't brought them the rewards of intimacy and reconciliation that they too want, because women don't know how to respond to men when they finally do deliver their feelings. Unconsciously men know this; they sense that should they expose themselves, women will be shocked, disgusted, or dismayed, and might abandon them.

For example, after being repeatedly scolded by his wife for not complimenting her, one man began consistently to tell her she looked beautiful, only to have her respond by saying, "you've got to be kidding; I look horrible," or, "how can you say that; I've got these giant bags under my eyes."

When he got discouraged by her negative responses, he stopped complimenting her, and she started complaining once again that he never complimented her. He explained that he'd been trying but she'd shut him down, that it felt awful to try when she wouldn't receive his praise, and that, as a result, he'd given up. "You don't understand," she said, "I only want you to tell me I look beautiful when I feel beautiful, otherwise it'll make me feel worse."

"You're asking the impossible," he said. "How can I possibly know when you're feeling beautiful? To me you're beautiful all the time. Besides, I want to express *my* feelings, not just rubber-stamp yours."

What I've discovered in talking to a great many men is that even when they do make their best efforts to communicate their feelings, their efforts often don't garner the kind of response they were led to believe they would get. This isn't just because of the ineptitude of men's attempts. For lurking below many women's seemingly straightforward request for more emotional expressiveness from men is a surprising dirty secret: women are actually ambivalent about men revealing their emotions.

While we may think we want to hear how a man feels about us—like the woman in the story who wanted compliments—we may have a limited capacity to receive what we finally get. Or we may be downright afraid to hear what a man may have to say about his life or himself. For at the same time we're asking men to be emotional, to open their submerged and tender vulnerabilities, we often really don't know how to deal with them when they accept the invitation and start spilling their guts.

For example, one woman who had sensed that for years her husband had been holding back because of some emotional secret, was horrified when, after years of prodding, he told her that in his adolescence he had a very strong sexual attraction to his younger sister. His feelings for her, which he had never acted out, had been the only emotions that he had been able to feel in his troubled family. Instead of feeling closer to him because of his sensitive revelation, his wife was disgusted, called him a pervert, and said she couldn't believe she had married someone with such a "filthy secret" in his past.

Another man, risking disclosure of his feelings of sexual

inadequacy, found himself immediately shut down by his wife. "How can you expect me to listen to such things and still think of you as a man?" she said. And another man, talking about the emptiness of his many sexual conquests in the past, was told point blank: "I don't want to hear this; I want to believe I'm the only woman you've ever made love to."

While disclosures of a sexual nature are invariably extremely sensitive to both men and women and need to be discussed with great care, they do constitute the locus of some of our deepest vulnerabilities and are a legitimate subject for deepening intimacy in relationships. But even when the topic is less volatile, men find themselves being repeatedly shut down.

A young man whose wife was always encouraging him to reveal his feelings told me, "I totally broke down when my wife told me she was pregnant. I felt overwhelmed about the huge responsibility and told her that, while I was thrilled, I was also feeling very scared. Would I be a good father? Could I make enough money? What would a baby do to our relationship? Before I could even finish, she had a fit that I was crying because she wanted me to be strong for all of us."

Later, when I spoke to his wife, she said to me privately, "It's strange. I fell in love with Steve because he wasn't a macho jerk like my father, but when he started to cry, I looked at him lying there on the bed and thought to myself, Why can't he be strong like my father? If he's such a wimp, who's going to protect me and our baby?"

Another man discussed his desire with his wife to go mountain climbing and was told point blank: "Forget it; I'm not sitting home every Saturday preparing to be a widow."

What these vignettes reveal is that despite women's stated desire for men to reveal their feelings, we tend to react in a way that insures that men will continue to play out the old male role of holding the world together and keeping their feelings in. We don't know what to do with the man who is weak, who cries, who has emotional needs. Should we comfort him, or should we reinforce his "manhood" by taking the age-old position that he should pull himself together and "behave like a man?"

This surprising truth, that women don't want men to be emotional, is one I encounter again and again in therapy. Women come in with their partners, begging them to "get in touch with their feelings" and then when the men begin to, they freak out. In fact, just recently another therapist revealed to me the same scenario. When the husband of a woman who had been begging him to "be real" and "get to his feelings" showed up in therapy and broke into wailing primal pain, she was so overwhelmed that she walked out of the session and decided to leave him the very same day.

Payoffs for Ambivalence

"In order to be kinder, I need a woman who can allow me to be kind."

-*Restaurateur, 43*

Women have difficulty with men's revelation of feelings because in general, we don't think of men's emotional disclosures as being like our own emotional outpourings—just an "expression of feelings." Instead, we tend to see men's emotional output either as a sort of aberrant behavior, a weird exception, or as a communication whose contents will definitely be enacted. This, of course, is because unconsciously (and often consciously) women view men (as men do too) as creatures of action. Thus when her husband threatens to leave her, a woman expects that he actually will, while that same woman may very likely see herself as merely "letting off steam" when she threatens to leave him.

The irony in this is that no matter what sort of feelings women express ("I'm so angry I'll never speak to your mother again," "I hate your guts; I'm going to have an affair") men are expected to hear them not as real threats but simply as "a woman expressing her feelings." Yet, when what is being expressed by a man is clearly only his feelings, when he's broken down because of fear or sorrow that is overwhelming or incomprehensible to him, it's often extremely difficult for women to listen or respond, to simply enter into the emotional experience with him.

One woman said that when her son was born with Down syndrome, "my husband went into a state of uncontrollable grief. He was so broken up. I didn't know what to do. I couldn't think of a single thing to say, or any way to be with him that could begin to touch his pain. I realized then that I had no idea whatsoever what a man needs to hear, or have done for him when he's in such an emotional state. I never did figure out how to comfort him."

Another woman spoke about the pain her husband went through when his twin brother died in Vietnam. Her husband had been able to avoid the draft because of a serious vision problem, and when his brother was killed he felt not only the loss of his brother, but also an overwhelming sense of guilt that he had "gotten away with not having to go to war." He became fixated on his brother's death, spending day after day at the cemetery, and coming home inconsolable. His wife didn't know what to do. "I'd never seen him like that," she said. "I was scared to death by his feelings. He was out of control. I felt totally useless. Finally, in desperation, I sent him to a therapist."

This woman's reaction summarizes how many women feel in the presence of men's feelings—and how, incidentally, many men have traditionally felt in the presence of women who are expressing what feels to men like an excess of feeling. Basically, none of us knows how to marshall the full range of empathy required by such situations, but in the past, because the male role demanded that men suppress their feelings, women have been spared encountering their sense of powerlessness in this regard. In some sense, it's been a relief for women to not have to deal with men and their feelings because we don't know what to do with the man who is feeling.

There are a number of reasons for this. One is that men have been so closed-mouthed about their feelings that women have had virtually no experience in dealing with men in an emotional state. While we've had a lot of experience consoling, counseling, and comforting our women friends in the throes of crisis, most of us haven't seen many men fall apart. As a result, we're not well schooled in responding to the man who is in the anguishing loss of grief, of professional crisis, of failing romance.

In general, we've assumed that the man in question wouldn't collapse or that, if he did, he'd pick himself up. That's what most of our fathers did, and so we really don't know how to respond when, physically or emotionally, a man breaks down in front of us.

But it's not just because women are unfamiliar with the rocky terrain of male emotions, that we're all thumbs when men become emotional. In a way most women can't acknowledge, we really don't want to be exposed to the full range of men's emotions. As a young male accountant lamented to me, "They want you to show them your feelings. But they only want you to show them the feelings they want you to show them."

Over and over men report to me that the women they love want to see only certain feelings—love, tenderness, admiration, minor work irritations, thoughtful concern about themselves and their children. Women don't want to hear, see, or be drawn into empathic engagement when men are terrified, angry, despairing, or trying to bear unbearable sorrows. Since we never imagined the depth and complexity of men's emotional underground, most of us are still ill-prepared to respond. Should we consciously contemplate what might be required to truly respond, we could then understand our own, at times, profound ambivalence, for just as we take men out of their depth emotionally, so they will certainly take us past ours.

Does She or Doesn't She?

"I wanted him to tell me everything, but when he broke down crying about his childhood for four hours on the plane from New York to San Francisco, I was sorry I'd ever asked."

-Woman executive, 31

When it comes to what women want about men and their feelings, we have in a sense fallen for our own P.R., telling ourselves that we want a feeling man without realizing what an unruly beast he may be, and how afraid and unprepared we may be to deal with him. Because in the course of our own evolution we've been acting big and strong and independent, we imagine that we've transcended all the old dependent, security-craving parts of ourselves and are actually ready to stand on an equal emotional footing with men. It's a wonderful idea, but it's impossible to wipe out thousands of years of male-female tradition with a single sweep of the sociological broom.

Thus we find ourselves in the embarrassing position of consciously asserting our independence while unconsciously still wanting to be protected by men. It's as if within every liberated woman there's a desperate, needy, insecure little girl who wants to be spoiled and looked after by daddy. And, because in general women aren't able to acknowledge their unconscious desire to keep men in the protector role or to realize how much emotional safety men's occupying that role has granted them, they find it almost impossible to listen to the kinds of feelings which, when men express them, seem to jeopardize their security.

The fact that men can't really protect women from all life's tragedies is at the root of women's inability to receive a great many of men's feelings. Women want men to keep them safe and to a great extent, women's inability to embrace men in their sensitivity is really an unwillingness to face their own existential situation. We like to think of men as our existential umbrellas, the protective covering that stands between us and the slings and arrows of outrageous fortune. Life is full of pain, suffering, and tragedy that goes beyond our ability to ameliorate or even to comprehend it, and we want men to somehow handle this for us, to provide us with the illusion that life isn't the way it really is.

Since constantly living in a state of feeling out of control to one degree or another is so unsettling, we are continually looking for solutions to this existential unrest. For women this often takes the form of expecting men to bring everything under control so we won't have to endure this endlessly unsettling feeling. The truth is that no one can make the world safe for anyone else. Yet until now, women have been unwilling to look at the fact that this is what they've been unconsciously expecting men to do.

As a result, women keep trapping men in a double bind. On one hand we say, "I want you to be sensitive, to show me your feelings, to cry." On the other hand we say: "Don't expect me to think of you as a real man if you do."

Riding the roller coaster of women's unconscious ambivalence, men just can't win. They can't win if they behave like the men of the past, silent sufferers who hold the world together because then they'll be judged for being unconscious unfeeling brutes, and they can't win if they try to become the sensitive men who express their feelings because women still haven't progressed far enough with their own transformation to be completely at ease with that either.

Since so many women are in denial about their subterranean ambivalence, men feel constantly tricked when they make what to them seem Herculean efforts to be vulnerable. They've been taught to believe that if only they'll show their feelings they'll be loved. But when they try, what they all too often experience is that they feel foolish and even more isolated than in the past when emotional isolation was their assumed condition. Rather than bringing them closer to women, their efforts at emotional transparency seem only to bring on another shower of criticism. "There is nothing I've wanted more," one man said to me, with a kind of ineffable longing, "than to be able to express my feelings to a woman. But, frankly, I haven't been able to find such a woman. For a man to be tender, a woman has to be vulnerable too. Ask me what's the Holy Grail for a man in the 90s and I'll tell you: a woman who can really listen, with her mind, with her body, with her heart. Show me a woman like that, and this war-weary knight will ride home singing."

Like men themselves, women haven't recognized men's pain about their emotional suppression. What women have noticed—and complained about—is what they keep missing with men—the emotional experience that could bind them deeply and feelingly to men. But instead of empathizing with men's loss, the one thing that could actually improve the situation, women just keep on being upset that men don't seem to have feelings.

All the while we complain about men's not being able to feel, we are also, without consciously being aware of it, counting

on men not to feel. Now we must humbly and honestly acknowledge that, in spite of our stated desire to the contrary, we have
not only participated in, but actually co-created the cut-off-
from-their-feelings male status quo. For we too are counting on
men to go to war without cracking up, to work every day of their
lives without flinching, to kiss off half their personal wealth and
give up the custody of their children in divorce without so much
as a flicker of an eyelash, and, in the day-to-day emotional realm,
to suppress whatever feelings of theirs that might not be
comfortable to us.

What is perhaps saddest of all about this is that women
continue to hold these expectations (unconscious though they
may be) without thinking about how these very demands can
have no other effect than to cement men in the position that so
totally frustrates women. Strung out by the double bind of
women's simultaneous hopes and fears, expectations and inca-
pacities, men feel personally defeated and utterly unwilling to
risk disclosing any feelings even if they could get in touch with
them. And so long as women count on men "to be men," for just
that long men will be deprived of the only thing that could bring
them closer to women.

6

More Tender Than We Know: The Myth of Male Insensitivity

"It can happen sometimes that a man is so sensitive that he has to become completely insensitive in order to survive."
                                                                -Hotelier, 53

As we've seen, early in life boys get the message that it isn't acceptable to have feelings and so they toss their emotions one by one into the rag and bone pile of their unconscious and start the long inexorable journey to becoming men. In a process known as repression—forgetting and then forgetting you forgot—they develop the emotion-suppressing characteristics that in time will define them as men.

But just because at some point men forget their feelings doesn't mean they stop having them. Instead they gradually, consistently, and thoroughly convince themselves that what hurt didn't hurt, what they were afraid of didn't scare them, and that their longings and heartbreaks were really no big deal.

Through repression, men eventually create an unconscious populated with a myriad of suppressed emotions, while their consciousness becomes ever more simplified and one-dimensional. That's because personality functions like a kind of emotional see-saw—the more the unconscious is weighed down by a diversity of feelings, the more the conscious, visible personality reveals a limited range of feelings. However, repression doesn't solve the problem of what men should do with their feelings. It may get their feelings out of the way for the moment, make them temporarily invisible, but rather than actually delivering men from the nagging inconvenience of emotions, repression actually makes their feelings more intense.

It's a basic psychological truth that when an emotion is repressed, rather than receding or dissipating, it actually gains power and becomes stronger. Like volcanic lava trapped between two layers of rock, a repressed emotion intensifies under pressure until finally it insists on finding release in one form or another. Thus anger, which at its inception might have been delivered as a forthright statement or even a loud-mouthed complaint becomes, in time, an abusive explosion; sorrow about the childhood loss of a parent, unspoken and unwept, becomes an adult depression of immense proportions; and joy about a particular talent, unnurtured and unacknowledged, becomes in adulthood a chronically sarcastic outlook.

Rather than providing any real measure of emotional relief, repression actually produces even more emotional consequences. It's as if the repressed emotions, like slightly anaesthetized mad dogs sleeping in some dark subterranean chamber, are ready to awaken at any moment and come out raging and barking.

The Rip-Off of Repression

*SHE: You feel as much as I do; you're just as sensitive as
I am; you just can't put it into words.*
HE: Yeah. Ain't it a bitch.

Since in the process of socialization men use the psychological defense of repression far more than women, it is men
who find it difficult to come to emotional resolution. Emotional
resolution is a psychological sequence in which feelings are
consciously felt, audibly expressed, and, as a consequence,
subsequently dissipated to such a degree that the person
regains a state of equilibrium. It is this active emotional process,
the cornerstone of personal emotional well-being and interpersonal intimacy, which women seem to engage in more easily
than men, that allows unresolved emotions to be cleared so that
an individual can experience subsequent feelings without a
back-log of unresolved emotions. Women seem to have the
capacity for emotional resolution, to restore themselves to
emotional homeostasis through dialogue; women know how to
"talk things through" until they "feel better," but because of
repression, men rarely get the relief of working through their
feelings and starting again with a clean emotional slate.

As a result, in some sense men are always in a state of
emotional double jeopardy. Since they repress their feelings so
effectively, women can easily assume they're feeling nothing,
when in truth they're feeling (or defending against feeling) not
only the emotions generated by a present event, but also all the
similar feelings which, because of repression, have been collect-
ing unresolved in their unconscious. This is difficult for women
because they often don't have a clue as to what they're missing
with men emotionally, and it's difficult for men because for a
man to feel *in the present moment* is also to open himself to the

vast array of feelings which, unwittingly, he has repressed in the past.

Unlike women, whose socialization allows them to gain immediate relief by expressing their feelings at the time, in opening to feeling men may well subject themselves to an onrush of feeling that seems purely overwhelming, for men have to deal not only with current emotions but also with all the feelings that through repression they have assiduously avoided. Emotionally, men are never up to date. This makes them significantly and distinctly more emotionally vulnerable than women.

While as a consequence of repression it may appear that men are one-dimensional cardboard cut-outs, it isn't true that they're insensitive, as women often mistakenly conclude. In fact, I believe that one of our greatest psychological secrets is that men are far more sensitive than women—not because they have the capacity to feel more, but, rather, since they're so cut off from identifying the feelings they do experience, their emotions tend to pool in the unconscious and become stronger than women's—precisely because they remain unexpressed.

While both men and women may choose to deny it, it has been my experience that unbeknownst to the perpetrator, men can be far more easily injured than women by the slightest word, glance, or sensation of neglect. This is simply because the full magnitude of their previously unrecognized and unacknowledged emotions lies just beneath the surface of their psyches, precariously poised, exquisitely vulnerable to the unexpected stimulus that can set it off.

Most women wouldn't imagine the extraordinary pains from childhood that some men still carry with them. Grieving the loss of intimacy with his wife, a successful Los Angeles businessman recalled to me in tears, "It's such an old, old pain. When I was little my mother always used to come in my room and touch my face in a certain way before I went to sleep. Then one day, when I was about six, she stopped. I was always afraid it was something I'd done to make her stop. I felt as if I'd been cut off from the one thing I could not live without. She broke my heart. I always wondered if my brother missed it as much as I did, but I was afraid to ask."

It is precisely because of the degree of feeling and amount of repression men must constantly live with that men act as emotionally invincible as they do. Since intuitively they're aware of the amount and intensity of feelings they've repressed, men fear that unlocking their repressions could deliver them to a torrent of feeling that could purely overwhelm them. Thus *men have to stay cut off emotionally* in order to protect themselves from the inadvertent release of their feelings and their perhaps unmanageable consequences. As a result, their only protection lies in strengthening their repression.

If degree of protection equals level of vulnerability—and I believe it does—then men's repression of their emotional lives should long ago have given us all a clue as to how extremely sensitive they are. As you will recall, a reaction formation is the acting out of a feeling opposite and in reaction to an emotion which the individual experiences as psychologically threatening. Thus, for example, bravado can be a reaction formation enlisted to dissipate the discomfort of inherent shyness, bragging to counteract a sense of insecurity, and over-effusiveness to compensate for an unacceptable feeling of dislike.

In the same manner, the myth that men are insensitive, indomitable, and just plain tough is one of the greatest reaction formations of all time. As a matter of fact, it is precisely because men are so sensitive that we all go around pretending they're so tough, and until very recently, both men and women have participated in an unconscious collusion to deny that men's sensitivity is really of such a magnitude that they have no choice but protect it.

It shouldn't be such a surprise to discover that men are so sensitive. Men's sensitivity is flagrantly revealed in their biology. A man's penis knows all, shows all, and tells all. A man's excitement and panic, interest and disinterest, guilt and passion are all most graphically registered by his sensitive, intelligent penis. Unlike a woman, a man can never fabricate or falsify his interest or his orgasm, and certainly sexually a man can never keep his feelings to himself. What his heart may not know and his mind may be unable to articulate, his penis will communicate quite readily.

In spite of this really quite graphic physiological statement, men have denied their emotional vulnerability for so long that by now both sexes as good as believe that it really doesn't exist. To the extent that men themselves are responsible for denying how sensitive they are, women certainly do have a right to be frustrated with them, and to complain about how inaccessible they are. It's true that men are remote; it's true they don't express themselves; it's true they come off like statues or barbarians, wise guys, condescending jerks or non-stop performance comedians.

Indeed it is precisely because women know that men are capable of sensitive, emotional responses that we are frustrated. We want to partake of the complexity of feeling, the rich texture of experience that, intuitively, we know is possible with men. Somewhere we know that men are holding out on us. So, of course we're angry. We are angry that men keep shutting us out, behaving as if they don't have any feelings. For somewhere every woman knows that, like the alcoholic, the longer a man denies his true condition, the longer she'll have to wait to have her real experience with him.

The tragedy in all this is that while women legitimately complain that men deny their sensitivity, there's also a part in women unwilling to acknowledge that male sensitivity does indeed exist. To a certain extent, women too would like to go on buying into the myth that men really don't have much in the way of feelings, that they're only interested in sex and/or power.

One of the reasons women hang on to this illusion is that men come out of their armor so rarely that it is genuinely difficult for women to get an idea, let alone maintain a consistent sense, of the emotional vulnerability that exists in every man. Women are shocked from time to time to discover that men too entertain the most intricate and sensitive emotions, that men are taken apart, baffled, or deeply touched by a whole array of what on the surface may appear to be totally inconsequential things.

Many of us can identify with the woman who said to me: "I'm always amazed when my husband tells me that some little thing I've said has totally devastated him. He acts so invincible- -it never seems possible that just my words could wound him." Women's inability to believe is so strong, in fact, that when men do tell us about their vulnerabilities, we often treat such disclosures as flukes or exceptions and not as an individual reflection of the whole range of feelings a man is consistently having, whether, of course, he is keeping conscious track of them or not.

Another woman told me that when she had trouble sleeping because of her husband's snoring, she would often take a blanket and sleep on the couch in the living room. One morning at breakfast her husband said, "It just kills me when you do that. I can't stand it. I'm so lonely in bed without you that I can never go back to sleep."

"I was flabbergasted," she said. "He's always so calm it never occurred to me that he could be so upset over this." Obviously this woman hadn't imagined that beneath her husband's placid exterior lay feelings of such exquisite vulnerability, nor had she ever understood that he suffered a fear of abandonment.

I myself had a lesson in this regard when, many years ago, in the anguishing throes of divorce, I was sitting with an insurance salesman who appeared to have everything together. As he went methodically over the term, life and paid up at sixty-five insurance options, I was thinking self-pityingly, "This guy doesn't know what misery is." Then, in response to a random question of mine, he gradually told me his whole life story: that his wife had had an affair with his brother, that she had gotten pregnant and had a son, that in time he had forgiven her and raised the boy as his own, that the boy, whom in time he had grown to love deeply, had died of leukemia was he was seventeen, that in his death he was left with a welter of confused and overwhelming feelings. By the time the man who was "all together" had finished his story, he was weeping openly and so was I. Like many other women I had been caught up in the notion that men stand somehow above, beyond, or outside human suffering, simply because for the most part they don't let on.

The Missing Piece: Emotional Truth

> *"I wish I could talk to someone about love. In this society, it seems inappropriate for guys to show their true feelings. This is sad."*
>
> *-High School Senior, 17*

Men *don't* let on; they don't allow us to see them in their suffering, don't help us to help them with the uncomfortable painfulness of what they are feeling. Rather they repress, avoid, deflect or convert their feelings, acting out instead of saying in words exactly what's going on with them. This endless emotional mime show of doing everything except verbalizing their feelings leaves women angry, baffled, and at a loss.

Elizabeth, who'd been warmly encouraged by her lover to go on a trip, was shocked when she came back to find that he was "too busy" to see her for almost a week. When they finally got together he admitted that her absence had been "almost unbearable" for him. "I know I wanted you to go," he said, "but when you were gone I couldn't stand it. I fell apart the minute you left town. I was so upset I felt as if I never wanted to see you again."

Elizabeth was lucky—her lover broke through to speaking his feelings. But all too often men omit the single piece of information—their emotional truth—that would reveal the sensitive structure of their inner being. For example, when asked "what's bothering you?" most men will answer first from their bodies: "I'm tired; I've got a backache; my shoulder hurts," rather than going to the emotional material: "Since I didn't get the raise, I'm worried sick about money"; "I'm afraid the lump under my arm *is* malignant"; "The thought of not seeing her ever again is breaking my heart." Such disclosures come often only after a ingenious mixture of delicacy and persistence on the inquiring woman's part. For, when it comes to their emotions, men are generally as closed up as clams. And unless women learn how to wield the emotional clam knife with great sensitivity, men will stay that way.

In the protected environment of psychotherapy, when men finally start to unravel their feelings, what they reveal shatters all male stereotypes. Men's hearts are tender and easily wounded, and often by the most surprising things. One man was devastated, for example, when he saw an ex-girlfriend at a cocktail party with another man. Even though he'd broken up with her two years ago, he couldn't handle it that she'd "replaced" him with another man. "I know this is ridiculous," he said, "but in some sense I really thought she'd be mine forever. The thought of not being the one who watches her wake up, who touches her face every morning. . . it's unthinkable."

Another man talked about how difficult it was for him to be a foreman on his job because he was so sensitive. "I have a terrible time when I have to fire someone," he said. "I can't stop thinking about what they're going through. I think about what this guy's going to have to say to his wife and children and it just tears me up." Yet another was so saddened by the break-up of his best friend's marriage that he went through weeks of sympathetic insomnia. "What can I say? What can I do? I see him falling apart, and I keep thinking, where are the words, what can I say that could even begin to touch him in his pain."

Alex, age forty-eight, and "all grown up," as he said, with grandchildren of his own, was devastated because his mother had chosen to go to his brother's house instead of his for Christmas dinner. In fact, just in talking about it, he broke down crying. "He always got the things I wanted from her," he said. "It's like I'm still waiting for her to be my mother."

Marshall had an irrational blow-out with his sister when she mentioned in passing that she wouldn't be able to attend his daughter's christening. "I just went berserk," he said. "It seems totally crazy now, but my baby girl's a miracle child; she almost died at birth; she's the most precious thing that's ever happened in my life and I needed so bad for my sister to celebrate with me."

These men are all reporting the remarkably intricate assaults from their emotional front lines, slings and arrows of ordinary life that profoundly affect them. Like women, men get upset about the teeniest things even if they—and we—don't believe it. And when it comes to the major issues—war, taxes, terminal illness—where women tend to assume men are solid and can bear up and bear on, men also often feel totally overwhelmed.

"When our son was dying of AIDS, my wife could just sit with him for hours, fixing his blankets, feeding him Jello, wiping his chin. Me, I'd walk into the room for a minute, look at him, crack up, and stumble into the hall just to keep from him seeing me crying. I couldn't do a thing for him, couldn't think of anything to say, I never did. It's been more than a year now; she's pretty much over his death, but I'm still cracking up. Whenever he comes to mind, I just fall apart crying."

Whether it's the serious illness of a child, the loss of a partner through divorce, or unresolved feelings over the death of a parent, men have a much more difficult time bouncing back. Because in an ongoing way men don't continually work through their emotions, they have a tendency to stay marooned at the scene of their last emotional shipwreck. This phenomenon becomes even more exaggerated when devastating life dramas are played out in their midst. In a crisis, men are suddenly thrown out into the lion's den of their emotions, opened up to the real depth of their sensitivity with virtually no preparation whatsoever. For many men emotional experiences of such magnitude are like trips to another planet, journeys to outer space they feel they can never come back from.

In fact, men simply don't recover easily from even the slightest emotional offense. I can't tell you the number of men who tell me how emotionally shredded they feel after a fight with their sweethearts or wives: "She blows up, yells and screams, gets it all off her chest and feels like a million dollars. I feel like I've died and been chopped up in a million pieces. Days, weeks later I'm still picking emotional shrapnel from the wound."

In addition to their suffering about the time it takes to recover, men are also in pain about the awkwardness of their emotional process. They feel a sense of futility in relationships because, since they're generally unacquainted with the process of emotional resolution, they feel as if they'll always be victims of emotions, their own or somebody else's. Although of course they generally can't express this, their frequently stymied or amputated efforts at expression give them an overall feeling of inadequacy, one that only serves to reinforce their instincts to stay away from emotions altogether.

To make matters worse, it is this sense of inadequacy that men fear the most. Thus, when it comes to their emotions, men are victims not only of their inability to feel, but also of the judgments they have about their emotional ineptitude—a most debilitating double whammy.

What further exacerbates the situation is that it's almost impossible for women to believe that men are such emotional basket cases. Because women tend to see men as unemotional, it never occurs to them that perhaps the reason men are so emotionally defended is that at some point they may have been so devastated that they're no longer able to take emotional risks.

We tend to think of men's shut-offness as simply "the way men are," and don't consider that their apparently unemotional state may be the result of an overwhelming emotional experience. "I was critical of my boss' endless over-emphasis on organization until I learned that his parents were killed in a plane crash when he was three. From then on, I understood dimly that somehow, against all odds, he was trying to keep what was left of his world in order." "I used to judge my brother for being so silent and withdrawn, until I learned that for years he'd been sexually abused by our uncle."

The original emotionally shattering experience may well not have been of the magnitude of the death of a parent or sexual abuse, but for a man any loss, disappointment, failure, or breach of trust, can, at any point in his history, have as profound an effect on him as it would on a woman; however, because he most likely will have handled it through repression of his feelings, the degree to which it would have affected him remains invisible to himself and those around him.

While some women are willing and able to divine the sensitivity that lurks behind the apparent closed-offness of men, this is a skill most women still don't have and others resent having to try to develop. As a result men and women together are forced to put up with—or worse yet, nurture, the male-has-no-feelings-mystique, with men suppressing and symbolically acting out their feelings, and women feeling left out in the cold or endlessly doing the translating for men. The net result is an impoverishment in relationship, with both men and women feeling distanced from one another and with a majority of the energy in relationships devoted to sorting out an endless array of undelivered or inappropriately delivered emotions.

What I am asking each woman to begin to do, when she encounters a man who is still unable to meet her with the range, depth and quality of emotional exchange she longs for, is not to assume it's because he's an unfeeling brute. Instead, we should all begin to ask ourselves—and very gently ask him—the kind of curious, open-ended questions which, in themselves, are an acknowledgement that there is more to men emotionally than ever meets the eye.

Women need to change their assumptions about men. We need to start being curious about what men may have suffered, about what causes them to close off. We also need to remember—and with a degree of compassion that our own frustration often robs from us—that men really don't know how to take the steps from emotional crisis to resolution. As a result they may well be trapped for years in an emotional holding pattern over something women could well have recovered from a long time before. In the end, in the middle and at the beginning, we need to finally acknowledge that men are far more sensitive and far more at the effect of their emotions than we ever realized.

7

Actions Speak Louder Than Words: Cracking the Male Communication Code

"Men have weird conversations, don't they? They only talk about things. Widgets and ball games, that's all they ever talk about. You never get to hear how they feel."

-Engineer's wife, 36

The fact that men can't articulate their feelings doesn't mean that one way or another they don't express them. Cryptic as their methods may seem to women, men *do* communicate what they feel. Unlike women, however, who tend to be verbal to the nth degree, the male vocabulary for feeling is action. For men actions speak louder than words. That's because, as we've seen, a man's way is to do; therefore unconsciously he presumes that what he does will say how he feels.

This is why, when a woman's upset, a man will buy her a present, repair the faucet she's been complaining about for months, or stay up all night driving her home from her mother's house where she's just had a terrible fight—but won't talk to her about how awful it must have been to argue with her mother. When a woman is still unhappy, after the gift, after the faucet's been fixed, when she's finally home safe after the nightmare visit with Mom, he can't understand why she is still upset. He *did* something, didn't he, so how can there still be a problem?

The problem is that women don't necessarily want action—women want "the words"; women want to be told how a man feels and to be asked how they feel. And women want an experience of empathy, the sense, through what a man has said, that he is feeling *with* them. But men tend to want to do and to solve, not to "talk about" the problem, and it's this male translation of feelings into action that is the chief reason women are continually frustrated in their interactions with men. Essentially, women are creatures of conversation; men are beings of action. To women, feeling *is* language, what counts is what gets said; if we haven't heard it, we don't believe it. Because we are so verbally oriented, we're often unable or unwilling to extrapolate the emotional content from men's seemingly cryptic verbal offerings. We don't want to have to interpret; we want men to meet us directly, on our own territory, with the right words and when they can't—or it appears won't—we are thwarted and stymied.

Although we can readily see how this discrepancy becomes the source of major difficulties, there's often a period early in courtship when women do understand and are even charmed by the fact that men act out their feelings. They're enchanted by all the things that men do: the trinkets, tokens and presents they buy, the proverbial dozen red roses, candlelight dinners, half-carat diamonds, unforgettably passionate lovemaking sessions, to say nothing of the promise of security all these portend. Here, at the inception of the relationship, women accept the actions-speak-louder-than-words behavior of their suitors, are willing to hear the "I love you" behind such actions whether or not a man has uttered the actual words.

But when the courtship is over and real life has set in, and a man continues to do instead of to say, when he starts pruning the shrubs, fixing the car, taking the dog to the vet, buying a new washing machine and expecting his wife or sweetheart to know that these actions too, are statements of love, a woman is often no longer enchanted. She wants something else: words, intimate conversation, a sense of herself and the man she loves through the two-way mirror of communication.

We want to know a man, feel him, have conversations and sweet interludes with him. Fixing the faucet doesn't say "I love you" quite like a dozen red roses, and the myriad other messages men are trying to deliver with what they continually do are as difficult to understand and as unromantic as crescent wrenches and axle grease for most women. So it is that, as time goes on and women's unmet expectations become more intense, the space they wish would be occupied with words becomes a heartbreaking vacancy, and the frustrating drama of men and women in intimate relationships begins.

Of course actions that say "I love you" represent only a small part of what men can't, don't, or won't say with words. For it isn't just love that men express through action—men also express grief, rage, and fear without words. Bowled over by sorrow, a man may go out and chop wood, run till he drops, or play a vicious game of handball. When a man's angry, he'll speed on the freeway, bash his fist through a wall, break the new lamp, or go out and get drunk. He may not know what he's angry about, before, during, or after acting out his anger; and even when there's an obvious connecting event, rather than talk about the emotion a man will most likely choose to act it out instead. "When I found out my daughter had cancer," Paul said, "I went up to the shooting range and blasted the target until it was black with holes."

In general, men's actions constitute a kind of code, an elaborate method of simultaneously revealing and concealing their true feelings. By performing an action, they manage to deliver a certain measure of their real feeling, enough to keep them in contact, but not so much as to leave them emotionally vulnerable. Men do something that's vaguely related to what they're feeling without really exposing themselves or anyone else to the real substance and content of their emotions.

To women's great frustration, men's emotions are endlessly permutated into action. Men *do* their emotions; they don't *say* them. Women watch these behaviors, intuit something's going on, and can only wonder what it is.

Much as women hate this behavior, because of male socialization and the immense discomfort men feel in the face of their emotions, men have almost no choice but to translate their feelings into the actions which symbolically carry their meaning. Thus we must deduce that the man doing dishes for his law student wife is saying "I love you; I support you; you're terrific," although he won't say the words; that the man who buys his daughter a sports car for graduation is saying he's proud of her, even though he doesn't bother to tell her; and that the man who endlessly polishes his dead son's motorcycle is grieving, although he can't talk about it with his wife.

Among men, these action-packed cryptograms tend to be understood. Men know when they're slapping each other with wet towels in the locker room that they're expressing their affection; that when they show off their new car they're asking for approval—not of the car, but of themselves; that when they walk into the party with a beautiful woman on their arm, they're asking to be recognized as powerful; that when they watch sports together they're seeking the solace of male bonding.

Even when they talk with one another, they talk about what they do, not how they feel. A man will talk about his achievements, acquisitions, salary, family, vacation, boat, retirement dinner, or the football game without saying how he feels about it, how it moved him, or what he still needs from it. And, in general, men feel comfortable in this mode with one another, able to make the translations or living as if they don't need them.

But the male penchant to demonstrate rather than articulate still baffles and frustrates women. Rebecca didn't really "get" this about her husband Frank until she'd lived with him for almost ten years. In the middle of a horrendous fight in which she was raving that he never said he loved her, Frank tossed back, "But don't you understand, when I go to work every day, when I put new tires on your car, when I fix the furnace, for Chrisakes, I'm *showing* you I love you. Why else would I do all these things?" She was shocked, incredulous, because she'd always thought he'd done all those things just because they had to be done. Understanding his code didn't necessarily make *her* feel more loved, but it did allow her to comprehend that this was how he was trying to love her.

In the actions-that-mean-I-love-you-category, most men view their financial support, in particular, to be the visible expression of their love. The mere fact that they get up every day and go to work to support their wives and children is for them the absolute proof that they love their family. That's why so many men are aggravated when the women in their lives keep saying to them, "*But tell* me that you love me." It feels to them as if nothing they've done means anything. They feel depressed, hopeless, and stupid because, without consciously being aware of it, they hoped and expected that the eight to ten hours a day they spend at work every week would be saying the "I love you" and they're shocked to discover that it hasn't.

In a sense, men bring their work mode home. Since at work they're valued for performance and accomplishment, they tend to assume that in their private lives, too, their actions will carry the day, whether they can express themselves verbally or not. Doggedly, pigheadedly and relentlessly, men trust that the people who love them will comprehend that their actions do indeed communicate their love. Rather than recognizing action isn't always the appropriate vehicle for expressing feelings, men tend to stick to what's familiar, to rely on actions all the time.

On an unconscious level men really believe that what they do for their wives—their work, their steadfastness, their taking out the garbage, their fixing things, their holding the little world of their families together—will tell their wives that they love them. Men really do believe that the actions indigenous to the male role will in themselves be sufficient to carry the message that they love their wives and families. But it isn't.

This is why a great many men, divorced by wives who complained because their husbands "didn't love" them—i.e., "didn't communicate," never "said the right thing" or "weren't sensitive enough"—are devastated to discover that the motivating factor behind their wife's departure was her affair with a man who "understands," i.e., communicates verbally with her. "But I did love you; I did everything for you and the kids" is the wounded wailing cry of so many men who offered their lives on the sacrificial altar of work and domestic fidelity for their families. Following society's rules, they believed that what they did would be enough—only to be told at the end that it wasn't, that their wives had wanted to be talked to and listened to instead.

For women, actions alone aren't enough. We need the words to understand the meaning of the actions. That this is true not only leaves women frustrated, but keeps us standing so far outside the male *modus operandi* that men are abandoned to a kind of emotional isolation most women can only barely perceive.

The Meaning of Inaction

HE: Love is an action.
SHE: Talking is an action.

Men's emotional expressions are so thoroughly linked to action that an emotional component can be discovered not only in men's intentional actions but also in their passive inactions, which can carry an opposite but equally profound significance. Thus, not-doing, not-performing, not-listening, and not-answering are all also very potent forms of "communication." This is particularly true when the non-action is in response to some agreed-upon thing in a relationship. For example, the man who's been asked a million times to pick up his socks from the floor but still doesn't do it; the man who doesn't pay his credit card bill before the late charge comes due, though he's assured his wife that he would; and the man who drags his feet about renting a tuxedo for his wedding, although he told his fiancee five times that he'd do it tomorrow—all are making powerful statements through what they are *not doing*.

These men are all being what we call passive-aggressive. Indirectly, they're expressing some hidden resentment, anger, or frustration. They're saying "something's bothering me," but they're not taking the emotional risk of actually verbalizing what it is. They probably don't even know what they're feeling, but whether they consciously know it or not, through being passive-aggressive, they are definitely communicating it.

Passive-aggressive behavior, unfortunately, often takes the leading edge in the male emotional repertoire. It is the expression of unidentified (and, as a result, unverbalized) anger through passive acts: not-doing, not-saying, not-participating. This means that an aggressive (angry, frustrated or negative) feeling is being felt, but rather than being directly verbalized, e.g., "I'm angry at you; I'm frustrated; I'm irritated," it is expressed passively through not-doing and not-communicating.

Passive aggression is indirect hostility, of a small or great degree. It's the silent treatment—slamming the door instead of expressing the gripe; the disappearing or not-appearing-when-you-said-you-would act that men so frequently indulge in. It is experienced as a sort of psychic pin-prick by women, a some-thing-just-happened-here-but-I'm-not-quite-sure-what-it-is phenomenon, where a woman feels vaguely attacked but can't quite identify the way in which she was.

This very common male behavior pattern is particularly frustrating to women because, as it plays itself out, women never quite know precisely what men are trying to communicate through their non-communication. Is he mad at me, the children or his boss? Or is he upset about something I don't know anything about? Sometimes you know and sometimes you haven't got the foggiest idea. As if this confusion weren't bad enough, one of the truly disturbing second generation consequences of male passive-aggressive behavior is that women, for no apparent reason, find themselves acting out anger which doesn't, in fact, originate with them.

Thus when a man doesn't say, do, or come through with whatever he's promised, when he acts out some red-flag but seemingly totally off-the-wall behavior, a woman may find herself blowing up, in effect expressing the anger the man in her proximity couldn't express, except through his passive-aggressive behavior. Often as not the result of this dynamic finds the woman enduring a condescending male response like, "There you go again, getting all upset and hysterical about nothing."

Substitute Behaviors

"Men do for women because they don't know how to be for women."

-*Entrepreneur, 38*

Among the numerous feelings men handle symbolically, by doing something which serves to stand in for the real but difficult-to-handle emotions, are their fears about aging and death. Since one of the things men aren't allowed to feel is how wobbly and fragile they are in the face of their own mortality, they find other ways to express their unacceptable fears. For, while the distinguished silver-haired man may be Madison Avenue's image of success, the real live man with graying temples is often scrambling to recover his sense of lost youth, to manage his fear of oncoming death.

But once again, instead of dealing with these feelings directly, men try to manage their panic: by taking up long-distance running at age sixty, buying a spiffy red sports car, washing the gray out of their hair, going on a sailing trip around the world, or precipitously trying to change careers. One lawyer, at forty-five feeling a vague discontent after twelve years of practice, decided to go back to school and become a dentist, because that's what he'd wanted to be when he was young, before he followed in his father's footsteps. Another man, a physician unhappy with the way twenty years had passed "in the twinkling of an eye," sold his practice, moved to a little town in the Midwest and opened a hardware store. Still another, an accountant, endlessly "frustrated" by his "meaning-less" work, tried real estate, the ministry, and contracting before he returned to his career in accounting.

Other evidence of this kind of emotional substitute behavior is the way many men in mid-life divorce, marry considerably younger women, and create another family. This isn't to say that mid-life divorces don't often have validity in themselves—relationships do fulfill their specific purposes and come to completion—but in many instances this trading in on a new model represents the action that embodies a range of inexpressible feelings. Rather than admitting they're scared about aging, these men seek to stave off their fear of death by starting over again, attempting to regain their lost youth by marrying it, defying the clock by doing in mid-life what they did (or didn't do) when they were young.

Men perform these emotional substitutions so consistently that it isn't just in life-and-death matters, when they're unconsciously terrified of being capsized by their emotions, that they replace their feelings with actions. Men do this with just about everything. It's as if it never occurs to a man to express a feeling directly.

Even though some women are starting to encourage men to express what they feel, most men still can't do it because often they're not even aware what they're feeling. A man came into my office recently, told me a story about a major career disappointment, then looked at me and said, "So tell me, what *am* I feeling?" In his hilariously revealing way, he was acknowledging the great male problem—that although he could articulate at length about the facts of the situation, he could neither discover nor express his feelings about it.

Because the language of feelings is still so foreign to men, they often somatize their feelings, that is, express them through some physical reaction: a pain in the back, an aching neck, an ulcer, a headache, a heart attack. Men may experience fear as a flutter in the pit of the stomach, sorrow as a constriction in the throat, anger as white-knuckled fists tap-tapping under the boardroom table. In a very real sense, men come into their emotions through their bodies. That is, their emotions are translated into symptoms or sensations that are enacted on a physical level; but the words that express these emotions never get attached to them. In short, men can't identify the aching back as rage at their boss, the headache as anger at their wife. Men don't know they're mad—they just hurt physically.

Whether men express their feelings through action or somatize them, they're always mediating their emotions through the physical dimension. Even when they're able to articulate their feelings to some limited degree, there's almost always a physical component. Men generally answer first from their bodies. If you ask a man how he *feels*, he'll most likely say, "tired," or "my back's out again," rather than saying, "I'm sad," "I'm discouraged," or "I'm in love." And since men's bodies are the medium *and* the message for their emotions, it's not surprising that the epitome of men's transmutation of feelings occurs in what they communicate through sex.

Men, Sex, and Emotions

> *"Men look for love with their pricks because they don't know how to love with their hearts."*
>
> -Businessman, 48

Men's seemingly overwhelming concern with sex and women's generalized notion that sex is the only thing men are really interested in is one of the broadly circulating misconceptions about men. To hold this view completely overlooks the fact that, for men, sex is a far more complex and emotionally loaded enterprise than both men and women ordinarily imagine.

In reality, sex isn't just a biological release for men, men's favorite pastime, or the only thing men are interested in.

But because of the way our culture is set up, it *is* virtually the only vehicle men have for emotional intimacy, for delivering and resolving the whole complex range of their unarticulated feelings.

In a sense, sex has to contain a man's entire emotional vocabulary. Whether or not men know what they're feeling, what they are saying, asking for, seeking and offering in sex is all the tenderness, fear, anger, excitement, sense of possibility, need for bonding, assuaging of sorrow, nurturing of the body and solace of spirit they can't put into words. It's precisely because men have to say so much through sex, that they themselves are so often confused about it.

That's why, for example, without quite understanding the reason, a man may want to get up and go home after having sex with a particular woman, and why, in another instance, he may wake up disgusted the next morning that he did make love to the woman he was with—the experience wasn't as much or as deep as he needed it to be; he wasn't able to express or she wasn't able to receive his "message." He feels sad, lonely, ashamed, or vulnerable after having tried to communicate something through sex. He can't put this into words, of course. He didn't know that that's what he was trying to do. He only knows that he wants to get out, to remove himself from the place and person to whom he couldn't speak his deeper needs.

It's this hidden male need to have sex serve as the container for such a great range of emotions which also explains why, sometimes without his consciously knowing it, a man may return again and again to the solace of a particular woman's body. He does so because he feels himself received so deeply, because in making love with her, something is being fulfilled: his unstated questions are answered, his feelings are felt and resolved without having to be consciously identified. "To me, making love with her is like being reborn every time," said a client who had just fallen in love.

Without discussing it among themselves or with women, men intuitively know the range of possibilities that sex includes. Men know that it's more than primate physical release, self-indulgence, aggression or oppression; that it is, in fact, the arena for the expression of their unexpressed emotions. Unconsciously, men know that sex must be their words, their medicine, the love they give, the love they need to get. This is why, on the grosser level, their words for sex range from "fucking," to "having sex" to "making love," and why their sexual experience varies depending on which woman and what feelings and circumstances encompass it. Even when men are bragging about their sexual conquests they often have a vague sick feeling which is the symptom of their regret that somehow they have been unable to communicate the many deep and specific things they need to express to the person with whom they are making love.

What a man cannot say with words to his wife he says with his body, what he feels unable in any other way to give her, he gives through making love to her, with the hope that she will hear him. The sense of communion and connection which often eludes him because of his verbal ineptitude, he gains through the sexual encounter.

Unfortunately, like smokers who use cigarettes to handle every emotion, every situation, many men also use sex to handle unmanageable emotions, to take the edge off feelings which, through being too intense in either a positive or negative direction, threaten to emotionally disrupt them. When a man's had a lousy day at the office, when he gets elected chairman of the board (or when he doesn't), when his son's been in a motorcycle accident, when his daughter's getting married, when he's making war or protesting it, when his team wins the World Series or loses, when he's happy and when he's miserable, he wants to have sex. Whether a man feels vulnerable or on top of the world, he will most likely choose to express it through sex.

In being men's virtually only vocabulary for feeling, sex can become the medium for expressing a host of undifferentiated, repressed male emotions, particularly unconscious aggression, disappointment, and resentment. Among other things, sex can be an act of domination for a man, whether this has to do with the physical position he assumes, the attitude in which he undertakes it, or with his intention that through it, if only momentarily, he is bringing another human being under his domination.

Domination sex is especially prevalent in men who have been emotionally dominated by either their fathers or mothers. People who have been dominated and abused, dominate and abuse in return, twistedly trying to gain a sense of their own individuality, efficacy, and power. When this need is expressed through sex, sex becomes an act of aggression and violation and its potential for healing and emotional bonding is completely obfuscated. When this is the unconscious drama that is being played out, women feel objectified and used in the sexual encounter; and it is essential that they protest when they are enlisted to participate in such acts of displaced and covert aggression.

Unfortunately sex does frequently carry the charge of unresolved male conflicts and suppressed aggression. This is why women so often complain about men's seeming detachment and selfishness in sex. One woman said that whenever her husband came home from seeing his mother, he would "attack" her in bed, while ordinarily he was a generous and compassionate lover; another that she could always tell precisely the condition of her husband's relationship to his boss by the position and tenderness (or lack thereof) with which he made love to her.

Along with using sex as an outlet for aggression, men

also often sexualize their pain. What I mean by this is that since they have no way of communicating their emotional pain directly, sex becomes the medium through which they release their frequently unidentified pain, whether it be loss, panic, terror, or insecurity. In the sexual bonding of skin upon skin a man is momentarily delivered from the appalling sense of aloneness he feels in the presence of his pain. Unconsciously, he also feels the magical potential of new life being stirred in the generative act and therefore he is unconsciously encouraged.

Since sex is the medium through which men express such a vast array of emotions, when men are sexually deprived or cut off, they often have extreme, though often not conscious, emotional reactions. They can become belligerent, abusive, critical, condescending, deprived little boys who punish in return. The exaggerated channeling of so many emotions into the sexual arena means that men can't help but experience sexual rejection as emotional rejection.

Thus when a man is denied sex he experiences it not as a missed sexual encounter, but as a complete rejection of himself. It's as if his deepest needs aren't going to be acknowledged. It's as if he himself has become unworthy of being received. He feels that his very essence is being denied. He can no longer speak; there's no longer anyone to listen. It's this feeling of rejection as himself, by the way, that a man is referring to when he tells the woman with whom he is having an affair, because he feels sexually deprived at home, "My wife doesn't understand me." He doesn't mean that, literally, his wife doesn't understand him. He means that in his experience of sexual deprivation he has come to feel emotionally disconnected, as if he doesn't exist.

Because sex is such a powerful communicator for men, something significant is also being communicated when men don't want to have sex. When men withdraw sexually, they are most often expressing anger passive aggressively. But they may also be acting out fear of being overwhelmed or the lack of a feeling of safety with a woman.

One man, so terrorized by his wife's hysterical outbursts by day, began gradually to withdraw from her sexually until he realized that their sex life had all but vanished. "I finally realized I was so emotionally battered that I never felt safe enough to approach her sexually," he said. "I was always wondering when the next bomb would go off—and, I suppose underneath wondering when she'd start attacking my sexual performance." Another man said that his wife's critical comments during and after lovemaking made him feel so totally inadequate that he simply couldn't take the risk of making love to her anymore. It wasn't until several years later when he had an affair with a woman who kept telling him what a wonderful lover he was that he not only regained his sexual confidence, but started expressing his feelings verbally.

Far more than we generally acknowledge, sex is a many splendored and multi-faceted phenomenon—especially for men. So, although it may be against our myths, our prejudice and even our individual experience, we need to remember that in the sexual encounter a great many things are always being transacted. With respect to our intimate relationships, instead of being judgmental or simple-minded, locked into black and white thinking, we need to be curious and inquiring about what men may be communicating through their sexual behavior. For, as women already know, there is always much more to sex than sex itself.

Everything but the Thing Itself

HE: Quit harping on me. You've told me all this a thousand times before.
SHE: I know, but you've never listened.
HE: How do you know?
SHE: Because you've never responded.
HE: How do you know?
SHE: Because you've never said *anything.*

Sex instead of verbal disclosure, displacement of emotions, and passive aggression all constitute ways men communicate in code. But even when it comes to verbal communication, men use the indirect method. Put simply, men don't say what they mean, even when they do speak. They may say something like what they mean, something close to (or entirely opposite of) what they mean, or something which only symbolically refers to what they mean.

Take, for example, the man who was totally emotionally devastated by the death of his boss, a man who was only a few years older than he. In his employer's untimely death, without quite consciously knowing it, he suddenly saw his own mortality. He saw that what he was aspiring to had killed his mentor, but of course he was unable to say this to his wife. Instead, shortly after the funeral, he started coming home and complaining about his job. "Things are awful at work," he'd say. "Everyone's picking on me and the business is going to hell."

These coded messages were so off the mark that although he continued to complain, his wife was unable to decipher them. The real emotional issue was never disclosed; he didn't have the foggiest idea of how to identify it and he certainly didn't know how to put it into words. Even if he could have known how he felt, being a man and having to hold his family's world together, he certainly couldn't come home and say, "I feel like I'm on a death trip, supporting you and the kids. Everything I've aspired to is pointing the way to my early demise." Frustrated, his wife encouraged him to work out his problems with his co-workers, which, eventually, he did. But when he continued to be depressed because the real emotional content still hadn't been addressed, his wife finally encouraged him into therapy where in time the real issues surfaced.

As this tale of male emotional elusiveness demonstrates, because men don't have the language to communicate their true feelings, women often have difficulty responding appropriately. Women are more than willing, even eager, to give men what they need, but without a clear directive, they're functioning like stymied mind readers, looking for clues as to how to proceed.

In fact, men's, at times, almost primitive verbal indirect ness creates immense frustration for both men and women. Men are so uneducated in the language of feelings that even when they're invited into the emotional arena by a woman's direct emotional expression, they often can't follow suit. A marketing executive, moved to tears, as he later told me, by the loving words on a birthday card from a woman he admired, couldn't even tell her how much her words had meant. The next time he saw her all he could say was, "That must have been an expensive card." He wasn't able to say what in fact he had felt: "I'm blown away you remembered my birthday; your words touched my heart; I appreciate your love."

Another man, too shy to ask a woman for a date, kept saying to her, "There are a couple of great movies in town. Have you heard about such and such?" Finally, he launched into a lengthy discussion of the various films, without ever asking her out. Not only could he not ask her for a date, but far more sophisticated and therefore entirely impossible in the communication realm, he couldn't tell her how much he really liked her. He was brokenhearted later, after having seen her out with another man, and I asked him why he hadn't expressed these things to her. He said simply, "I felt them; I just couldn't put them into words."

Since much male communication is often so pitifully indirect, even men can't be sure what they're talking about. In their most vulnerable moments, they will sometimes open up about their own frustration over the male predicament of communication by code, whichever form it may be.

One man regretted never having had "a real conversation" with his best friend who was dying of leukemia. "All we did was watch videos of old movies; then he died." Another was terrified of expressing his feeling of indebtedness to some neighbors who took him in during his divorce. "I sent them a basket of fruit for Christmas and just signed my name; I didn't even include a note." Another man, weeping, revealed, "My father never told me he loved me but I always figured he did since I was the one he'd take to the baseball games. Still there was always that little nagging doubt because he never actually said the words. I wish just once he could have *said* I love you." Whatever the subject or relationship, men feel crippled by not being able to say or have said to them the things they need to have put into words.

Words or Actions: Which Will it Be?

"When I get close to a man, I wonder how women have ever managed to be related to them. They wouldn't recognize a feeling unless they could take it to the bank."

-Woman escrow officer, 42

Yet another difficult consequence of men's inability to express feelings directly is that it creates a void in relationships in which women's feelings seem to take precedence. Since women generally have much more immediate access to the words for their feelings, they tend to think that theirs are the only feelings around. It's as if the female theory is, the more words produced, the stronger and truer the feelings. As a result, it becomes all too easy for women to forget that men are expressing their feelings through their many cryptic codes: action, inaction, substitution, and symbolic communication, and that to date men still haven't developed a very sophisticated language for expressing their feelings because they're still in the process of trying to divine precisely what those feelings are.

Thus it is that men can neither hear the words nor find the words that refer to their emotional experience. When it comes to what they've heard they've had to shut down and, as it were, stop up their ears with wax. When it comes to what they might say, they've never found the language for the feelings which, in the big-boys-don't-cry school of thought, they've had to suppress and squelch. They literally can't tell us how they feel because they do not know.

As a result of this ongoing imbalance between inarticulate men and emotionally expressive women, the real argument between the sexes is: What is to be the language for expressing feelings? Will it be words, as women prefer, or actions, as men insist? This is the conundrum that men and women have been stranded in forever, the hallmark of the conflict between the sexes.

What women need to understand to break the deadlock is that, when it comes to our insistence on verbal communication, it's as if we're inviting men to explicitly female territory. For, in asking a man to express his feelings directly, women are, in effect, asking that he become, for the moment at least, more like a woman. If Professor Higgins in his somewhat self-serving tutorial efforts was asking, "Why can't a woman be more like a man?," women, in their efforts to get men to talk about their feelings are, in effect, asking, "Why can't a man be more like a woman?"

Women are asking men to adopt an essentially feminine mode, the mode of verbal expressiveness. Men not only resent this, they're terrified. They usually feel, and to some degree rightly so, that it's unfair that *they* should be the only ones who have to change. Why can't women "just understand" what they mean?

In some sense, verbal communication does represent the broadest common denominator in human interactions. Both men and women use language to conduct their business, whether it be emotional business or the larger, more complex transactions of running the world. For the most part, we all know the meaning of a given word, and because of these agreed-upon meanings, words are generally much easier to interpret than actions. In a sense, words are the universal code.

Thus, while it is true that male communication by code does carry emotional meanings that women should learn to divine, it is also true that men need to learn how to use language, the preferred communication medium of women. Communication by code can never cover the range nor equal the power, the intricacy, and the beauty that can be created through the use of a common language. If men want satisfying relationships with women, they will have to start venturing out from their familiar position of communicating in code and practice the art of direct verbal expressiveness that women already know to be so rewarding.

And if we are ever to really diminish the rift between the sexes, women will also need to discover that the language beyond language expressed in motion, action, gesture, and posture also has a validity and meaning of its own. Perhaps as women move more and more into the traditionally male arena of action in the world, they will also become more familiar with the vocabulary of behavior and begin to comprehend that actions, too, embody emotional statements.

To the extent that women become able to do this, and to the degree that they can discover in themselves the actions that carry deep meaning, they will be able to view the male approach more sympathetically. This will open the way for men to let down their guard, to begin the painstaking process of learning words, the language of women. But insofar as men and women are unable to acknowledge the validity of the male approach or the need for liberating men from the burden of living only by code, the abyss between the sexes can only deepen and the intimacy we all desire will continue to elude us.

8

The Bogeyman in the Closet: Men's Fear of Not Being Enough

"She's always complaining. About me. About life. About her work. The implication of course is that I should make it all right. I'm her husband. I'm supposed to hold the whole damn world together. Provide and protect. If I can't, I'm no good."

-Professor, 38

Women and men have kept men so consistently, so tidily in their role that what is in fact the central emotional motivation for men remains essentially invisible. While men are holding the world together and doing such a magnificent job of suppressing their feelings, at the core their lives are governed by an only vaguely repressed fear that constantly hounds them.

At bottom, what most men are afraid of is not being

enough. In more ways than women can ever imagine, men are afraid of being revealed to be inadequate. Men are afraid they're not strong enough, handsome enough, or rich enough, that they won't be good enough lovers, won't achieve enough in their lives, won't provide well enough for their families, won't gain the respect of their children, won't be able to hold their own with their colleagues and friends, won't be good enough fathers, won't leave a mark at the end. And when it comes to the inner circle of intimate relationships, men fear they will love too much and be abandoned, or not as much as the woman who loves them and be suffocated or overwhelmed. They're afraid they can't equal or manage a woman's feelings and that, as a result, there will be devastating consequences.

In fact, much of the male behavior that mystifies or annoys women springs from this basic fear of inadequacy, a man's sense that somehow he won't be enough. Most of us don't know this about men because they do such a good job of obscuring it by reaction formations, denial, and passive aggression. Thus the man who is terrified his girlfriend won't choose him boasts of his sexual conquests; the man who's afraid his wife will abandon him furiously denies such a thought ever crossed his mind; the man who feels inadequate as a provider complains his wife spends too much on groceries.

Although it may seem mind-boggling to women, men constantly report to me their fear that in one crucial area or another they won't be able to measure up, and the attendant fear that the area in which they can't will immediately make them unacceptable and ultimately destroy their entire sense of adequacy as men, especially in the eyes of women.

Because of the male code of competition, men feel as if they have to succeed, have to have all the answers, have to be better than everyone else, have to do everything right—and all the time. Thus the fear that they haven't or won't continually dogs them. Because of this indwelling fear of inadequacy, the cornerstone of a man's identity is, in a sense, his endless attempts to be adequate in the face of his fears of inadequacy. A man sees himself as existing to hold himself, his wife, his children, and his world together. To the extent that he is able to do this he feels adequate, i.e., like a real man, and to the degree he's afraid he can't or is, in fact, unable to, he feels inadequate, i.e., less than a man. Like the emperor in "The Emperor's New Clothes," men live with the constant fear that while they're trying to run the world, they'll be discovered to be standing out in public stark naked.

Women have difficulty understanding men's fear of inadequacy not only because the male identity requires that men suppress it, but also because it is not a female fear. Not only are women allowed to be afraid, they've traditionally been encouraged to reveal their weaknesses—to swoon at spiders, to shriek at the sight of blood. Even now that these stereotypes have broken down, women still don't have to do everything right. We can say, without losing face, "I'm scared; I can't do this, I'm not even going to try." Fear and retreat because of fear are acceptable stances for women, and failure may lead to specific disappointment, but it's never a total reflection of their value as women.

To be a woman is to be permitted (for good and ill) the luxury of being able to feel inadequate. It's all right for a woman to talk about how insecure she feels. In fact one of the great social pastimes of women is to talk about their inadequacies. Talking about our fat thighs, our lousy haircut, our loneliness, our desire for a man, our fear of power, or our disappointments about our jobs are all legitimate topics: "I'm going nuts"; "I just can't handle it being alone one more day"; "I'm depressed, I don't know what to do with myself"; "I could never go on vacation alone; I'm too scared." "I'm having a terrible time at work; my boss got me so upset I started bawling and ended up going home early."

Men, on the other hand, can rarely confide such things; if they were to talk about such fears or feelings of inadequacy, their sense of male identity would be immediately eroded.

The Roots of Inadequacy

"My fear in love? I'm afraid I won't be able to give her enough so she'll love me as much as I love her and if she doesn't love me as much as I love her, she'll leave me."
                                                    -Grocery store manager, 42

Men's inherent fear of inadequacy stems from the central fact that they can't bear children. Unconsciously men are overwhelmed by the fact that women have the capacity to deliver new life to the world, while they themselves do not. In fact, men are so overwhelmed by women's ability to bear children that they're afraid *nothing* they can do will ever equal it. In relation to that incredible achievement, *all* male achievement pales, becomes in some sense an unconscious effort to measure up. Because men can't give birth, they try to do everything else, as if through an endless string of achievements they could finally close the gap between all they can achieve and the single achievement they can never make. For men this ongoing labor of trying to measure up is a gigantic undertaking, and is the real reason men constantly worry about whether or not they're enough.

Thus, like a full-time low-grade fever, men constantly experience a vague but haunting sense of inadequacy in the presence of women. It's as if the very experience of being related to a woman drops a man off at the doorstep to an awareness of his own limitations by unconsciously but continuously reminding him that he can't bear children while she can. But in addition to this primary source of discomfort, the specific things a man is required to do, give, and be in relationship to a woman further expose him to his feeling of inadequacy.

Because of their complex emotional lives, women remain a mystery to men, seeming to be forever engaged in a process that eludes, baffles, and often denigrates men. Being in the presence of a woman's emotions brings men face to face with the fact that they themselves really don't know how to function emotionally. Being invited into commitment with a woman throws them up against an array of responsibilities that, once again, they fear they may be unable to fulfill. Either way, in relation to women, men are delivered inescapably to a frustrating, albeit unconscious, awareness of their own limitations.

Keeping Up Emotionally

"What's my greatest fear in a relationship: not being able to answer a woman's needs."

-Body builder, 36

Among the bogeymen in the male inadequacy arena are the fears men encounter in the presence of women's emotions. Women have no idea how really scared men are of their emotions. They tend to think men are so strong and durable that nothing will affect them.

This rather simple-minded fantasy is supported, of course, by the fact that women rarely see men being affected by the emotions women produce. Women certainly don't see men reacting in the same highly emotional way that women react to one another. What men do emotionally seems to be very low key indeed (except, of course, when it comes to anger).

Because of the bind they're in—needing to be strong to maintain their male identity—men are in no position to acknowledge how terrified they are of women's feelings. It isn't manly to be intimidated by women, so men really can't admit that they are. Once again the operative definition of maleness imposes a restriction on the very kind of communication that might open a channel between men and women.

Can you imagine a man saying, "You scare me to death when you cry like that. I can't handle it. I don't know what to do." It's an embarrassing thing for a man to acknowledge. Men aren't supposed to be afraid at all—and they're certainly not supposed to be afraid of women. But the truth is that often when women express their feelings, and especially when they express them in a volatile manner, men find themselves feeling totally out of control, unconsciously scared and enraged.

One man, for years overwhelmed by his wife's emotional outbursts, told me, "It took me four years before I could even imagine that I would survive. At the beginning when she'd go off on one of her wild binges, I'd just stand there and think, 'My God, there's no way I'm ever going to live through this.'"

Another young man, being treated to his first round of emotional episodes with his new bride, was amazed to discover the degree to which his wife's depression affected him. "I'm blown away," he said. "I can't stand it. She cries. She says all these despairing things. I do everything I can to try and cheer her up but nothing works. I just want to throw up my hands and scream: NO MORE EMOTIONS!"

Men are afraid of women's emotions for several reasons. First, because they have almost no skills with which to navigate their own emotional Scylla and Charybdis, men are afraid they don't have what it takes to operate on the emotional level. For a man, dealing emotionally with anyone is like setting out on the open sea toward a continent which, so far as he's concerned, may not even really exist. He isn't sure he's going to be able to cross this mysterious ocean and he has serious doubts as to whether he'll ever reach a safe harbor. Furthermore, since the feelings to which men are so frequently exposed aren't those that would inspire them to learn the art of verbal emotional communication, men would just as soon that women find some other way of handling their feelings than by verbally expressing them.

In the face of threats to their power, men traditionally functioned either by subduing through physical force or, through patience and fortitude, enduring whatever onslaught had occurred. But in the emotional arena, a man knows instinctively that neither of these methods will likely be effective. He isn't supposed to use force and he doesn't know if he can endure; and in the specific moment of emotional upheaval he doesn't know whether he'll be able to calm the woman down or wait out her onslaught. No matter which method men use, what's clear is that men are at a loss about how to occupy some middle ground when it comes to women's emotions.

Thus, to the powerlessness men already feel in relation to a woman's procreative ability is added the powerlessness they feel about being forced to participate in the emotional arena. Whether still outside it looking in, or already inside and caught up in the fray, men fear they'll be overtaken by women's emotions, sucked deeper and deeper into an experience for which they have no capability.

Because of this, in some sense, the specific content of the encounter is irrelevant—men fear they'll be unable to handle the emotional experience no matter what it's about. As one man said, "I feel as if her emotionality is going to kill me, whether or not I win or lose any particular fight."

Since men really don't know how to come forward with emotional expression, and since they're afraid that, should they try, women will discover them to be inept, they often say insensitive things such as, "It's ridiculous for you to get upset," or "Just calm down, there's nothing to be so hysterical about." Often, a man's first—and usually unconscious—reaction is to try and shut down a woman's emotional production so she won't find out that he can't deal with such a highly-charged emotional encounter.

Men also dismiss women emotionally because they're afraid they'll be discovered to be inadequate in dealing with the demands, complaints, and judgments inherent or stated in women's emotional expressions. When a woman is yelling about how for years her husband hasn't fixed the roof, for example, he's worried not only about how he's going to live through the tirade, but also how he's going to find the time and money to fix the roof. When a man is being complained at because he hasn't made love to his wife for five weeks, he's not just wondering if or when she'll shut up, he's also wondering if or when he'll feel safe enough to approach her sexually again.

In either case, a man fears that whether he responds to a woman's emotional explosion or to the request contained in it, he'll discover himself to be ineffective—and this, for men who define themselves through effectiveness, is the worst experience they can have. Their entire male identity is on the line.

In order to begin to change the situation, we need to remember that in their dealings with women, men are not only coping with the emotional unpredictability of women, they are also constantly trying to manage the monster of their own unacknowledged fears of inadequacy. When it comes to their emotional lives with women, men are doing their best just to keep their souls above water.

Men's Fear of Commitment

"To me, being a man is finding the balance point between love and power, between responsibility and freedom."
            -Real estate developer, 53

It's no earth-shattering news that women are more willing than men to make emotional commitments. In college and beyond, women are not only ready, but eager to make the commitment of marriage that men seem more reluctant, if not downright resistant, to making. Contrary to most women's notion that men are just flighty Peter Pans who refuse to grow up or dance-away lovers who like to torture women with their marital ambivalence, the male resistance to commitment is a manifestation of men's fears of inadequacy with women.

Unconsciously men know that in marrying they will put themselves back into the very situation that has always terrified them–namely, a relationship in which on a daily basis they may be totally unsuccessful in dealing with the emotions of a woman. Given all this, a man is naturally reluctant to recreate the situation from which, for a brief time in young adulthood, he may have escaped.

For the truth is that countless numbers of men have, in effect, been forced into the role of husband through the death or absence of their fathers or simply because their mothers preferred their sons to the men they married. Indeed, so many boys have been taken advantage of in this way, been taken on as surrogate husbands and emotional nursemaids, that by the time they reach adulthood, the time when women expect they should be willing to make a commitment, they feel as if they've already endured a lifetime of commitment. No wonder that they're not eager to jump back into the fray.

One 38-year-old man, harassed by his sweetheart to get

married, went berserk one night when she asked him to pick up some lettuce on his way home from work. "That's it, we're not getting married. You're just like my mother. I had to bring home everything for her. We lived right across the street from the market and she never once in fifteen years went into it. I was her slave. I had to get everything for her, right down to her panty hose and Kotex. I am *never* doing that again," he raved, then broke down crying in uncontrollable sobs.

Another reluctant committer said, "My mother had this thing about neatness. It was the only thing that made her happy. I guess her life was so empty that having everything in order was the only thing that mattered to her. She used to police my room. When everything was clean—and I mean *everything*—she was happy. When there was one thing out of place she would take it like a personal assault. I had *no* privacy. She wanted to know what everything was, why I had it, what I was going to do with it, when it would be worn out, and where I was going to keep it in the meantime. I finally found a way to take the cardboard bottom off one of the lamps in my room. I kept some condoms in there and a few other things. Frankly, I don't know how I kept it together until I finally escaped to college at eighteen."

A third young man said, point blank: "I've always been my mother's husband, the one she could cry to, her escort when my father was gone, the one she complained to about her own mother. It wasn't that my father wasn't willing. It was just that she liked me better. When I was little I liked it; I felt special. When I got older, I started to hate it; she wouldn't let me go. She'd have some kind of trauma every time I had a great date. She'd make me come into her room afterward and kiss her good-night. It was creepy. Now I can't stand it when women get attached to me. I always have one main girlfriend and a couple of others on the side. The thought of being stuck with one woman is absolutely terrifying to me."

As these examples demonstrate, many men resist commitment not because they don't love women, but because their initial male-female relationship was not the comforting sanctuary we epitomize the mother-child relationship to be, but a battlefield in which the boy's physical and emotional energies were surreptitiously mobilized on his mother's behalf.

For, far from being fully equipped to be mothers, to give the one-directional generosity that motherhood at its best requires, a great many mothers are emotionally in need themselves. Whether this is by virtue of childhood deprivation ("My mother was an orphan; her mother and father had both abandoned her by the time she was two") or their own disappointing marriages ("My mother loved my father, but he was a doctor and never came home"), many women engage in motherhood as deprived little girls, or women still unfulfilled in romance. As a result, many mothers appropriate their sons as husbands, lovers, business advisors, household slaves, and emotional confidantes, delivering them to adulthood with an often unidentified but nevertheless internally seething rage toward women.

In their adult relationships, men seek refuge in the feminine sanctuary that was originally denied them, but once coming into its presence, they also come in contact with their suppressed rage at their mothers. This makes them wince and eventually turn away (with any excuse whatsoever) from the women who desire commitment from them.

What makes matters worse is that women don't understand where men in this situation are coming from. They're appalled by men's anger at their mothers, or, in observing men's "thoughtfulness" to their mothers, the way men dotingly or devotedly meet their mother's every need, want to capitalize on it for themselves. ("He's so good to his mother; I thought he'd be good to me." "He calls his mother every night. I thought he'd make a great husband." "He pays his mother's dentist bills; he just bought her a new upper bridge; I knew he'd be a wonderful provider.") Whether women are put off by men's repressed rage at their mothers or enchanted by men's service to them, rather than understanding the pain men suffer in these unresolved emotional attachments, women want what they want from men, and feeling disappointed and rejected, blindly judge the men who are reluctant to make a commitment to them.

While many women are keenly aware of the pressures their mothers put on them—to give them emotional solace, to make their dreams vicariously come true (by being the prom queen, by marrying the rich man)—we often aren't aware that counterpart tragedies have befallen men nor that these tragedies have affected a man's capacity for commitment. Because of gender this situation affects men and women very differently. For, in marrying, a woman gets away from the woman in her life, while for a man marriage represents the substitution of one potentially overwhelming woman (his wife) for the original overpowering woman in his life (his mother).

Feeling Responsible for it All

> *"I'm tired of being THE MAN; I'm tired of having to play God. I'm not responsible for meeting your expectations; I'm not responsible for not meeting your expectations. I'm just a person on a journey."*
>
> *-City planner, 43*

Even when men haven't been so obviously psychologically abused, they often have trouble making a commitment. This is because they fear that in the intimate proximity of an adult romantic relationship, not only will they have to deal with their fears of inadequacy, but they will also come face to face with real responsibilities the male role requires. As one young man said: "I'm scared to death of relationships; I'd like to fall in love, but I've never made enough money for any woman to want me. I'm pretty good looking so a lot of women fall for me, but when they find out I don't have what most women want: money, a house, job security, they lose interest. I'm just a fling, a good idea. I know I deserve to be loved for myself, and not just for being a billfold, but when I come away from these romantic episodes, I feel like a failure at relationships."

Women are virtually unaware of the hidden psychological blueprint by which a man's unconscious is programmed with the message that choosing a woman means that he instantly and endlessly becomes responsible for her, the guardian of her dreams, the architect of her reality.

From time immemorial, men have been biologically, sociologically, and psychologically groomed for the job of making the world safe for women. Traditionally in marriage, a woman, in effect, turns her life over to a man for safekeeping. She is delivered and protected; he becomes totally responsible. And the minute he feels his responsibility, he also faces his fears. Will he be able to provide at the level she needs and wants? Will she be happy? Will he be able to make the house payment? What if he loses his job? What if he gets tired of it all? No wonder he runs.

While it is no longer completely true in the present epoch of emerging female equality that men are responsible for women, women who are still troubled by male reluctance to commit need only take note of the fact that the paradigm of male responsibility is embedded in any romantic relationship. Even now, when women's roles have been dramatically revised, women expect men to take the initiative. It's the man who must take the emotional and economic risks in courting a woman. It's still most often the man who asks the woman out on a date, the man who pays for it, the man who initiates sex, and the man who does or doesn't call again. Except for the rarest of exceptions, men send women flowers, and not vice versa. A man embraces a woman when she sleeps; she puts her head on his chest, cries on his shoulder, leans on him when she's loosing her footing— on the ski trail or in life.

It is these male-as-protector rituals which, in courtship, set the tone for the vast array of security-providing services men will have to perform. Romance, marriage, and so called "real life" all present men with the overwhelming montage of responsibilities that a man has no choice but fulfill.

In spite of external changes, at the unconscious level, both men and women assume that men will pay the rent, take care of the car, the plumbing, the taxes, the future, and his mother-in-law. Of course he'll also want children, and of course he'll be happy to provide for them. Before he even sets foot in marriage, a man already knows this and, internally, he cringes. What if he can't get a good enough job? What if he gets fired, what if his wife finds out that he doesn't know how to be a good father, what if, in times of crisis, he turns out to be a coward? Of course most men aren't consciously thinking about all this, but on an unconscious level their decisions are being designed according to this awareness. On an unconscious level they always sense the oncoming endless array of inexorable male responsibilities.

This, by the way, is the secret, invisible reason men have bachelor parties. In a sense, a bachelor party is a wake for male freedom. Men don't get together just to celebrate the good fortune of the groom, to indulge in one last hurrah of male-bonding revelry, but to bid farewell to a man's independence, to his right to irresponsibility, to the time in which, for him, the world was young. As one libatious celebrant said: "We got together; we got drunk; we laughed our heads off, and then we sent him to the noose." What this young man was intuitively acknowledging is that the groom is moving on from the state of being footloose and fancy free, to the state of taking on the awesome burdens of making a woman happy. For, whether he consciously admits it or not, every man knows that to be married is to be—across the board—responsible.

In general, women have no conception of, and certainly little empathy for, what it means psychologically for men to have to live out the myth that they must be the ultimate source of security for women. Even now, with women working along-side men in virtually every male profession, women can still just barely imagine what it means to live—as men do—by the centuries-old male tradition of knowing that you are the one who inescapably, always, and without question must provide and protect. This is by now such a deeply ingrained part of male consciousness that in general, neither men nor women take note of it—it's simply the way things are.

Some years ago, my sweetheart and I were camping in the wilderness when some thieves broke into our campground at night. The minute he heard the noise, my sweetheart jumped up—as I expected he would—to scare the marauders away. It wasn't until sometime afterward that I realized it had never occurred to me that he wouldn't get up to protect me. In fact, both of us had immediately assumed that he would face the danger alone. He was the man; that was his job. He was the man, so, whether or not he was scared to death (as he later told me he had been), he was the one who would stumble up out of his sleep to protect us. No matter where they are or what they're doing, whether they're on vacation, whether it's midnight, whether they're at home or in a strange land—whether or not they're shaking in their boots; men are there to protect.

The male-as-protector, male-will-do-everything myth is

so intrinsic that it operates in even some of the smallest gestures men offer to women. One woman told me her new boyfriend insisted that she trade places with him in bed. The reason for this, he explained, was that where she'd been sleeping was closer to the door. He wanted to sleep there, so, if anyone tried to break into the house, he would be occupying the place between her and the oncoming danger.

Such an instinctive offering of male physical protection is but one small everyday example of the total sense of responsibility men feel all the time. In fact, the psychological vocation of bearing all burdens is so intrinsic to the male identity that to whatever degree a man feels scared or resentful about it, he either sublimates it or criticizes himself. Men judge themselves harshly for being ambivalent about taking on the male role, or for feeling inadequate to carry its burdens and responsibilities. To the extent that men don't instinctively jump to pursue it, they feel odd or wrong as men. "There must be something wrong with me. I don't really want to get married," they say, or "There must be something wrong with me. I'm sick of taking care of my wife and children."

Women don't realize that even though they have made contributory strides in taking on certain responsibilities (women do now contribute to the family coffers, sometimes even more than the men in their lives; women do take the car to be fixed, call the plumber, and mow the lawn), men still haven't been relieved of the psychological burden of responsibility. They still *feel* responsible, still operate from the internal notion that it's their job to hold the world together. When it comes to the traditional male responsibilities of providing and protecting, men are still the court of the last resort.

The way men feel about their responsibilities is comparable to the way women feel about being the psychological parent, the court of the last resort when it comes to physically and emotionally nurturing children. To be the psychological parent is the uniquely female burden. As most women know, even when a man is changing diapers, wiping away tears, taking the kids to preschool, or helping with homework, psychologically, it's still the mother who feels like the "real" parent.

Just as men have internalized their sense of responsibility for providing and protecting, women have internalized the responsibility for childrearing. It's the mother who sleeps with one ear cocked when her child is ailing, it's the mother who knows intuitively when her son has had a bad day at school, when her daughter's been jilted by a friend. It is women who are the choreographers of relationship, the interpersonal peacemakers. They make peace between their husbands and children, their children and one another, their children and their children's friends. It's a mother's job, and everyone knows it, to make sure that her children are happy. To be the psychological parent is to know at every turn that you are responsible for how your child feels about himself, for what she is doing at any given moment, and for how in the end he or she will turn out.

Although we have come a long way in sharing these male and female burdens, the changes we've made still haven't been integrated at the unconscious level where we can express them as new psychological attitudes. Both men and women have revised what they are doing—women now work and men now change diapers—but we still haven't changed the way our collective social unconscious views our respective responsibilities. In our hearts, women are still the nurturers and men are still responsible for everything else.

Support in the Inadequacy Department

"If only I could have a real feeling with a woman without still having to be the protector for just one minute."
                                                            -Engineer, 38

Men don't get the idea that they're responsible from nowhere. In fact, even now, when women have assumed responsibility for themselves, and in many cases also their children, we still tend to think of men as the heroes who, no matter what the crisis, will solve the problem. Consciously and unconsciously, we look to men not only to be the grantors of family environmental safety and economic security, but also to give us a sense of our own womanhood by loving and providing for us, and these expectations set up another scenario in which men try to succeed but fear they will fail.

In spite of our own liberation, on an unconscious level we still look to men as the ones who, no matter what has befallen, will rescue and provide. For example, Monica, a successful junior college administrator, endlessly complained that her husband, a university professor, "wasn't a provider" because she "still had to work." She completely ignored the fact that she enjoyed her job, that she and her husband had exorbitantly expensive tastes, traveled extensively, and that her expectations were ridiculous given the fact that for their own aesthetic pleasure they had taken on the burden of owning a house that was far beyond their means. In other words, no matter whether their financial needs were a consequence of necessity or outrageous self-indulgence, she expected that her husband, all by himself, would provide for them.

These expectations are really nothing more than barely camouflaged father fantasies. Some women come right out and say that they want "some big strong guy" to protect them just the way Daddy did, and even when this longing isn't so boldly articulated, many women carry it as an unformed unconscious expectation. Women hope and believe that like the mythical perfect father, a man will do it all for them.

Women's own evolution has done much to explode the myth of the omnipotent man who fulfills every need, and has even instructed women in how to provide for and protect themselves. But in our collective unconscious there's still a residue of the myth that Daddy will come along once again and take care of everything. No matter how individually successful a woman may be, she may still dream in some secret chamber of her heart of the millionaire who will sweep her off her feet and take care of her.

As a case in point, Jan is a 47-year-old widow who's been supporting herself and her two children very comfortably for ten years. She owns her own house and loves her work as a real estate agent, but she's still avidly waiting for the man of her dreams to show up and "rescue her" financially. What's so interesting about her position is that she isn't waiting for a man to give her love, companionship, or sexual excitement—all of which she says she has enough of in her life. When she talks about her situation and its solution, she invariably speaks of her need for "economic rescue."

Obviously, in spite of her considerable financial success, she sees her own adequacy as an aberration, an achievement made inescapable through some error of the fates, a career she'll give up when the right man comes along. Although she obviously doesn't need a man for financial security, she continues to fantasize she does. In so doing, she typifies a great many women who in reality have transcended their need for male deliverance, but are still psychologically bound to the myth that men must rescue and provide.

Because there is still an immense disparity between what

women are capable of doing and what they secretly desire, women send men a double message. Thus, in addition to men's own natural tendency to feel responsible, they also sense women's desire for them to continue to be responsible. This is how women collude with men to keep men on the job—and to keep them in terror that they may fail.

As a consequence, women's real contributions have little impact on men's overweening sense of responsibility and their concomitant fear of not being enough. The result of all this is that, rather than freeing men to explore themselves, to become acquainted with the very sensitivities and emotions most women claim they are longing to have men share with them, women (albeit unwittingly) hold men in the place of being in-charge-of-it-all. And since a highly developed sense of responsibility is the utter antithesis of psychological vulnerability, it is almost impossible for men to go exploring in the emotional realm when they're still stuck in the responsibility mode.

But because women's collusion is so subtle, it's very difficult to see that, without our consciously intending to, we're requiring men to continue to carry the burdens of male responsibility. The sad thing is that, not being able to see our collusion, we can't help men get beyond the demands of their burden. Instead, we keep men chained to it.

As for men, they continue to be haunted by the fear that in trying to keep women happy and to fulfill their huge responsibilities they will be discovered to be inadequate, partial or total failures. Since to be responsible is to have no choice but *to be responsible*, men can't open up their emotional knapsacks and spread out the wares of their fears. Since they can't, they're forever in the position of deluding themselves and women about what's really going on with them. They have no choice but to continue to deny, repress, and project their fears. This separates them not only from what is deep in themselves but also from the rich and nourishing emotional communion they might have with women.

Because men feel they are responsible, they can't break down and break into themselves and consequently, women can't receive the conscious aliveness and sensitivity they desire from men. Thus the burden of men's overwhelming sense of responsibility continues to be a nightmare from which men can't wake up, and a daydream in which women hope for the impossible.

Is there a way out? Something is being asked here of both men and women. In order to get the real change we seek in our relationships, women will have to grow up, give up the Daddy-will-do-it-all myth, and stop colluding with men in their hero-designate trips. And men will have to give up their pride, stop being ashamed of their fears, and start risking the sensitive revelations that will eventually gain them access to women's respect and empathy.

This requires that women remember and men acknowledge that men are afraid of being inadequate. For both men and women to stand in the light of living with men's fears—their fear of failure, their fear of not being enough—is the beginning of a healing that is the necessary precondition for a whole new age between men and women, one not divided by gender, but united by the truer bonds of human joy and human suffering. Recognizing these truths will lead us to the place where we can meet men democratically, face to face in the intimacy where all our vulnerabilities can blossom, all our empathy can grow.

More than We Ever Imagined: Men Need Women So Much

9

"Men need women because women have already got what men still need."

-Screenwriter, 39

One of the best kept secrets about men is that men need women so much. Our social mythology, of course, is that women need men so much. Women have to trick and trap men into wanting them, because, so the myth goes, women need men so desperately and men don't need women at all. Women have to be gorgeous, sexy, intelligent, charming, submissive, and irresistible, so they can get a man—the man who, supposedly, can live without them but whom they can't possibly live without.

In this view, men are stalwart, sturdy and strong; they do what they want; they have all the power, all the money, and all the opportunity. They can have any woman they want; they can leave any woman they're tired of and replace her within five minutes, because to a man a woman is just an object and it doesn't really matter which woman a man is attached to. That's the myth, anyway. But the truth is that men need women far more than women imagine, and in a much deeper way.

Men need women to love them, to give their lives meaning, to prove to themselves they're real men, to give them a place to come home to. Men need women in order to approach their own emotional experience: to recreate the nurturing bond that was broken with their mothers, to grant the withheld blessing from their fathers, to replicate the affection of their sisters, to erase the competition with their brothers.

Men need women to love them so they don't feel abandoned, so they can feel their feelings vicariously, so they can get their emotional needs met without having to express them in words, so they can be connected to the spiritual, so they can feel human. Far from being the powerful, omnipotent heroes women fantasize them to be, men are emotionally fragile.

Vulnerability is the sense that you are weaker than that which surrounds you and has the potential to overtake you, the sense that you might not be equal to what you're called upon to do, or that your mental or physical strength won't be sufficient to the demands that may be placed upon you. Vulnerability leads to the need for protection. Just as the little boy who's afraid of the barky German Shepherd on the corner needs his mother to walk him to school, whenever and wherever we're vulnerable we need to enlist an outsider's help: if we're sick, the person who can bring the chicken soup; if we're physically frail, someone to lean on; if discouraged, an optimist to cheer us up.

Even scheming high school students know that if you're afraid of flunking the test, you should sit next to someone who's smart and writes big. Vulnerability implies the need for assistance.

But when it comes to their emotional vulnerabilities, men are the disenfranchised. They can't exhibit their fears and limitations; it isn't manly. Instead of being able to discover and articulate their vulnerabilities, men are stuck with them like an ever-growing pile of dirty laundry they keep jamming back into the closet. Since they are, in effect, psychologically cornered in this way, many men try to talk or numb themselves out of their own vulnerability. It's almost as if in a desperate, camouflaged effort to prove to themselves that they're not vulnerable, men deal with everyone else's needs in a kind of insane wild hope that by taking care of their wives, children, bosses, the IRS, and their mothers-in-law, their own needs, fears, and frailties will somehow disappear.

In acting out the quintessence of the male role in this way, men engage in what I call the Everything-But Syndrome. Like the blind person who does everything but learn Braille, the fat person who does everything but diet, the alcoholic who tries everything but AA, men work too hard; say too little; cry not at all; drink, smoke, and watch television too much—in short, do *everything* but admit they're in need.

Since the male role prohibits men from asking for assistance because they're supposed to be the ones who grant assistance, they've had to develop alternative methods of getting their real needs satisfied. One of these, as we have already seen, is through passive aggression, the male form of emotional manipulation. Another is a kind of primitive level expression, emotionally grunting as it were, Ralph Cramden style: coming home and bellowing if the dinner's not on the table, threatening their wives with abandonment. Yet another—and although unconscious, perhaps the healthiest method of trying to get their needs met—is by putting themselves in emotional proximity to women.

Men go to women in order to be in the presence of what is still undeveloped in themselves. Since, in relation to their own emotions, men are still so unformed, they are drawn toward women in order to be in the presence of what, at the level of their unconscious intuition, they know they must come to possess. For it's only through their proximity to women, who are already allowed to admit their emotional vulnerabilities, that men have even a shred of a chance of unearthing their own. In the same way as, by being in the neighborhood, you can pick up the fragrance of the autumn leaves the guy up the street is burning, by being in the presence of a woman's emotions a man hopes, by osmosis, to take on a few of his own.

To the degree men live by this unconscious emotional homing instinct, they can either use their proximity to women as an opportunity to develop their emotions, or, should they prefer to be lazy, as an opportunity to have a vicarious emotional experience they don't have to generate themselves. Historically, men have frequently done the latter, becoming emotional peeping toms who ride piggy-back on a woman's emotions. By watching the emotional performance of women, they almost feel as if they've had an emotional experience themselves.

This acquisition by proximity is a familiar human behavior. In each of us there are a number of attributes and possibilities which, for one reason or another, remain unformed. To the degree that we've lost touch with or never fulfilled our individual potentials, we have the possibility of gaining possession of them through proximal experience. Thus each of us chooses someone to love at least partially because he or she is in possession of what we need. So long as we're in the presence of a person who embodies what we seek to develop, we have an opportunity to experience it vicariously and, through a process of awakening and assimilation, to gradually take it on and incorporate it in ourselves.

This is what we mean, for example, when we say of another person: he's so funny, when I'm with him I get funny myself; she's so sensitive, when I'm around her I feel so tender; or, he's so calm, when I'm in his presence, I settle down. This is why, for example, we see long term friends beginning to mimic or adopt the mannerisms and speech patterns of one another, and why long-married couples begin to look, talk, and act like one another.

Since for men what is most often repressed are aspects of their feminine dimension—sensitivity, tenderness, the full range of emotions and the language with which to communicate them—it is only in the presence of women, who possess these attributes in full embodiment, that men have a chance to gain or regain those precious aspects of themselves.

Men, simply by virtue of being men, can't provide this emotional opening for one another. They can give each other male bonding. They can show each other how to be brave, courageous, steadfast, and proud; but they cannot, given what it still is to be a man in this culture, lead one another to the intricacies of their emotions, which, in our culture can still be fully enacted and expressed only by women.

Women possess in realization what men possess only as the shadow of a possibility, an incomplete dream. In the presence of a woman a man can feel what it is to feel. The way a woman lives out and embodies her own emotions inspires the initiation of emotion in him.

That's why, although some men have already taken a forward leap into the deep waters of their own sensitivity, it is still for the most part only in conjunction with a woman that a man can begin to experience the full richness and fluidity of his emotions. Through a woman a man can see, and eventually come to embody, the softer, more translucent aspects of himself, acquire access to his sensitive, feminine dimension, to his feelings, to his true capacity for tenderness. Through living in the presence of her feelings, a man can discover the richness and complexity of his own. In a woman a man can discover the submerged exquisite components of himself; apart from a woman, he can only conform to the tenets of the male identity. A woman provides the light in which a man can see himself, holds the mirror in which the depth of his true image in all its intricate exquisiteness can finally be revealed. In the presence of the emotional atmosphere a woman carries within her, a man can finally gain access to the deeply emotional in himself.

While this may be possible in theory, unfortunately, even when men are close to women, they can't always be successful in this process of emotional osmosis. For not only does male emotional expression go against the myth that men don't need anything, but precisely because of this myth women have never learned how to help men feel safe enough to do the emotional spelunking required to bring men emotionally home.

Thus, to the degree men consciously or unconsciously seek their own emotional development, mere proximity isn't enough. Because of both men's and women's fears about dismantling the male role, not only must a man be in a woman's emotional field, but women must also be strong enough to hold the emotional ground while men are going through the process of claiming their own submerged emotions. The man who would learn to expose his vulnerabilities needs a woman's emotional strength to make him feel safe enough to reveal them. In a sense, a woman must become temporarily like a man. She must set aside her own emotions (as men have always done) so that a man can feel his. Unconsciously most men know that this is the necessary precondition of their own emotional exploring, but neither men nor women yet know how to create the conditions by which this could happen.

The Refuge of Women

"I feel like a king when I'm with her—purposeful, proud, and whole."

-Consultant, 42

Men also need women so they can perform their manly feats on the tightrope of life. In order to go out in the workplace men have to be tough, mean, lean, competitive, heartless, aggressive machines. Like a suit of armor, a man has to put on his masculinity to meet the expectations of society, to do his work in the world. But when he is intimately in a woman's presence, he becomes availed of the possibility of casting off his armor and gaining access to the softer reaches of himself. As one high-powered political consultant said to his wife, "Of course I can't show my feelings at work. It's absurd. Can you imagine me teary-eyed in front of the state legislature? I'd be carted off in a van. The only place I can be tender is here with you at home."

Women are often surprised at this seeming doppelganger male persona—the man who's a raging lion in public, but a sweet, kind pussycat at home. One woman said she was always embarrassed to go to parties with her husband because he was so aggressive and obnoxious out in public, especially to other men. He'd disagree with them, make fools of them, insult them directly; she was sure that the people who saw him when they were out socializing could never imagine what a loving and tenderhearted man he was at home.

It is precisely because men have to be so fierce in the outside world that they need women so much. Stranded in the male competitive world and separated from women, men can only be warriors and heroes. Only at home can they even begin to be pussycats. Only at home can they possibly let down their hair. Only in contact with women can they be reminded that beneath the crunch of their armor lie the softer, more elegant aspects of themselves.

The Sanctuary of a Woman's Body

"Her body was the pool in which I learned to swim, in which I poured my tears."

-*Violinist, 75*

Surprisingly, men often come into these softer aspects of themselves through their connection with women's bodies. We all need the blessing of the human touch, need to be in the presence of another human body. For all of us, physical contact is our earliest experience of connection and belonging. In intimate physical proximity, our souls are nourished; we feel loved. The solace of another human body, the simple comforts of the human flesh—these are basic human needs.

Through contact with the female body, men receive solace at a primal level. Not only are they having a feeling experience in the moment, but they are physically drawn back to the memory of the connection they felt with their mothers in infancy, when, before language and before the noose of the male role was lowered upon them, they could still have feelings.

This is why men so often remark about the softness of women's bodies, why the physical embrace and sensual communion a woman offers is like a homecoming to him. When men extol women's physical attributes they are not only making a literal observation but also a metaphoric one, acknowledging that in physical contact with women, they are being called back from the edgy hardness of life that being a man always is, to the place where, as at the beginning of life in contact with their mothers' bodies, they could have a feeling experience. In a sense, sex and affectionate contact with a woman's body are the only forms of solace a man can legitimately seek to redress his daily sufferings from having to be a man.

This male need for physical connection is also quite visibly expressed in the male physiology, where because of the external penis, men constantly experience themselves as "being on the outside trying to get in." In a sense, a man is always looking for a place to put himself, a place where he can finally belong. As one man said, "When I'm outside I'm lonely, when I'm inside I've come home."

Men constantly seek the union that will diminish their sense of isolation, the feeling that they must be solitary, self-sufficient and strong. Union with the female body offers men consolation about the solitariness of physical incarnation itself

Men also seek physical union with women because whether or not they are consciously able to articulate it, sex also gives them a direct experience of the feminine, of that which complements maleness by embodying its opposite. Furthermore, in the sexual act, a man not only encounters the receptive feminine, he is actually received into it. In the process of being received, he has a firsthand experience of the receptive state which, at its ultimate, is the mystic feminine. On a physical level, he apprehends that to be receptive is to take in, to feel deeply, to be transformed. On a spiritual level, he is invited into his own transformation, for in this encounter with the feminine a man comes as close to his own femininity as he can possibly get without actually having to dive headlong into it for himself.

This is a gift. Through the woman's body, a man is given an example and invitation. Men aren't always aware of this, of course, and because of their own limitations, women don't always truly offer this. Indeed, for all of us, sex can be an act of spontaneous physical immediacy or a physical metaphor for the deepest meanings of our existence. Since it is a bonding which invites the erasure of ego, it puts us momentarily in the experience of being that single point of awareness which is the point of view of spiritual reality. In this sense, sex brings us in contact with the transcendent, the numinous. It places us in the presence of our own power in the universe, the capacity to be the mediums for the creation of human life while at the same time it acquaints us with our utter powerlessness. Sex illumines our connection with all who have come before us, all who will come after.

Thus in the sexual act, men as well as women become connected to life, to their power to create, effect, and transform. In some primary way, sex is, for men too, a connection with the energetic essence of life. For while men experience women as being directly in touch with the life force, mystically connected to the ultimate patterns and elements of life, and at the apogee of their generative power in the miracle of giving birth, in the procreative act men, too, can feel, if only momentarily, their own participation in the generative act. Through sex, men can be brought into the presence of the holy.

The History of Men's Need

> *"Inexplicably I found myself on the floor wailing 'Mommy, Mommy, Mommy.' I can't describe the pain. It was at once searing and healing. I felt as if I'd been torn from the bosom of life."*
>
> *-Therapy client, 34*

Men's need for women is formed in the womb, since it is a woman's life and body which sustains a man-child even before he is born. Men perceive the world before their birth and enter it at their birth through a woman's body. Male children are brought to the world, then wrapped, carried, and nurtured by their mothers' hands, and breasts, and arms.

In a sense, a man's first love is his mother. Whether that love was disappointing in some way—because of the devastation of abandonment or betrayal—or whether it was a blissful bondedness, a boy's relationship with his mother imprints on him the image of what it is to be connected.

Early on, in the happy days of infancy and childhood, a boy is allowed to indulge his physical and emotional attachment to his mother, to suckle her breast, to kiss her and be kissed by her, to cry and not be ashamed. He can break down and sob with her over a broken toy, a skinned knee, a playmate's harsh words. A boy can be babied and nurtured, seek refuge in her body, tell her his troubles without having his dignity compromised. He is allowed, unabashedly, to want her and the solace she provides. In short, with pure feeling, with his as yet unsuppressed feminine sensitivity, he can find consolation in hers.

But at a certain point, a boy is required to separate himself from his mother because it's time for him to become "a big boy." Through a series of subtle behavioral reinforcements he is gradually instructed to withdraw physically and emotionally from his mother so he can develop the hairy toughness which will eventually turn him into a real man. This process of individuation is very painful for the little boy and later the young man, although he's usually unaware of it. On a conscious level, he's simply doing all the things that boys and young men do: going to bed without hugs and kisses, playing sports, having fights, winning, going out and breaking windows, defying school principals and fathers. These are the cultural emotional rituals through which, in time, without even quite knowing he has done so, a young man leaves his mother behind.

But it's not only what he must do to become "a big boy" that separates him from his mother. It is also what his mother does to him. Knowing she must separate from him and following the unwritten rules of training him to be "a real boy," she also gradually withdraws from him.

As one man said, "When I was very little, my mother used to have this wonderful way of just sitting for what seemed like hours, in a big old armchair in the living room. I would go up to her and put my head on her lap and she would rub my neck and scratch my back. Then, one day, she said I couldn't do it anymore because I was 'a big boy now.' Now, whenever I feel a woman's fingernails along my back I feel a strange mixture of pleasure and an aching kind of sorrow."

Another man said that when he was two and his father lost his job and his mother had to go back to work he would drag himself to his parents' bed and sleep horizontally at the bottom, believing that if he could throw himself across his mother's feet she would never get up and leave him again.

Whatever the particular circumstances in this developmental rite of passage, a boy is gradually pushed away by his mother. It is assumed that, because he's a boy, these separations won't have a negative emotional effect on him. To the extent that he might experience his mother's absence as a loss, he has to camouflage his pain. Instead of feeling it and expressing it in words, he must sublimate his grief and rage in acceptable male undertakings—school success or athletic prowess—or by acting out, becoming a juvenile delinquent.

Since this emotional rite of passage is neither consciously acknowledged nor openly discussed in our culture, to whatever degree a boy vaguely senses his loss, he can't talk about it, and the pain of his separation, because it remains unarticulated, continues in adulthood as a deep internal wound. Thus there is always a mystery, a pain of incompletion, that surrounds a young man's breaking away from his mother. Although boys must and usually do complete this separation, it is felt as the small ongoing interior sorrow that men are endlessly trying to redress through intimate contact with a woman.

Thus we see that in defining themselves as male, men have no choice but to submit to this process of separation in which they must give up their connection to the feminine. Later in adulthood, however, after this individuation process has been completed and male identity is firmly established, men want to recreate the close connection with a woman which feels like an island of safety for them. Instinctively they know that their lives will be incomplete, their functioning impaired if they aren't once again connected to the nurturing feminine.

Abandonment Redux

"I keep picking women who are always running off somewhere—to business meetings, to friends' houses, to their mothers. And I'm always mad they're leaving."
-*Massage Therapist, 29*

Once having found the love they seek, however, still other difficulties arise, for since their mothers were the ones who, of necessity, both gave love and took it away, adult men have a very ambivalent relationship to women. On one hand they seek the warmth, love, and nurturing they experienced (or wish they had experienced) with their mothers; on the other they still carry the rage of betrayal that this nurturance was taken away (or never given).

This terrible ambivalence is dropped off at the doorstep of the women they love. Men want to recreate that sense of nurturance and protection through a relationship with a woman, yet at the same time they resent the woman's power to take her love away. As an adult, a man lives in terror that his heartbreaking childhood drama will be enacted again with the woman he loves, and unconsciously, he's angry about it.

In a sense, it's as if a man says to himself, "Oh, I know how this story goes: First I feel close and protected. She loves me; I can put my head on her lap, and everything's wonderful. Then one day I wake up and all of it's taken away." In telling himself this story a man almost preconditions himself to write it again in his love affairs and marriages. Often by expecting that once again he will be abandoned, he indulges in behaviors which create the very distance and separation he fears will be inevitable.

These feelings of fear of abandonment, transferred from childhood to adult experience, are one of the reasons why men feel so frustrated with women and why women seem powerful and mercurial to them. In men's perception, women leave, and if they haven't left yet, they might soon. Since men never know whether women are going to stay or go, or if what they do can influence whether women stay or go, men see women as having all the control and themselves as having to constantly adapt their behavior so women won't leave them.

But there is yet another complex component to men's ambivalence about women and their concomitant fear of abandonment. When a child experiences abandonment, he always interprets it as somehow being his fault. He can't actually conceptualize that circumstances—either the requirements of his own maturation process or the specific deprivations caused by the birth of a brother or sister, a mother's illness, or economic hardships—could be the cause of his abandonment. He can only imagine that it was somehow because he himself was wrong, inadequate or bad, that he was deprived of his mother's love. As a result, many men unconsciously feel as if their abandonment by their mothers—whether physical or emotional—is somehow their own fault. Since they feel guilty about their own imagined precipitation of their mother's withdrawal, they constantly live in terror that in adulthood they will do something or fail to do something which will result in their being abandoned again.

Thus for every man, developing something he can offer to a woman is always the thing he wants to do most. He will do anything, try anything, be anything, in an effort to make a woman happy. If he can make her happy, he reasons, she won't leave, she won't get cold, disappear, withdraw, take her body away from him. He does this if the woman is kind and good—so she will stay and bestow her feminine riches on him—and also if she is cold, or difficult. In this case, where the woman already embodies a man's worst fears, or is a reincarnation of his emotionally distant mother, he will attempt to sweeten her up, to turn her into the woman he hopes will ultimately be able to nurture and receive him.

But these efforts are always underwritten by a profound sense of insecurity. Will they work? Will it last? Will what he has done be enough? Within each man is the cowering abandoned boy who wonders if what he does or is will be sufficient to keep him in the loving nurturing proximity of the woman he loves. Whatever he offers—financial security, the comfort of his physical protection, his sexual fidelity, the outcome of his work, his feeble attempts at being emotional—underlying all his efforts to please a woman is the memory that long ago, for some mysterious reason—because of something he did or didn't do—he was separated from his mother. Thus his fear is that with the woman of the present, the loss will occur once again.

Why Does He Always Leave?

*"One day he's here and he's all lovey-dovey, talking about
the Bahamas and getting married. The next day he leaves
a message on my machine that he's going out of town for
three weeks and I never hear from him again."*

-Magazine editor, 34

It is this fear of abandonment that also explains a great
many of men's approach/avoidance behaviors. What I mean by
this is that, as many women know all too well, men can establish
very intimate contact with women and then, seemingly for no
reason, withdraw—fail to call, resist moving in, promote hostility, threaten to leave, or disappear for days at a time. One
woman remarked that whenever she had had a particularly
warm experience with her husband, the next night he would
disappear "with the boys" and not come home until so late that
when he finally did she was totally enraged. She'd wake up and
blow up at him, thus creating the emotional distance he
unconsciously feared might surface at any time for any inexpli-
cable reason.

Another woman told about spending a beautiful day in
the country with a wonderful man; he wined her and dined her,
took her to bed and very tenderly made love to her, then didn't
call her for two weeks. When he finally did, he referred to her
as a "buddy." It later came out in therapy that his mother had
died when he was three, that his single memory of her was of
standing at the foot of her hospital bed toward the end of her
illness. The morning after his beautiful experience, the man
had gotten up early, and seeing the woman asleep in his bed,
had remembered his final painful encounter with his mother,
and, unconsciously imagining another imminent loss, had
quietly pushed the woman away.

Such passive-aggressive behaviors can either provoke the feared abandonment or dilute the level of intimacy to the point where—as a "buddy" for example, rather than as a lover—the degree of intimacy is no longer scary to a man. In other words, the man has devolved the intimacy to the point where it no longer feels so precious that to lose it would be a significant loss. By diminishing the quality of the experience, he himself creates the dissolution of the emotional bond so that he can't be unexpectedly victimized by its disappearance. As long as a man feels he can leave without being devastated himself, he feels as if he's safe in a relationship.

Another way men compensate for their fear of abandonment is by calling up the handy-dandy defense of reaction formation, becoming bullying, macho, he-men, threatening to abandon women in order to protect themselves from the fear of their own potential loss. Here, once again, instead of coming forward with a direct verbal expression of their fear, they convert their own anxiety into an attack on women, pretending they're not afraid, and trying to get women to be scared in their place. Here the paradigm is: so long as the woman is scared, the man can relax. She won't leave him if she's scared that he'll leave her.

One woman said that for years every time she and her husband had a fight he would get in his truck and, spewing gravel, drive away. For years she would lie awake scared to death he would never come back. Finally, she got so sick of his abusive disappearing act, which she had always believed represented a real threat, that she decided to leave him. Instantly he turned into a desperate whimpering baby, begging her not to leave, telling her he couldn't live without her, that all those times he'd driven off he really had no intention of leaving.

Like passive aggression, this compensatory behavior does nothing to solve the real underlying problem and often only exaggerates men's fears by putting women off, and causing women to indeed withdraw. However, what women need to know, remember, and address in their own behavior is that however a man may choose to handle his insecurity, whenever he approaches a woman to get his needs met, he is internally juggling his ancient fear that he will lose her.

While it is unglamorous and perhaps even disconcerting for both men and women to contemplate the fragility and magnitude of men's fears, it's high time the notion that only women fear abandonment be discarded. Men, too, are afraid of separation, of being abandoned. For a man, too, losing his partner can feel like the end of the world, like emotional death. In order for men and women to come closer to one another we all need to remember that, rather than being the exclusive privilege of women, the fear of abandonment is a primal human emotion.

Men Want to Give Something Women Can Receive

"If she takes what I give her, I know she's happy and then I feel happy too. I know she won't leave."

-Salesman, 36

Because of their need for women, men want to give to the women they love. When a woman receives and values what a man gives, she is, in effect, acknowledging her need for him, and he knows he has a place with her. This makes him feel safe and connected, worthy in turn of receiving what he needs from her. This is why men bring women flowers, why they buy their wives fur coats or take them to Europe, why a man feels a sense of well-being when he can build a house for his wife or buy his sweetheart a car.

As one man said, "My mother would never let me help

her—pay the bills, protect her from my alcoholic father, rescue her from the piles of kids. She had ten children and she was always exhausted and depressed. She worked herself to the bone, and then died when I was eighteen. To me the message was, if you can't reach a woman with what you have to give, she'll die, she'll leave. How can I get a woman to take what I want to give her so she won't have to leave?—that's my eternal question."

In their adult romantic relationships men instinctively know there's an unwritten law of balance operating beneath the surface. Only if they have satisfied the woman in their life will they be able to get what they need in return: sex, conversation, companionship, a place to come home.

Men also want to give what women will receive because they need to experience themselves as loving, as being capable of generating the bonding and tenderness that comes from giving to the women they love. This is particularly true in sex, for when a woman expresses through her orgasm that she has received what a man has given, a man feels potent, worthy, competent, and connected. Since a man is always afraid of losing his connection to a woman, he's not only happy, but relieved when he can give her something she will receive. He senses, for a time at least, that his union with her is secure; and to the degree that a woman can be consistent in receiving what he has to offer—sex, presents, physical and financial support— to that degree only can he be free from his haunting fear of abandonment.

Women need to know how delighted and gratified men are when they can nurture, pamper, indulge, protect, and defend their sweethearts, wives, and lovers. When the women they love receive what they give, men are at peace and in joy. As one man put it, quite simply: "Why do I love her? Because she receives my love." To a man a woman's receiving is the recognition of who he is.

Still Out in the Cold

"Intimacy. Intimacy. Intimacy. That's all I really want. But I don't know how to get it and I don't even know if I'd be able to recognize it if it showed up. Only a woman can show me what it is."

                                              -Boutique owner, 33

What is so paradoxical and sad is that, in spite of their seemingly endless efforts, men's need for women remains so great. This is because it continues to be almost totally unacknowledged by both men and women. Whereas a woman can openly acknowledge her need for a man—women can freely admit to one another that they're "looking for someone special," that they want to be taken care of, or that they're desperate for a relationship—men still need to keep their relationship desperation under their hats. Women are allowed to cry on one another's shoulders about not having a Friday night date, not finding a husband, not getting what they need from the husbands they have; but men are expected to act as if such "trivial" matters are irrelevant to them. In being permitted to be forthright about their need, women, in a sense, have the legitimacy of their needs confirmed. They also get the benefit of the emotional release that comes from venting frustration when their needs aren't being met; but because they can't even admit what their true needs are, men's needs remain consistently unacknowledged and therefore unaddressed.

For anyone, an unaddressed need is always exaggerated by an overlay of panic. This is because the person with the unmet need is experiencing not only his need, but also his terror that his need may never be met. Thus an unexpressed need, rather than receding, becomes more and more developed and intense. So it is that as men continue to deny their deep need for what they can receive only from women, they find themselves unconsciously and paradoxically in even greater need of it.

Tragically, despite men's great need for women, at this moment in history, rather than feeling connected and worthy, men are feeling singularly disconnected from women. Although they may not be vociferous about it, men really do want to love us. In the most profound sense, men want to be taken back in—to the nest, to the heart, to the emotional and spiritual sanctuary that only women can offer them. Men have been out in the cold for so long that unless women come out to them and take them very tenderly by the hand, they will never be able to find their way home.

Aching for Wholeness: Men and the Feminine Consciousness

10

"*Basically men are useless in relationships unless they've developed their female side.*"

-Computer executive, 36

If Freud's unforgettable question of the 1890s was "What do women want?" then the antiphonal question for the 1990s is "What do men need?" I believe the perennial attempt to answer Freud's question stems from the unconscious hope that if only, or if ever, men could figure out what women need and could satisfy them, then finally they could discover their own needs too. In a sense, men have been living in emotional poverty, for, as we have seen, until very recently their emotional needs, both collective and individual, have been virtually unidentified, unacknowledged, and unaddressed.

What *do* men need? Men need to be emotionally healed. Men need to be released from their roles as women's enemies and saviors. Men need to gain access to the sensitivity women claim they want them to exhibit; men need to be freed from their own limiting definitions of what it is to be a man. Men need to have an internal, as well as an external life, to be able to feel as well as to do, to express as well as suppress, to contemplate as well as perform. In short, men need to have an emotional life, to be able to communicate—with words, with tears, with tender gestures—with women and with one another about the various rich and difficult inner contents of their lives.

As we have seen, however, rather than being given or guided into an emotional life, men have been trapped in the role of being provider-protectors, heroes, and automatons, and they literally do not have access to the emotional materials and techniques with which to create the emotional experience they need. As things stand now, they are delivering all they can from their limited repertoire, and the fact that they're willing to give women everything except the emotional encounter is itself a proof of what they don't possess.

It's not for lack of good will that they continue to disappoint women; they simply can't deliver what they still don't know they have, the invisible component to which men have always held title but have never gained possession.

This mysterious vacancy in a man's psyche is what we may call the feminine consciousness. By feminine consciousness I refer to those qualities of personality, whether they reside in men or women, that are in essence receptive, intuitive, caritative, and visionary. By receptive I mean able to take in, to be acted upon; by intuitive, able to sense by extra-ordinary and specifically nonverbal means; by caritative, feeling, nurturing, responsive to that which is in need or pain; and by visionary, partaking of the capacity to see the unseen, imagine the impossible, connect with the universal, the mysterious, the divine. The feminine consciousness is the consciousness of union, of peace, of sensitivity. It is the consciousness that has as its essence the seeking of similarity, rather than difference. In all of us, it is the force that binds, not divides, that is willing to undergo transformation, rather than defend the status quo.

In the past, these luminous qualities have been seen as primarily pertaining to or residing in women, hence we call them feminine. Indeed, in general it is true that women have been the carriers of the feminine consciousness in the world. We all look to women to nourish our bodies and spirits, to console us in the dark hours, to nurture our children, to express our collective anguish at the wailing wall, to apprehend the truth beyond language that intuition embodies.

The Whole of Personality

"From now on, I'm going to make the important decisions in my life according to my feelings, my intuition, my logic, and my best self-interest."

-Divorcing entrepreneur, 42

It is precisely this feminine dimension men need to incorporate now. To know their woundedness, to be able to grieve, long for, and want; to desire, to tend, to console—these aspects of feminine consciousness which have always before been seen to be the exclusive province of women must now become the familiar stomping grounds of men.

If we think of the totality of a person's consciousness, we may say that, as in some alchemical formula, it is composed of a certain number of parts which we call masculine and others which we call feminine. Each of us is a blend of the masculine and feminine aspects, with men, of course, tending to contain more of the masculine and women more of the feminine.

The degree to which a man embodies what we call the masculine consciousness, for example, is the degree to which he embodies the male aspects of ego, male pride, identification through work, the suppression and displacement of his feelings, an analytical mind, and reliance on his physical strength. To the extent a man is in possession of his feminine aspects, he is able to cry, to express his emotions verbally, to rely on his intuition.

In spite of what has changed, at the emotional level we are all still acting out the same old sex roles. Most men are still locked in the position of expressing only their masculine attributes and are still so unfamiliar and uncomfortable with the feminine that they're trying to hide or deny it, while men who are blessed (or cursed) with possessing it already are struggling to find a culturally acceptable outlet for it without being punished for possessing it.

As an engineer said, "In my profession the lack of recognition for my sensitivity has felt like a lifelong condemnation for being 'the wrong kind of man.'" Another, a products designer, said, "I only know how to be vulnerable. Everything affects me. There are times I wish there were some other way I could be. It would make my life a whole lot easier." Yet another man told the horror story of being accused of molesting a young boy because, at his father's funeral when the boy had burst into tears, this man had kneeled down and taken him into his arms to comfort him.

The sad truth is that whether men already possess the feminine to some degree—and have to deal with it as an aberration—or don't acknowledge it at all, they still aren't able to move comfortably with it in their lives. Men are still living the horrible fallout of having disowned the internal feminine and women are still angry at them because they have.

Some men are beginning to become aware of this. But awareness—simple diagnosis—is a breathtakingly long distance from transformation, healing, and change. To know what has wounded you, even to name the wound, is still not to have been healed, still not to be, though scarred, reborn.

So what can men do about their pain? The problem of course is that men's pain is an emotional phenomenon. It occurs in precisely the venue in which men are unable to help themselves. Emotional pain, and emotions—the psychological antidote with which to heal it—are off limits for men. If only they could cry—but men can't cry. If only they could collapse—but men can't collapse. Instead they're stuck with their grief.

The process of emotional healing for men requires that a man be given the vision with which to apprehend his own wounds: to identify them, mourn them, shed tears over them and, in the end, be cleansed of them. This process of identifying, grieving, and being cleansed is, if you will, an essentially feminine process. It is feminine because it is receptive in essence. The person being healed must be in possession of the pain that needs to be alchemized. He must receive it to the point where he can feel it, and having taken it in, then and only then can he begin to grieve and release it. Only when he has mourned will his eyes be washed so that he can see his own suffering, so that he can become compassionate not only with himself, but also with women.

The Approach of Change

"I want to become more spiritually and emotionally connected. I would welcome knowing that part in me. It's a good part, and I want it to come out."

-Band manager, 45

A number of men and women on the forefront of developing consciousness have watched as men have been standing on tip-toe, tap-tapping outside the gates of their own unexplored feminine dimension. Men are talking more, taking more time for themselves and with one another. But nowhere is the emerging feminine more readily apparent than in men's willingness to take a more active role in the rearing of children, and in women's encouragement of them to do so.

This trend of male participation in childrearing is just one piece of evidence that intuitively we're all beginning to agree it's time for men to gain access to the feminine. In spite of not openly acknowledging this, we are shyly creating opportunities for it to occur and in the protected emotional environment of a man's relationship with his children, we do allow a man to get in touch with the softer, more vulnerable aspects of himself. Through nurturing his children—holding, rocking, and feeding them—a man can begin to gain access to his feminine self without shame, contempt, or embarrassment.

In spite of, or perhaps specifically because of such changes, it's difficult to comprehend the degree to which men are still terrified of the feminine in themselves. Most men can't even face how afraid they are of their own feminine aspects, and even men who are aware of their fear and trying to overcome it are having a difficult time. As a friend acknowledged to me, "I want to be sensitive, warm, and loving, but I have to admit when I see men hugging each other, I'm really put off."

The truth is that, although some men are exploring their sensitivity through therapy or men's groups, most men are still stranded in the outback of male consciousness and have miles to go before they meet women on the common ground of the conscious feminine. What this means is that although they may be venturing a peek at their emotions, men still haven't gotten acquainted or comfortable enough with them to use them as the medium of their connection with women.

Why Men Are Stuck

> *"Somehow I know that my capacity to feel will change when I get the words to describe my feelings. But I don't know how to do that."*
>
> *-Graduate student, 30*

Men haven't raced downtown to buy admission tickets to the conscious feminine because dismantling and reassembling male consciousness is a terrifying proposition. Embracing the feminine is a process that will require the profoundest revision of male sensibilities and self definitions. For a man to take on the feminine dimension doesn't mean simply putting on—as he would a three-piece suit, a carpenter's belt, a hard hat or gun— a different outfit called "the feminine." It means, rather, that he will have to see that in the very deepest reaches of himself, he is not only capable of acting and performing, as men have always done, but that he is also capable of feeling while acting, and of feeling instead of performing.

Men will have to discover that they have a purely receptive feminine, feeling function, as well as an aggressive masculine performing function—and that the feminine function will not disrupt the organic functioning of their masculinity. They will also need to claim this as their true and integrated male possession, for there is also the very complex problem of orchestrating a whole new repertoire of behaviors and feelings.

Therefore taking on the feminine means a man will have to be able to feel instead of act—if feeling is the appropriate response to a given situation—but that he will have to learn when to move from acting to feeling (or vice versa), and when to do both at once. This in itself is an elaborate level of emotional discernment not readily familiar to men. To integrate the feminine means profoundly understanding that being in the feeling state could actually enhance the way they hold up the world.

Contemplating embracing the feminine also brings men face to face with some of their worst fears, because to be emotional is, above all, to be vulnerable. To be vulnerable is to be open, to be able to be wounded. It is the capacity to undergo, to be affected by an emotion or experience, and, once having been affected, to be transformed by it. Thus, to be vulnerable is to be able to be deeply changed.

For a woman, the ultimate experience of this vulnerability is the transformation of her body during pregnancy. In it, a woman takes in a man, undergoes the rearrangement of her physical structure, and with the birth of her child, completely revises the physical and psychological function of her life.

Since the defining characteristics of male consciousness are the embodiment of power, action, and control, for a man, vulnerability—this potential total rearrangement—in any form is frightening. To be male is to be the agent, not the object, of change. Men want to act upon, to assert, aggress, and enforce. Whereas the essence of the feminine is to be affected by, it is the masculine essence to try to remain unaffected.

Taking on the seemingly infinite capacity of the feminine to undergo change is terrifying to men. Yet in even the simplest of emotional encounters, women are asking essentially that men develop vulnerability, which represents the antithesis of everything men have always been told to be as men. This consciousness is a totally new undertaking for men, one which, it seems to them, will compromise their entire male identity, and they're scared to death of it.

For men, opening to feeling necessitates not only developing the ability to have a new experience, it also requires giving up a level of protection that has been a great source of comfort to them. In a nutshell, in being emotionally vulnerable, men will have to give up being invulnerable, and in so doing, to develop a whole new male archetype. While from women's perspective, invulnerability is a defensive second-rate emotional stance, for men it represents the protected sanctuary from which, precisely, they have been able to function—and function on women's behalf. Occupying this place they have also been spared the anguishing sorrows, emotional convolutions, and importunate outpourings women have always been prey to.

In this regard it should be mentioned that women have never particularly wanted to see that there are advantages to being unfeeling—but there are. Being able to proceed in heart-breaking circumstances without being yanked off course by the distracting pull of emotions—going into the burning house to save the child without getting hysterical in advance, wielding the knife on the operating table without having your hands immobilized by the fear of failure, being able to work twelve hours a day for your wife and children without getting bogged down in self-pity—all this is of great advantage to the man who must do so, and to those who benefit from his so-called insensitivity. A man instinctively knows that what women receive through his being cut off from his feelings is of great value.

Evolution of any kind takes sacrifice. Thus it is that even in unconsciously contemplating becoming vulnerable, a man intuits that he will lose something of importance, something precious, something he values in himself; and he fears that it won't be replaced by something of equal value.

This fear is made even more palpable by his instinctual recognition that in having an emotional life, he will not only come into the presence of his positive feelings, but also of his terror, rage, and sorrow. He fears he will do the impossible thing—be vulnerable, go out of control—and that once having done it, he will encounter not only his joy, but also a shocking immensity of monstrous, negative feelings. As one man said, "It's bad enough to be vulnerable, without having to feel all this sadness too. If I have to get into the feeling state, at least I should get to have a good feeling."

The unconscious recognition of what being vulnerable would mean is so threatening to men as to make the emotional undertaking almost the last thing any man would want to do. In fact, most men would rather do almost anything else than get in touch with their feelings. They would far rather double or triple their efforts at what they're already doing: working, providing, protecting, paying (the Everything-But Syndrome again); disappoint the women in their lives by boldly insisting they don't have a need to communicate; fool themselves into thinking they're already in touch with their sensitivity; despise, deny, and disown their emotional vulnerability; or insist they don't need to change. At the level of the collective male unconscious, it is so unbelievably threatening for men to contemplate this change that even though there have been invitations galore from women, most men are still hiding out and waffling.

Although it is extremely difficult for men to submit to the state of vulnerability in order to learn, if they are going to take on their emotional lives, they must. What they need to remember, however, is that vulnerability, as modelled by women, is also power, for when the woman is most changed, as when her body is transformed in pregnancy, she also becomes most powerful.

Accepting the feminine in themselves also means that men must acknowledge that in some sense they have always been incomplete. Facing this incompleteness is one of the most difficult things a man can do. For as we have seen, men believe that they must be everything for everyone, and their attendant greatest fear is that they won't be enough. Allowing themselves to see that in some sense they aren't enough is the most frightening thing they could contemplate. Seeing themselves as having a lack—in this case, the lack of the ability for emotional experience—is a nightmare discovery for most men, and another reason that, no matter how much they may unconsciously desire it, they resist incorporating the feminine. In short, men hate to see that something is missing in them.

Yet the paradox is always the location of the miracle; the moment of terror is the moment of possibility. The courage required to embrace the feminine proves a man's masculinity, for only a very strong man has the strength to be so very vulnerable. In disclosing his fear of being weak, a man becomes beautifully strong; in being open and receptive, he becomes authentically protected. The man who can say he's afraid can begin, instantly, to receive the solace he needs; no longer must he bear his fear alone. The man who can weep can have his tears wiped away. The man who can open to his fragility can finally embrace his true power.

In short, the man who integrates his feminine self becomes more wholly masculine because he is all that he is. He is no longer a shadow of himself, half there, living an as-if life of emotional suppression and passive-aggressive defensiveness. He is finally born whole. As one young man, embarking on his healing journey in psychotherapy, put it so beautifully, "I'm scared to death to be here, but I'm here because I don't want to live my whole life as somebody else." Intuitively he knew that there was so much more to him than he had already experienced or would ever discover if he continued to follow the path of being a man that had been so narrowly laid out for him. This is the same young man who said, when he completed his healing journey, "I feel stronger than I ever imagined possible, but in a completely different way. Now I know how I feel–for me that *is* being a man."

The Age of Androgyny

> "*Sometimes I not only think but know in my bones that in our hearts there's really no difference between men and women.*"
>
> *-Painter, 44*

If our male-female relationships are to survive and transform, and indeed they must, then somehow men must come to feel safe with this unspeakable process. Men must do this—not only for the women who want them to, but for themselves—and for the future of relationship itself.

We all yearn for union. Instinctively, we all seek reconciliation. When men begin the work of incorporating the feminine dimension, it will move us all in the direction of androgyny—the emotional state in which a person has fully incorporated all his or her masculine and feminine aspects and, in which, therefore, none are projected onto the opposite sex. The changes women have made have already catapulted us into the trajectory of a transformational process from which there is no return. Whether we like it or not, the transposition of attributes once deemed solely the property of either sex is already well underway, the move toward androgyny is already shaping the future of both male and female psychosexual identities.

Through their incorporation of the feminine, men must now balance the maleness that women have already begun to balance in themselves. In doing so, they will not only join women at the androgynous frontier, but will advance us all toward the spiritually provocative landscapes of the future. With the initiation of the feminine consciousness in men, both men and women can be powerful, logical, aggressive, and direct, as well as intuitive, nurturing, empathetic, and sensitive.

These territories are beyond the merely psychological. They point to the spiritual cosmos and represent not only what we can newly expect our relationships to be—union, communion, healing, and transformation—but embody the highest truth, that in its essence and ours there is no division or separation, no opposite or antithesis, no male or female. We are all one.

Panic in Androgynyville

"Men dominate, provide, protect, and accomplish. We are so far behind women that we have to dig even deeper to be open."

-*Owner of video store, 38*

Still, all this melting of boundaries is immensely scary, for it is through maintaining distinctions, and particularly gender distinctions, that we preserve a sense of order. In general we prefer rules to chance, sameness to change. We feel safer living in the illusion that things will continue as they are, than we do entertaining the possibility that our boundaries will be jiggled, expanded, or violated to a degree that will ask us to change more than we feel we can.

For, although in a subtle sense, the androgynous has already begun to be incorporated into our culture—unisex fashion, women with chopped-off hair and men with hair to their waistlines were early clues; women in every kind of job at every level and men at home pushing babies in strollers are no longer weird exceptions. Nevertheless, at the level of our collective unconscious, we still carry an exorbitant fear about androgyny. The excessive reactions to the whole cafeteria of sex role blurrings—coed dorms, shaved heads for women, the abolition of clubs for men only, women in the workplace, the marketplace, and the state legislature, and, above all, to male and female homosexuality—all reveal our fears, our deep internal need to keep things psychosexually "in place."

So even though androgyny is already galloping toward us, we are all still afraid of its arrival. In spite of the fact that both men and women would immediately gain greater access to themselves and one another in the further dissolving of gender boundaries, and that we would open a gateway to the spiritual level, on a psychological level we still fear it.

What both men and women need to bear in mind as they undertake these changes, however, is that androgyny does not imply that women will become men and men, women. Rather, it invites both sexes to draw as many cards as they like from a deck that spans the entire psychosexual and psychospiritual spectrum. When people are at ease with the full range of their emotions, embarrassed by neither the masculine nor the feminine in themselves, they approach life with a much greater sense of excitement, fulfillment, and possibility; they are more able to have an ecstatic experience of themselves and of others.

Nowhere is there a greater payoff for this than in intimate relationships. For it is precisely to the extent that we relax gender boundaries, that men will be able to approach women through their sensitivity and meet women in the place of real emotional exchange. In the ways we've missed men the most, we'll finally have the experience we've always desired, the relationships we've always longed for and men have never dreamed of.

For, to the degree that men become comfortable with their own femininity, they will also develop the capacity for empathy, the feeling-with-others that until now has been the special privilege of women. This will enable men to identify with women in their suffering rather than simply trying to solve women's problems. In knowing what women suffer, what frustrates them, what brings them happiness and satisfaction, both men and women will feel less alone. Finally men will be able to give women something women *can* wholeheartedly receive.

In some larger, more mystical sense, for men to take on the full range of emotions will also have the effect of mitigating the polarization between the sexes. For, when a man can see the feminine in himself, no matter how it expresses itself—whether in creativity, in the verbal expression of his emotions, in his compassion for his wife, in his tenderness with his children, or in his awareness of his fear of death—he can far more readily honor these sensitivities in a woman.

Conversely, the woman who has embraced the masculine in herself can be far more appreciative when she encounters in a man the hallmark male attributes of aggression, logic, emotional detachment, and power. Instead of denigrating these, as women so often unconsciously do, we can then fully and beautifully honor the gifts of the masculine.

Androgyny, this blending of sex roles, is an exquisite kind of mirroring. For when we can see ourselves in each other, we no longer judge; we begin to love. This is the beginning of the healing we all need.

In the development of the feminine consciousness in men lies the blueprint for the end of the battle between the sexes. For, so long as we view one another as opposites, representatives of totally antithetical camps, we will all keep facing each other off across the emotional barbed wire barriers that keep us prisoners in a brutal sexist cold war.

Women's enormous discontent will be assuaged only when men have integrated enough of the feminine that women can resonate with it. Then and only then will women feel encouraged to appreciate men in their incontrovertible masculinity, and to further enrich both the masculine and feminine aspects in themselves.

11

Our Holy Work: Initiating Men into the Feminine Consciousness

"Who is going to be with our men when their pain comes out of them?"

-*Therapist, 49*

What becomes indelibly and eloquently clear is that men need to be delivered from the masculine to the feminine forms: of living, of loving women, of creating the sexual, emotional, and spiritual intimacy that elevates and transforms relationships. But the only way they will ever be able to integrate the feminine is if women offer the safety net of their womanhood, their own deeply integrated feminine, to encourage men into these heart-opening changes. If men could do it themselves, the project at hand would already have been accomplished, this book would not have been written, and women would already have stopped complaining.

Indeed, the thing women have missed in complaining about the way men are is that complaints in themselves don't provide the inspiration for change. Since change always originates from the deepest interior sensing of the person undertaking it, until men feel their own need for change, the changes they need, and women want, will continue to elude them. Unfortunately, since men are still so separated from their feelings, they are also disconnected from the very emotions that could let them know how much they want to change.

Since to be male is to make do with what is, to preserve the status quo, men have been so busy defending themselves from changing that they have neither cleared a space in the woods of male identity for the change to occur, nor have they been offered the clearing in which to contemplate what they desire. Discovery can only take place in a protected environment, in a state of emotional security, and men who are being continually harassed about changing can't possibly enter the fluid exploratory state that is the absolute requirement for emotional transformation. As a consequence, at present, men can offer only women the mechanical knee-jerk reactions born of being terrorized. Women must finally and thoroughly comprehend this, for only then will we be willing to give ourselves to this process.

Why Men Can't Help Themselves

"You women have it all together. We need to learn from you."

-Petroleum company executive, 56

Women are brought inescapably to this task because men don't have what they need to do it for themselves. Indeed it is exactly the thing men lack that is required in their transformational process. For, as we've seen, the male role, like a closed-circuit television, only goes round and round within its limited parameters of repression, conversion, passive aggression, and communication in code, in such a way that on their own men have no way to reach out into the emotional stratosphere and call in the feminine consciousness.

Men are also hobbled in whatever efforts they might put forth because, unlike women, they have neither the emotional experience nor the history of emotional supportiveness that would enable them to evoke the missing feminine in one another. They've had to live by the secret contract of competition which has required that at every level of social encounter with one another, they remain heroes or adversaries, staying emotionally guarded and even helping one another to suppress any feeling that might emerge by ridicule or a reminder to "take it like a man."

Men can't really talk to each other. They certainly can't embrace one another, can't wipe away each other's tears, can't offer consoling, tender, palliative words. They can only buck up and tell each other to buck up and carry on.

Men's predicament is further exacerbated by a generalized homophobia and deeply-ingrained male pride. As one client said to me when I suggested he join a men's group, "Go to a workshop for men only? No way. I don't want to listen to some guy sobbing about his troubles. And I sure don't want to tell a bunch of guys about mine. With most men I'd feel bored and with the rest I'd be threatened."

While women may deplore the fact that men need women to help them, the truth is that men can't recreate themselves alone. As one man acknowledged to me, "You want men to talk to each other?–get a woman to help them."

Say it Isn't So

"You want to know how I feel about men? Fed up. What have men ever done for us?"

-Secretary, 44

Exhausted as women are, we may well ask ourselves why it is, after all we've already done for men and have had to do for ourselves, that the liberation of the male psyche must also be women's work? Why, after the long hard labor of birthing ourselves, must we now also be the midwives to men? The answer is elegantly simple and terribly difficult: because only women now live in the state of consciousness that men must enter in order to complete themselves, because only women, who occupy the feminine domain, which defines the parameters of emotional aliveness and interpersonal intimacy have fully realized relationship capacity, and because it is only women, with our intuitive gifts for nurturing, our familiarity with the language of emotion, and our gift for calling forth life, who possess the capacity for evoking what is missing in men.

We may resent this call to our new role as initiators of the feminine consciousness in men, and we have every right to do so. We're tired. We've been through the mill. Women's liberation was long hard work, and as we contemplate yet another exhausting undertaking–delivering men to the feminine consciousness—we may well do so not with a sense of excitement but with more than a little resentment.

In the past we've been housewives, mothers, unpaid assistants, and general underlings to men. From these unglamorous beginnings we've clawed our way up the male ladder, only to stumble onto the discovery that now we must bring to consciousness the men who have always denigrated us. We look at the probable future and feel overwhelmed and resentful that at the very time of our rise to the apogee of our power, men still need something from us.

We're angry because it's time for us to enjoy ourselves, to bask in the rewards of our accomplishments. We've put in our time—when will we ever get to relax and enjoy ourselves? We've put them through graduate school, supported them while they were establishing careers, comforted them about their destructive, competitive fathers, mothered them in their sicknesses, soothed them about their ex-wives and girlfriends. We're tired of being men's helpmates, whatever the form, and are no more ready than Eve to embark on yet another male rescue project; it used to be dinner on the table and picking the socks up from the floor and now it's the feeling life of a man.

That's why the change hasn't occurred so far. It's as if, collectively, women have been saying, "We have to do more? We have to be the initiators of men's feminine consciousness too! It's not fair!" This feeling of unfairness isn't just rooted in self-indulgence. It *isn't* fair. It would be so much nicer—in fact it would be wonderful—if men could just pull themselves up by their own emotional bootstraps and join us as emotional equals in a vibrant emotional democracy. But they can't. We do have to help them. Until now, we've just been avoiding it and the situation has only deteriorated.

If women assume, as in a sense we have by asking, begging, and pleading, that men can develop emotional lives on their own, we're being totally unrealistic. It's as if men are blind and we are asking them to see the sky without being able to offer them the miracle by which their sight might be restored.

The incorporation of the feminine dimension can only be learned in relationship with a woman. This means, in a sense, that every woman who truly desires a relationship with a man must become a miracle worker on his behalf. She must see herself not as having a request to make but a holy obligation to fulfill. For, the unfortunate, blessed and stunning truth is that, if women are ever to experience the deep and satisfying relationships with men that they have always said they desire, then they have no choice but accept the work and begin.

To the extent that any woman is willing to undertake this work, to reframe her own expectations of what can occur between her and a man, to that extent she will initiate the process which will ultimately reward her with the experience of a genuine relationship with an authentically-feeling male human being.

A Word of Encouragement

> *"Once in a while I get a man to have a feeling with me. Miraculous. Then suddenly I get a glimpse of what a real relationship could be."*
>
> *-Marketing executive, 37*

Although the task may seem overwhelming, women are better equipped than ever before for this Herculean undertaking. First of all, we do know how to do it. We are initiating men into emotional consciousness and encouraging them to develop relationship capacity, which we have always invariably practiced, if not with men, then certainly with one another. For, even though we may have never been able to have the emotional intimacy we desire with men, we've certainly had it with other women. Our history is the blueprint for what we seek to build with men.

Additionally, because we have gained access to male roles, we're finally in a position to feel a measure of the isolation, pressure, and burdens men have always felt. To a significant degree, women are now having the male experience, rather than simply observing it. We now know what it feels like to set aside your own emotions in favor of what you're trying to accomplish—to put up and shut up, to bottle your tears and bury your feelings, to keep your nose to the grindstone while keeping your chin up and having a stiff upper lip.

As a consequence, our capacity for empathizing with men has been developed to a greater degree than ever before. In a sense, we've become spies in the house of love, in the prison of male suffering. From this new perspective—and nothing teaches like the crucible of raw experience—we can now understand men better and perhaps, as a result, also deliver what we have to offer in a way that men can more easily receive.

The challenge here is for us to undertake the work with men with kindheartedness and grace, to do it without being judgmental or demanding immediate results. Most important of all, we must invite men into the emotional arena without robbing them of their dignity, without patting their faces like imbecile children, poking them verbally, or insisting that they cry. We must allow them the luxury of exploring their sensitivity in a delicate moseying way, one that not only permits them to become more compassionate with themselves, but opens them to the possibility of greater intimate interchange with the women and men they love.

To do this, we must comprehend that men absolutely do have feelings and have been denied the opportunity to explore them in the way they can—which is gently, gradually, and on terms that are comfortable for them, not necessarily for us.

The changes that have already occurred with women are a prophecy of the possibilities to come. The fact that we have all arrived here makes this all the more hallowed a moment and asks that we reach for the best in ourselves as, terrified but optimistic, we move courageously forward.

Accepting The Burden

"We are really in our infancy, we men. We need to be cradled. Why not cradle men?"

-*Businessman, 48*

For women to come to terms with the burden of initiating men will invite us to change, to revise our myths about ourselves. We will have to accept that we are far bigger than we have ever imagined ourselves to be. And we will have to overcome our anger about what men have done to us, about what our fathers and brothers and uncles and bosses have perpetrated on us with their power trips born of insecurity, their silences, and their arrogance—so that we *can* be of assistance. We will need to remember—and forgive—all the transgressions men have made against us and this in itself will be a huge work of the heart for most women.

What will make this new burden bearable is to approach it with a fresh awareness. What will allow us to be generous in the undertaking is the discovery that this is not only an inescapable chore, but also a very deep privilege. For as the possessors of the feminine consciousness, we not only embody its blessing, but carry the high obligation of revealing its full power and using it in behalf of the emotional evolution of the human species.

Furthermore, it represents a beautiful redefinition of

women's roles as women. It moves us from the posture of serving to loving. It delivers us from enacting the tedious roles of housewife, secretary, and assistant (serving men from the one-down position) and elevates us into the roles of healer, mediator, and initiator.

Women have always had access to the feminine consciousness but because it has always been so much our essence, it has in a sense also always been invisible. Whatever one possesses in great measure—money, beauty, intelligence, opportunity—becomes almost impossible to see when you are totally submerged in it. Thus the power of the feminine consciousness, which has been so intrinsic to women's own function, has been almost impossible for women to hold in objective awareness. In a sense we haven't even noticed that we possess it, and as a consequence, we have unwittingly treated it as a capacity equally available to both men and women. As a result, instead of helping men, we have, in effect, continued to keep men away from their feelings. By expecting men to be sensitive, instead of creating the safety necessary for the nurturing of their sensitivity, women have denied not only the disenfranchisement that men have always endured, but also the power that lies in our own deep feminine essence.

Since time immemorial women have been the keepers of the emotional largess, and this must be the season of our generosity. Without sparing, without regret or resentment for what we have already suffered, without compromising what we have already accomplished with such long and bitter effort, we must move forward—delicately, patiently, steadfastly—doing the complex, painstaking, tender work of delivering men to the feeling life. For it is only insofar as we can be generous with the possession that is uniquely ours to give, that we will be able to heal the men we love and bring them into a true experience, not only of themselves, but also of ourselves.

The Last Thing We Ever Wanted to Do: Women's Resistance to Initiating Men

12

"If we're going to change the consciousness of the planet, we'll have to raise the children and the men."

-Female college administrator, 40

If it's so obvious that women must help men with the integration of the feminine, a transformation that would also be of infinite benefit to us, why have we waited so long? At the most elementary level, we haven't helped because we didn't believe we had to. We've hoped that one way or another, by luck, osmosis, or their own initiative, men would accomplish their emotional revolution without us. It's as if we imagined that men knew the way, that for some perverted or stubborn reason they were just holding out on us. It never occurred to us that the journey they needed to make was one in which they didn't even know how to take the first step.

In addition, in spite of our profound discontent and understandable impatience, we also have considerable resentment because, without being actually aware of it, we have already been serving this role for men. We've begged men to talk to us, we've encouraged them to share their feelings, we've asked them to be more sensitive. But the process of male emotional evolution has been conducted at a completely unconscious level, with neither men nor women facing what is really going on. Thus we're angry about what we've already given to men, and feel unwilling to contribute any more.

Paradoxically, however, it's developing an awareness of what we've been doing that could change the situation. For if we could consciously undertake this process as the mission that is ours to do, we would feel very differently about it (and might even get better results). But because we haven't done this yet, we stay locked in our anger and resentment.

In addition, we're also reluctant to help men because of our own deep-seated fears. For, when it comes to the possible transformation of men, there are two very difficult issues women must face: Do we really want men to change? What will it mean for us to go through the process with them? We think we want them to change, but surprisingly enough, as we shall see, for psychological reasons of our own, women, too, would just as soon have men stay in emotional limbo-land. No less than men, women are afraid of going through the process of male transformation.

Fear They Can't Change

What are these fears? First, when it comes right down to it, women are afraid men can't change. It's as if, in spite of our longing, in our heart of hearts we don't really believe men want an emotional life or that they would willingly go on a journey of emotional transformation. In addition, we've been told in countless books that it's neurotic for us to hope men will change, that we're masochistic, self-denigrating co-dependents if we imagine men could change or venture to assist them. Since we've been told this so strongly and so often, and since we haven't known how to make it happen anyway, we don't make the effort and, in effect, close off the possibility of ever having the kind of relationships we really want.

In a sense, women have given up on men. Far from being an acceptance of men's limitations, our giving up is a profound sabotage of the possibility of any future emotional interchange with men. Women need to support men with our loving expectations, to hold the hope that men will change. Hope is a memory of the future, the belief that what we want now will be true when time has moved on. Women must give men that hope, our willingness to go through the process, and the deep conviction of our hearts that when the future has arrived, the thing we longed for so desperately in the past will already have been accomplished.

And no matter how long we've waited—and it has been very long—or how hard the task—and it will be hard—we need to remember that we're not fools for wanting men to change. Our wanting, our passionate desire, our obvious impatience, is the expression of our deepest love and truest need for men. It is us saying from our souls that because they share the planet with us, we cannot be wholly human without them.

Fear that Men Can't Do it Right

Along with just plain giving up and therefore not being too intrigued with the task at hand, a great many women are also emotionally prejudiced. They have an internalized compendium of notions about the unfeeling nature of men that goes very deep. These ideas run the gamut from "they couldn't have an emotional life if they tried" to "I can't believe he has a caring emotional bone in his body." Such notions cause women to evaluate all male behaviors according to their own pre-determined, internalized female stereotypes. Rather than being able to read each man as an individual human being, let alone perceive his particular emotional nuances, (the feelings under his words, for example, or his kinesthetic behavioral code), women dismiss men as being emotionally incompetent, essentially unfeeling. In short, women are just as guilty of sexist ideas about men as men are about women. Like male prejudice, their stereotyped thinking about men does nothing but exaggerate the problem.

Although we don't come right out and say this, we do believe it. We express it by continuing to have our significant emotional relationships with other women. It's as if knowing that men are still lacking in relationship capacity, we don't want to diminish the quality of our experience by leaving it open to male novices or to what in our more uncharitable moments we consider to be emotional incompetents. Since we're familiar with the generally high caliber of emotional intensity we experience with other women, anything that doesn't come up to this level doesn't register on a woman's chart of what a real emotional experience should be. Since women know they can have a great emotional encounter with one another, why should they bother trying to get something half or a quarter as good with a man? As one woman said of her best friend, "She's perfect; I just wish she were a man."

But the underlying preference of women for each other's emotional company does nothing to move us all forward. With men still watching Monday Night Football in the living room while their wives talk to one another on the phone, men and women aren't getting any closer. It's a basic law of human behavior that the frequency of an action increases when it gets a positive response, and decreases when it gets little or no response. And, since women are so highly developed in giving each other an emotional response, their emotional behaviors continue to be reinforced and developed, while men continue to languish in verbal ineptitude.

Since men rarely get the kinds of positive responses (from either men or women) that would encourage them to further develop their inchoate emotional behaviors, they appear to be incapable of developing them. That's why women continue to prefer to have their emotional relationships with other women. In short, it's easy with women, difficult with men, and we've all become resigned to it.

But women need to recognize that so long as we continue to believe men can't express their emotions (and therefore don't give them a chance to practice), we ensure the frustrating status quo, and in effect, tie a noose around our own emotional necks.

Fear of Losing Emotional Pre-Eminence

Perhaps the most surprising reason women are afraid men might actually change is that women don't really want to give up their status as the gender who holds the position of emotional curators in relationships. As much as women say they're tired of acting out all the emotions, that they wish men would be more emotional, we really don't want to give up our place as the reigning emotion sovereigns.

Since for women, playing this role has always represented a significant portion of our self definition (we're the
ones who are in touch with feelings, who know what's really
going on in our relationships; we're the ones with the intuition),
women are unconsciously afraid of losing—or sharing—this
identity. Who will women be if not the ones who have a corner
on emotions? Although we have happily incorporated many
male aspects, we still revel in the identity of being the emotional
experts. In a sense, getting men to the place where they too can
feel, where they also have intuition, is like putting women out
of a job.

Paradoxically, even though women seem to be saying
that they want men to get their emotions together, at a basic,
subliminal level we're terrified men might. This is why we cling
to the belief that we'll always be better than men in any
emotional transaction. Even though we're asking men to become, in a sense, more like us, because of our unconscious
desire to sabotage men's access to the hallowed emotional
ground we're also saying, "but you'll never be as good at it as we
are." Unconsciously, we keep men in a double bind; far more
than we'd like to admit, we're afraid men might encroach upon
our area of expertise and rob us of our feminine uniqueness.

When it comes to our emotional pre-eminence, women
have never acknowledged that vis à vis men, we really don't want
to give up control. So long as we insist on our own emotional
primacy, we will unconsciously fight to keep men inept, to limit
the male emotional repertoire.

Our reluctance to give up our crowns in the kingdom of
emotions quite handily dovetails into the male ambivalence at
taking on the feminine. Thus we collude not only to allow, but
unconsciously to insist, that women retain emotional primacy.
This gives women the comfort of knowing they can retain
power, and men the consolation of having their frightening

transformation delayed. For the process to move forward, women must be willing to give up the glories of their traditional position in order to experience the riches of emotional democracy. Otherwise men and women will continue to ensure that the changes women insist they want and men so desperately need will not come to pass.

Fear of Giving Up the Martyr Role

Underlying women's refusal to help men lies another dirty secret: women are afraid of losing the martyr position they've always occupied. It's almost as if we've been operating by the motto: if the misery fits, wear it. Martyrs are committed to the expectation that the situation is hopeless and will never improve. And so far as the situation with men is concerned, this is precisely the place that many women still find themselves.

As wretched a role as it is, as shoddy as its rewards may be, the martyr role does offer certain gratifications. The martyred woman can focus on her identity as a doormat, how much she has given with no recompense, who she once was, or could be now, were it not for the *him* or the *them* who have taken such unfair advantage of her. In detailing the length and breadth of her doormathood, she comes to a sense of her own identity (warped though it may be).

In the past women were martyrs to their husbands and families: ("I ironed sixteen shirts and he didn't even thank me", "The kids walked all over my clean kitchen floor and didn't even notice") and now we're martyrs to the double masters of work and family: "I worked all day and I still had to make the dinner;" "My boss bawls me out for being late to work and my husband's mad because we didn't make love this morning."

So long as women continue to be miserable, and men continue to be unable to meet their needs, women can retain the position of being deprived underdogs whose needs don't get met and whose dreams are perennially unfulfilled. But should women help men into a full emotional life, then perhaps men actually will meet women's needs. Where will women be then? Somewhere different. Somewhere frighteningly unfamiliar.

But why would we want to be martyrs and why is the martyr role so hard to give up? The martyr role is a defense against women's fear that we'll never get what we want, a kind of emotional insurance policy against the possibility that, like our fathers and brothers, our husbands and lovers will disappoint us. Unconsciously many women are afraid that no man will ever really please them. Since this is so painfully difficult to face, they will do almost anything to prevent themselves from being vulnerable to possible disappointment. As one woman said, "I didn't even remind him a week ago that it was my birthday, because if I knew he knew and then forgot, it would have been totally devastating. Since he didn't really know, it's no big deal. I never get what I want from him anyway."

Should women actually make themselves available to the possibility that a man could make them happy, they might be disappointed at an even more devastating level. There's a certain comfort that comes from knowing you'll never being able to get what you want—you're protected from disappointment—"I'd never expect him to give me a diamond"; "Of course he's not good with the children"; "Of course I fake orgasm, what else is new?" The "Poor Me" Syndrome (I do everything for everyone else and never get anything for myself) is a safe hiding place for the many women who would rather feel continually deprived than feel exquisite disappointment in the single instance in which they really had their hopes up. From the martyr stance, it's as if we're saying, "I don't want to go through the disappointment of experiencing that men can't meet my emotional needs, so I'm going to protect myself by assuming they can't. Being a little disappointed all the time is better than being devastatingly disappointed even once."

Paradoxically, what starts out as being protection against being disappointed ensures that we'll never get what we want. For needs to be met, they have to be articulated, and when, because of being martyrs, women give up before they begin, they ensure that even the needs men could happily meet for them will never be fulfilled. Since fundamentally women haven't believed men could change, we've been unwilling to give up the martyr role, to take our chances in the high stakes emotional lottery of intimate relationships.

We need to give up the martyr role now—for men and for ourselves. For unless we're straightforward with our own needs, we can't reasonably expect men to do likewise. We need to begin to take the risk of asking for what we want directly, and bear the anguish of disappointment should our requests not be fulfilled. We'll also have to be strong enough to listen when men express their needs.

In discussing the martyr role, I don't mean to imply that women haven't suffered, nor do I wish to deny the magnitude of our real pain; but we all need to remember that playing the martyr is one thing and true suffering quite another. We will do better, for men and for ourselves, when we learn to communicate our pain, to give up the shallow payoffs of the martyr role for the genuine rewards that will come when we dare to ask for what we need.

Fear of Our Own Masculinity

Another component in women's reluctance to deliver men to their emotional selves is an unwillingness to further embrace our own masculine dimension. Intuitively we all know that in any relationship there is an inherent balance between the

masculine and the feminine. The balance can either be distrib-
uted in such a way that men represent the masculine components and women the feminine, or in such a way that the
partners, no matter what their biological sex, embody the
masculine and feminine components to some unequal degree
which between them represents the entire androgynous totality.

Thus in any relationship the male components may be
divided with the man embodying, say, 80 percent of the masculine attributes, and the woman the remaining 20, or with the
woman carrying 60 percent of the masculine energy and the
man only 40 percent. No matter what the distribution in any
given relationship, a man and a woman embody the totality of
both the male and female energies. Instinctively we know that
for a relationship to function successfully, either men must
remain men and women, women in all the traditional ways, or
both sexes must incorporate a balance of male and female
attributes. Thus, for men to operate more from their feminine
dimension would require that women take on more of the
masculine.

Without consciously being aware of it, women are afraid
that if men do, indeed, become more in touch with their
feelings, women will have to incorporate more rationality into
their emotional repertoires. Emotionality always requires the
steadying force of a rational counterpart, and to the degree that
men develop their emotional expressiveness, women will have
to develop their rationality to balance the interpersonal equation. For men to become emotionally expressive will require
that women hold the steadying, rational place of strength that
men once did.

To women, this feels like a kind of loss. We will have to
give up the great free-for-all of indulging feelings and develop
a more balanced emotional curriculum. This will require effort,

a plunge into the unfamiliar. Setting aside our emotions (that seemingly most precious part of ourselves) in order to be cool-headed, reasonable, and analytic is difficult for most women even to contemplate.

Ironically, the female privilege of luxuriating in emotions is one of the curious consequences of male oppression. For it's a truism that the underdog always glorifies what the oppressor has denigrated. Thus African-Americans developed Black pride; Ingrid Bergman, under attack for being single and pregnant, became an example of women's sexual freedom; and women, accused of being overly emotional, have claimed the castle of emotions as their stronghold. Since in the past they couldn't achieve the rewards of male power in the world, they elevated their emotions to the status of icons, deciding that having and expressing feelings was of much greater value than anything men did.

Even now, as we take on our power in the male environment, women continue to cling to this belief, just as men have maintained a grip on the classical male identity of being silent heroes. In a way, women have artificially exaggerated the value of emotions in order to have a meaningful identity, and, like a familiar but destructive habit, we don't want to give it up.

Like men, women are afraid that if they take the strong, rational position, they won't be able to move back and forth between the rational and emotional states. In order to put this fear to rest women need to be reassured that they can both feel *and* function. Just as we've learned in the working world to be able to move comfortably between our functional and emotional states, we must now learn to move from emotions to rationality in our relationships with men.

Women's fear of taking on the masculine also explains why we've been unwilling to see what desperate shape men are actually in. Curiously, this lack of empathy doesn't spring from women's frustration with playing the female supporting role. Rather, it is born of the unconscious fear of what may ultimately be required of us in taking on the male role. We don't want to see the pain inherent in men's situation because, unconsciously, we're afraid that the same abuses men have always endured may now befall us.

Such psychological disowning is typical of us all when we are called upon to bear witness to overwhelming pain. We don't want to visit the terminally ill patient because we have to face our own mortality. We don't want to commiserate with the friend going through the ugly divorce because we don't want to face the fact that our own marriage, too, may be fragile. We don't want to talk about a colleague's bankruptcy because we don't want to be reminded that our own economic security could be jeopardized at any moment.

In the same way, women would just as soon that men's predicament be left to men. If women were to consciously acknowledge what men have always been going through, then women would see that should we take on even a bit more of the male role, we ourselves might face new and overwhelming difficulties.

In some secret part of ourselves, we have sensed how difficult it is to carry the male burdens. This is precisely why, although we're willing to dabble with the prestige and power of stepping into male opportunity, we still don't really want to assume the whole nine yards of male burdens. Instead, we prefer to pick and choose the parts of the male role that suit us-- professional identities, money of our own, diversion from domestic servitude—without admitting that these rewards are unalterably embedded in the male role matrix of heartless responsibility and vicious competition.

Fear of Abandonment

In addition to not wanting to face the whole of the male predicament, being more in possession of our masculinity leads women to the doorstep of our greatest fear in this regard— namely, that if we are strong, we will be alone. For women secretly believe, and, indeed, historically it has been true, that when women can give themselves the things they have always expected men to provide—financial and physical security, for example—men won't want them, because they won't have anything to offer these strong, self-sufficient women. As we recall, the male ego is nourished when a man can give a woman something she can receive; hence a woman's self-sufficiency does change what she needs from a man, and many men do, indeed, encounter a sense of their own inadequacy when faced with a powerful woman.

Since up till now what men have had to offer to women is their money and protection, when a man can't offer a woman these things, he may wonder why a strong woman would want or need him. Thus, women's fear of being abandoned should they assume their own power isn't just a paranoid fantasy. For, to the degree a woman can provide for herself in any area, to that degree, precisely, she does rob a man of an opportunity to experience his traditional male identity with her.

On an unconscious level, both men and women know this. That's why women are leery of becoming too strong, and why some men avoid the women who are. Indeed, in regard to their own liberation, this is the greatest of women's fears. Over and over, women express their anxiety that if they get too strong, the man they have will leave—or no man will ever choose them.

Interestingly enough, it is to precisely the degree that we can become responsible for ourselves that men will be enjoined to discover new reasons to be involved with us, and new ways of expressing their connection. While further taking on the masculine consciousness does bring women face to face with some of our greatest fears, it also, paradoxically, delivers us to the possibility of receiving our greatest reward: relationships based not on economic necessity, but on authentic emotional interchange.

Fear of Our Femininity

Women are also reluctant to nurture men into their emotions because, hard as it is to believe, in their own way women are afraid of emotions too. Everybody's afraid of emotions being out of control, and women are almost as afraid of this as men are. Even women who appear to be in touch with their emotions—hysterical women, for example, or women who have no trouble talking about what's bothering them—often aren't in touch with their authentic emotions, the depth of sorrow, the soul-level fear, the submerged rage, that their seeming emotional expressiveness blurs or buries.

As a consequence of using their own emotional performances as a smokescreen for their deeper, more difficult emotions, women too have a fear of their authentic emotions. Women intuitively know that there's much more to emotions than meets the eye and so we're afraid of opening men to their emotional depths. We know that a man's emotions may include monster feelings from the deep, or roaring feelings from the jungles of men's souls, and we're scared to contemplate what might happen if men let them out.

Women don't think about this on a conscious level, of course—what am I going to do if my darling breaks down and starts howling?—but on an unconscious level we keep sending men the message that, emotionally, they'd better keep it together. For example, when her husband comes home looking ragged and devastated from work, a woman may invite him to talk about it, but if he isn't able to immediately in a way she can easily comprehend as an attempt, might offer him a cocktail instead.

In a certain way women haven't wanted to deal with men's feelings at all, and as we've gotten more comfortable with our own masculine traits, our reluctance has become even more pronounced. In a sense, in taking on the male dimension, we've virtually abandoned our own deep femininity, the very intuitive, caritative, nurturing instincts that were our one true possession in the first place.

In a way, we're afraid of having to call upon the depths of our own femininity, of discovering that we ourselves may be emotionally incomplete, that our own emotional repertoire may not include the capacity to truly empathize with men. Knowing that to some degree we've fooled ourselves about our own emotional lives, our unconscious fear is that men will ask us to do something we can't really do. To the degree that we've denied our own deep feelings, we're unequipped to deal with men. Because if we haven't felt it ourselves, we're certainly not going to allow men to feel it. We'd be too scared.

Because even emotional women are incomplete emotionally, there is some legitimacy to our fear that in the emotional arena, where we're supposed to be experts, we'll fail in our mission of assisting men. Just as men fear that what they have to offer to women won't be enough, so women fear that their gift to men may also be insufficient.

This is why, above all, women must do their own emotional work, must take responsibility for their own deep authentic emotions. This is our first gift to men—and to ourselves. Only from it can spring the riches of our gifts to men, the true joy of emotional interchange, the deep compassion of empathy. For empathy is at once the subtlest and most highly developed emotional intervention, and only the person who has suffered can suffer with; only the person who has mourned can share the mourning.

Fear of Our Common Vulnerability

In addition to not being prepared, women are also reluctant to see how afraid, how needy, now breakable, how capable of shattering men really are, because we don't want to face how vulnerable we all are—to recognize that vulnerability is the human condition. We're afraid that if we experience a man's feelings, we'll have to go to a depth of vulnerability that goes far beyond what even we as women allow ourselves to feel.

This fear of the monster of male emotions is also not unfounded, for it is women's unconscious perception of that great psychological truth—that emotions, repressed, become all the more magnified and powerful. Thus, without consciously being aware of it, women know that what men haven't faced, once faced, may be truly overwhelming.

In addition, in any true emotional interchange, we are all suddenly opened to levels of our own vulnerability we don't know how to manage. In another's pain, we may have to explore a submerged pain of our own; in another's exultation we may come face to face with our own sense of failure. Any emotional disclosure on someone else's part can unearth a devastating counterpart feeling in our own emotional museum. When we are in the presence of someone else's feeling, our own similar emotions come up to be felt. To listen deeply, face to face, to another human being means first, and perhaps most frightening, that we will have to encounter ourselves.

Therefore, although it results in a shabby representation of our true feelings, we often prefer to occupy an extreme, exaggerated or artificially polarized position rather than engage in the kind of lucent confrontation that could inevitably reveal us to ourselves. This is the way women have consistently though unconsciously behaved in the presence of men. For example, instead of saying, "Tell me how you felt when your father died," we don't ask because we don't want to deal with our feelings about our own father's death.

That's why, when it comes to assisting men in opening to their feelings, women generally prefer to manage men's feelings, rather than to openheartedly witness whatever authentic feelings may want to emerge. A woman doesn't really want a man to reveal how upset he is, because then she'll have to empathize with him; and in the act of empathy she herself may become upset. Then there will be nobody to be strong for anyone, especially for her. So, instead of really putting themselves on the line as high witnesses and midwives to men's feelings, women generally collude with men in agreeing that men have no feelings. Thus women don't have to be in the uncomfortable position of seeing that men are as fragile, if not more so, than they are.

So long as women collude with men in suppressing their emotions, women deny men the benefit of their uniquely feminine power, their familiarity with emotions. In so doing, women can perpetuate the emotional suppression they complain about in men, and insofar as they do, they are operating from the worst traits they observe in men: the denial of emotion, the unwillingness to come from vulnerability.

If we are all to move forward now, women will have to embrace the prophetic dimensions of their own deep femininity and trust that their capacity to feel will be sufficient to meet men's needs on the journey. For if women can believe and trust in this, then it surely will be so.

Fear of Union

Without realizing it, even as women passionately long for union with men, there is a part in us that equally hopes the wish will not be fulfilled. That's because, at the deepest levels of our psyches, we are all profoundly ambivalent about union. For all of us, living in harmony is extremely difficult. Theoretically we all want peace and love. Yet we continue to conduct our lives in ways which sabotage the very possibility of loving connection. Even if in some way we have discovered peace and love, we certainly aren't living them out to the degree we say we desire. It is a sad but amusing perversity of the human condition that in a sense, we're all afraid of getting what we want, of really having our dreams come true, of the overwhelmingly positive experience.

Not surprisingly, stress research shows that positive as well as negative experiences up-end our psychological balance and create the preconditions for physical illness. On an emotional level, good outcomes as well as bad ones upset our equilibrium. We're afraid of getting what we want, because the moment we experience deep attachment, we're also confronted with the possibility of loss. What we possess we can lose, while what we imagine we want we can endlessly fantasize about having. Thus it is that while on a conscious level we are seeking intimacy, on an unconscious level we are constantly finding ways of sabotaging our intimate connections in order to protect ourselves from the losses we fear may occur.

At the highest level this ambivalence expresses itself in the question of whether we will choose life over death, a drama we play out constantly through the choices we make, through our habits and addictions, through both our nourishing and destructive patterns. As we pass through life's vicissitudes, we are given a choice at every moment to be conscious, participating human beings, to be healthy or destroy our bodies, to do our emotional work or to check out by anaesthetizing ourselves, to seek our existential identity or to fritter our lives away. At any given moment, the particular choices we make move us inexorably in the direction of life or death.

These choices are how we act out the ambivalence we feel because in embracing life, we always confront the inevitability of death. In experiencing joy, we open ourselves to sorrow. In discovering union, we are brought face to face with the possibility of separation. Thus even though we long for relationships that draw us close, once inside them we tend to stand back at least one step in self-protection, constantly trying to avoid the tragedy we feel is inevitable. By maintaining a certain distracting level of discord, we insure ourselves against the awareness of potential loss. By keeping our relationships shallow, we obviate the possibility of being wounded at the depths.

This is the real reason why the union we desire so often eludes us. We can never pursue a relationship with undivided intention or with a whole heart because our hopes about what is possible are always clouded by poignant fears that our realized hopes will eventually be dashed.

This ambivalence pervades the entire human condition. On the social and political levels, too, we seek connection and communion, while at the same time we make a point of emphasizing our individuality and uniqueness. Maintaining a sense of our differences is one of the ways we don't do the boundary-melting necessary for deep union, but, instead, define ourselves over against one another. The emphasis on individuality is an attempt to overcome our existential terror of being diminished or extinguished by being absorbed into the whole. For if we are not defined by our differences, then what is it that makes us unique?

This struggle for identity is such a difficult issue that we want to artificially promote the differences between us. Because if we were to admit how similar we are, if we were to come together, then we would be brought to a level of spiritual refinement in which the male/female distinction and even personal identity itself would, in some sense, become totally irrelevant—and this is very frightening to us.

In a culture in which we constantly talk about the individual identity, and the importance of the self, to erase individual distinctions is to plunge ourselves into the throes of an existential crisis. As a people, we have applauded and pursued everything that further defines our peculiar individuality, and because we have elevated the concept of the individual to an almost godlike position, we want to maintain distinctions at all costs. The blurring of differences, the recognition of our common humanity—indeed the search for union itself—is threatening. It competes with the very notion that we as a people have taken centuries to develop, and conflicts with the essential underpinnings of our society to date. Thus our inherent psychological predilection to avoid intimacy is further confirmed and supported by the cultural milieu. Paradoxically, while the fear of loss of individuality is great, it is in the very experience of such diminishment that we would be catapulted into the recognition of the unity, the totality, the beauty, and the ultimate congruity of everything and everyone.

The more we become aware of our ambivalence and its impact on our relationships, the more we will be able to move through it. As long as we pretend we are unequivocally seeking union, it will elude us. But the more we can admit that we are uncomfortably, ambivalently struggling toward it, the sooner it will unexpectedly appear.

To look at the struggle between men and women in this light is to comprehend it in a very different way—to perceive it not as a conflict of men against women or vice versa, but as a symbol of the fact that in a haunted and very deep place in each of us, we are all afraid of what brings us together. To see the conflict in this new way is to discover its deeper meaning, and to invite us into a solution that reaches beyond the trivial and joins us all in the labor of evolution and healing.

Reshaping Ourselves: The Transformational Attitudes

13

"My father told me: Marry a good woman and do whatever she tells you."

-Engineering professor, 70

If the notion of men who can feel and deliver their feelings to women is to be more than just a romantic idea, the rhetoric of a catchy though unfulfillable promise, it will require some demanding transformations of consciousness on our part. We will have to develop or enhance the qualities of peace-making, patience, flexibility, trust, humility, reverence, empathy, open-heartedness, acceptance, maturity, masculinity, femininity, and gratitude. And we will have to cultivate these attributes as a labor of love and in a spirit of commitment.

Developing such transformational attitudes may seem

like a formidable undertaking, and it is; but if we accept we have the power to change our dog-eared, intimacy-defeating notions about men then the process will be almost magical in its simplicity and the rewards we desire will be surprisingly forthcoming.

Changing an attitude is a subtle undertaking, like turning your head a few degrees. Just as a photographer turns his camera ever so slightly to obtain a slightly different image, so women must alter the angle from which they contemplate men. Instead of continuing to focus on our discontents—whether legitimate or totally unfounded—we need to position ourselves so we can start perceiving men as good human beings who have loved and suffered with us. For only when men are embraced by perceptions that honor them will they be able to change.

Peace-Making

The first, and perhaps most important, quality we need to develop is peace-making. Instead of continuing to regard men as opposites or enemies, we have to start seeing them as fellow creatures in need of solace and illumination, as human beings who need to be delivered to their own transformation. We have to give up our focus on piddly little issues—why he forgot to bring home the butter, when he'll start washing the dishes without being asked—and use our energies to reach for the higher undertaking: developing a blueprint for the creation of feminine consciousness in men.

In helping men to this next level of development, we need to remember that the doing-it-all, paying-for-it-all, and even the he-man protection and security-providing men offered was, for most women, not really the reward we wanted. Women wanted and want—as men also want, without always actually knowing it—the sense of emotional and spiritual intimacy that can only occur when both men and women live in the conscious presence of their feelings. Remembering this, holding this as a vision, is the inspiration women will need so they can rise to the occasion of this momentous epoch in human emotional evolution.

Patience

Perhaps the most difficult attribute women will need to invoke is patience. Right now, precisely when we're sick and tired, fed up, exhausted, and inclined to abandon men altogether, we must marshal the new and impassioned patience that will allow us to come forward with our exquisite assistance. This isn't the passive patience of waiting and seeing, but the aggressive patience of expectation and involvement. This patience is qualitatively different from the patience we extend to our children. It asks that we wait for, and have the audacity to await with joy, the transformation of those whom we never expected to change.

To be patient will be to see men's changes as a process of unfolding, and not, as we might imagine from watching them function in the rest of their lives, something they can just decide to do and then immediately enact. Having patience means that we understand we are engaging men in an emotional process, that we'll have to go with them every step of the way, and that it will take them longer than we ever dreamed to move from one step to another. It means that we will have to tolerate, withstand, and wait out their fears of possessing and expressing their emotions as they take one tiny tentative step into the emotional arena, then reverse that very step before they move forward again.

In cultivating patience, we must, above all, hold the awareness of how difficult this process will be for men. For example, women often invite men to talk about their feelings by simply saying, "Tell me how you feel." They expect that just because he's been invited, a man can drop down to the emotional level and produce an answer. They don't realize that this is usually impossible, that for most men, this means mining territory they have not only assiduously avoided, but have imagined doesn't even exist. When we invite men to talk about their feelings, no matter how seemingly innocent the question, we're asking them to go to the no-man's-land of authentic verbal emotional communication without realizing that this is the last place in the world most men would ever want to go.

If we wonder how long we should be patient with men, we should consider how long it has taken us to accomplish changes in our own lives. We're still in the process of our own evolution and it behooves us to remember that the habits of role and gender, whether internal or external, can be unbelievably slow to reconfigure.

The discipline of patience will be somewhat easier if we can acknowledge that we ourselves have just put men through the psychosocial wringer. We've asked men to live with the fallout of our liberation, to get comfortable with a social structure that robbed them of the underpinnings of their old identities. Even though these changes were necessary and will ultimately be of tremendous value to men—because they shattered the incarcerating boundaries of sex roles—it's still true that men have suffered greatly because of them. Remembering this will give us an unexpected measure of patience.

Flexibility

Another shift women need to make is to become flexible, specifically to revise our unconscious expectations that men are going to change in exactly the ways we'd like. That men won't will be easier to stomach if we remember that our own changes weren't exactly altruistically motivated. What we did, we didn't "do for love." We changed because we were suffering; we changed to deliver ourselves from the unbearably constricting, oppressive situations in which we found ourselves. We *had* to get out, and, in the process, weren't particularly mindful of how men would feel—whether or not our sweethearts and husbands would be comfortable, let alone overjoyed, with the shifting sands of our identities.

In the same way, the changes men need to make won't necessarily satisfy all our fantasies of what ought to happen to men. Men won't be women's puppets, won't dance the way women want while women hold the strings. We're not just going to bring men up to snuff, as we see it. Male transformation can't be simply a women-placating operation. It has to be an authentic male metamorphosis, one that serves the deep, real, and long-unacknowledged needs of men.

Subtle though it may be, at bottom women really do hope, imagine and believe that when men finally get it together, they'll be exactly like women—except in men's bodies. But men are not exactly like women and they never will be. Men will never feel the same way women do, and no matter how much men incorporate the feminine, to some degree men's feelings will always be expressed more through power, forward movement, aggression, and action than women's. This is one of a number of incontrovertible differences between the sexes; differences which, no matter how much both the sexes may change, must still be profoundly respected. For, when the dust has fallen, and both men and women have changed, what will emerge are the clean-washed images of what the truly immutable characteristics of both men and women will always be.

Because we know this is a journey, and there is a destination—though we don't know what it is—women need to be willing to go the distance with men without knowing the outcome. We must keep an open attitude, be willing to risk it all. For, only if we give ourselves fully to the unknown can we possibly create the condition in which we might get even a little bit more of what we've always wanted. So long as we have an investment in the outcome, want men to change in such and such a way, by this or that date, men will resist in order to preserve their core of incontrovertible maleness, their masculine dignity.

As the process of transformation unfolds, women must bear in mind that, like it or not, their most deeply-embedded expectations—of men and of themselves—will be radically revised.

Trust

Women will also need to trust that the outcome will be worth the effort in some ultimate sense. Trust is the antithesis of expectation. It is commitment to the invisible possibility without being attached to the results. It is the relinquishment of control, the willingness to live in the state of emotional suspension where you don't know what will happen, yet still believe that something good will transpire.

Trust imagines the best, even when the situation looks hopeless. In this new undertaking with men, we must believe that, in spite of the mutual long history of discontent and disappointment, real transformation can actually occur. Trust is expecting that it will.

Trust is the courage to reach beyond the petty, into the larger arena, not of what is going to change tonight, after dinner, but of what is going to be possible in our whole lives and in the lives of those who are affected by knowing us. Trust is believing that what occurs will be more and better than what we asked for, will change not only our specific circumstances but the very atmosphere in which we live. As women watch the fabric of their notions about what men should be being shredded, tattered and torn, they must hold the trust that after time, tears, effort, and compassion, the cloth will be beautifully rewoven.

Humility

We'll also need to be humble. Humility is the grace of having a gift and using it without being overly impressed with its value. In women's undertaking to birth the feminine consciousness in men, humility will consist of giving up the emotional know-it-all position. Men can't learn from critical, self-satisfied, or condescending teachers, nor can they be expected to give up their hero-protector status to become apple-cheeked freshmen in the academy of emotions. If any real changes are to occur, women will have to stop playing the role of emotional know-it-alls and be willing to put their certainty on trial in the courtroom of emotional exploration. Only in a climate of mutual discovery can anyone feel safe enough to learn; and in regard to their emotional lives, men must feel absolute safety in order to move forward.

For women to have humility in leading men into the emotional arena means that we will not presume that we always know the right way to reach them. Rather, it is to be quietly and continually engaged in the process in good faith. In humility we will wait to see what occurs and do the best we can, knowing that we too will sometimes fail. Because we are venturing into unknown territory—not the territory of emotions, but the territory of being a guide to the emotions, we won't always know what to do; humility is living the acceptance of that fact.

Reverence

While men are coming into the presence of their emotional selves, women need to honor them for who they've always been, for what they've always done. Instead of denigrating men for being men, for disappointing us in the ways they always have, in the very midst of acknowledging their limitations, women must absolutely validate and celebrate them. This even means applauding men for having lived out the traditional emotionally-inaccessible male roles, for being soldiers and protectors, for holding the world together economically. For, only if men are honored can they maintain their dignity, and only if they maintain their dignity will they feel safe enough to embark on the, to them, absolutely frightening process of emotional exploration.

When we continue to honor men for their strengths, we give men hope, for in not behaving as if the only thing worth doing is the thing we're trying to get men to do, we create a safe matrix for them. In remembering that what men have always done has great value, we won't be tempted to offer our own gifts from the condescending, exploration-defeating one-up position. When we see men as our equals in giving, men can feel it in their hearts, and it will become easier for them to receive what we have to offer.

Empathy

In order to be compassionate midwives in this process of male liberation, women will also need to be powerfully empathetic. We can start to develop our empathy immediately simply by remembering that every man was once a little boy—the little boy who cried in the night because his mommy went to heaven, the boy who curled up in his mommy's lap, the six-year-old kid who was afraid of getting beaten up at school, the boy who fell out of the tree and broke his arm and had no one to hold him.

Remember that the man whose emotional emergence you are trying to facilitate was once (and in some sense still is) a scared, small, needy, little boy who longed to be held and loved, and who, like you, when it came to being loved was miserably shortchanged. Then, when you're inclined to become unreasonably demanding, to expect the man you're shepherding to be sturdy enough to take what you're dishing out, to do, this minute, what you're asking—instead of browbeating him into submission, you'll be patient and understanding.

Open-heartedness

Although we tend to think otherwise, the truth is that at the core men's and women's emotional needs aren't really very different. They are human needs, needs of the spirit in each of us. Just like women, men need to feel loved. Just like a woman, a man needs to be touched, to be nourished with physical affection, to feel he has been apprehended in the fullness of his spirit, to feel he is worthy of being received.

Because this is above all a *human* process, a man's emotional opening invites both men and women to discover the essential similarity between them. For as a woman begins to see into the farther reaches of a man's soul—when she sees his need, his fear, his sorrow—she will see how much like her he is and will be all the more willing to go through the transformational process with him.

As women meet men in their pain, in their sorrow and intense fragility, their resentments about having to help men will be gradually erased. What will remain is a sense of each man's beautiful uniqueness, his tragic and wonderful participation in the human condition and your loving connection to him.

Acceptance

In order for women to genuinely be able to assist in the process of transformation, we will also have to cultivate acceptance by giving up complaining. If we really want men to change, we'll have to give up this immature, knee-jerk reaction to men and look at the pain that cements men in the position of doing the things that eventually lead women to complain.

This isn't to say that women don't have the right to complain about real issues—unequal access to employment opportunities, lack of day care, domestic violence, unequal pay. But unfortunately we've gotten stuck in the process of complaining. Instead of reacting only to real, specific issues, women often cavalierly blame men for almost everything.

But complaining only makes men even more uninterested in risking the sort of dialogue that women really want, for when women complain, men feel judged and abused. Instead of opening up, they despair and withdraw, thus widening the emotional breach. Only to the degree that women can get off the easy road of complaining and reach for the language that communicates our real needs, hopes, and appreciations, our genuine desire for compassion, tenderness, and love, will we gain access to men's authentic feelings.

It takes maturity to get beyond the tit-for-tat view of life: you've oppressed me for five millennia and now I'm going to do the same to you. To transcend the revenge mode is to take on the larger and distinctly more compassionate view of those who have wounded us. Acceptance is a very deep, spiritual enterprise. It is to see that we have all been wounded and betrayed, that we have all inflicted wounds and been betrayers. It is to shift the focus from what divides and differentiates us to what knits us all together, to discover that at our depth and in our midst we are all one.

Maturity

Women will also have to stop wishing men would solve all our problems and to start assuming more responsibility for our own lives and fears. To do this, we'll have to stop treating men like the Platonic ideal of the perfect daddy: dartboards and firing range targets on the one hand and wizards and magicians on the other. We'll have to get over the notion that whatever's wrong with life is because of, or can be solved by, a man; if a woman doesn't have a man, that's why she's miserable, and if she does, whatever's wrong with her life is because of his inadequacies.

Women need to grow up. We need to come into our maturity and recognize that it's life itself that's scary, that both men and women are afraid. We will never experience the sensitive, revealing, emotional part of men so long as we keep insisting that men take on all our existential fears and real life problems.

Life isn't perfectible, even when we're in love. Nobody—and no man—can fix it all. In truth, the best we can expect from our relationships is that they will bring us into a deep experience of ourselves, and an opportunity to discover another human being in his woundedness, in his charming imperfection.

To the extent that the myth of the male hero-protector has broken down, women have had to come face to face with the precariousness of the human situation. While this opens the possibility for a new kind of union, we've often taken the easy path of remaining resentful, nagging and hoping, rather than joining with men to embrace a new unified vision of the tragedy and majesty of life. If we could step out of our old, by now really quite threadbare and inappropriate expectations, we could stumble into the presence of the truth that while not all our dreams will be fulfilled, there can be a genuine reconciliation between the sexes, one that enables both men and women to be true allies for one another.

Masculinity

If men are really going to be able to take on their emotions, the greatest transformational task for women will be to incorporate the male in themselves in ways and to a degree they never have before. In order to draw men out, women will have to adopt the male role not only in work, but also in holding the male place of suppressing emotions.

This means that a woman will have to rein in her own emotions, clearing the space in which, in safety, a man's deeply buried, barely formed emotions may gradually emerge. This means taming the tongue, squashing the impulse to have an instantaneous outburst. It will also mean that along with mod-elling the expression of emotions as women have always done, women will need to start using the male aspects of their minds, to analyze and organize the content of a man's emotions so that she can give them back to him in the linear logical form that he can understand.

Femininity

Paradoxically, to engage the feminine in men, we must also bring every scrap of femininity we have to bear on the situation, to draw on all our intuitive, deep feminine powers. We need to be valiantly, softly feminine, willing to take on and translate the feeble, somewhat unformed (and to us perhaps ridiculously infantile) attempts at expressing emotions that men have to offer, while at the same resisting the temptation to be too male, by pushing, demanding, insisting.

For it is only when we have deeply integrated our own deep feminine essence that we'll be able to encourage men to enter that fragile sphere in which, as men see it, they will have to risk everything. In order to make it safe for men, a journey of discovery, and not a mere capitulation to a hatful of women's demands, we have to awaken and strengthen our own receptive powers so we can truly take in—without prejudice, judgment, or rejection—what men are delivering to us emotionally.

For women to provide the matrix in which men can incorporate their own receptive feminine, women must be able to occupy the feminine position with, in effect, masculine strength. We must be powerfully receptive, able to receive whatever befalls us emotionally and to know we can withstand it, without shutting down or shutting out whatever is being revealed.

Gratitude

Perhaps the most difficult step in nurturing male emotional evolution will be for women to come from a place of appreciating men. For us to be grateful will be to live as if we are pleased with the men in our lives. To throw off the old rags of discontent and put on the ball gown of gratitude will mean that instead of endlessly harping on men because they don't meet all our needs, we acknowledge our great indebtedness to them.

It's scary for us to be aware of how much we actually do owe men. It's like opening a trap door to our own vulnerability, to what, in asking men to protect us, we have exacted from them.

Strangely enough, we're also afraid to see the improvement when men do change, because then we'll be indebted in a whole new way. Not only have men done what men have always done for women; they've tried to do even more, had the courage to live in the sex-role chaos that women have created. In this sense men truly are heroes; they deserve our undying love, our conscious intelligent gratitude. Because, for a man to give up being a man in the old sense takes the greatest male courage of all.

Gratitude is the ultimate female emotion for it embodies the ultimate feminine stance of total receptivity, the state of spiritual surrender. To realize that without what men have given us, life would not only not be so sweet, so convenient and protected, but, that in fact, we all may not have survived at all, that is the state of very deep vulnerability indeed.

In this way, even women don't want to be feminine. It's too frightening to be aware of the vast dimension of our own need. To be grateful means that we have allowed ourselves to be changed, to be acted upon, that we've given up being in charge. Even for women, this loss of control is a very difficult thing.

Being grateful would totally and categorically revise the chemistry of male-female relationships. For starters, it would immediately bring women down from the shabby pedestals of our passivity-oriented power, the power of the underdog, slave, and martyr, and acknowledge that men have pleased us and desire to please us.

Living in the state of gratitude would open us to receive something different from men—their feelings instead of their actions. In fact, it could move male-female relationships from the ridiculous stalemate in which only the contents of their roles can be passed between men and women. So long as we judge we are locked in the dungeon of self-righteousness; only when we are grateful are we open to receive. Gratitude is a huge, open doorway that invites us into an experience of one another infinitely more complex, demanding, and ultimately rewarding than the cluttered back room of anger, resentment, and regret women have always occupied vis à vis men. It is the portal through which we could all perhaps finally enter the great hall of authentic intimate relationships.

14

Evoking Men's Emotions: A Step by Step Approach

He drew a circle that shut me out
Heretic, rebel, a thing to flout
But love and I had the wit to win:
We drew a circle that took him in.

-Edgar Lee Masters

Not only have women been unaware that initiating men into the feminine consciousness was to be one of their tasks, but until now, we haven't known how to assist men in this process. We haven't known what to say, how to behave, what to do, even what to envision in order to bring men to the place of feeling. Of all the thankless jobs women have taken on for men, this one, in particular, has never had a job description.

Men are still in the boondocks emotionally, not because women have failed them in the past, but because only now has the sociological and emotional climate matured to the point where this transformation can occur at a conscious, premeditated level. Now it's time to begin. Time for women to get on the job by initiating certain behaviors, and time for men to learn the precepts, language, and behaviors that will develop their relationship capacity.

Where Are We Going?

> *"What would be the words for this? Can you give me some words for this?"*
>
> *-Computer rep, 35, trying to talk about his childhood abuse by his mother*

What, exactly, are women trying to do? What is the outcome we seek? How, when, and under what circumstances will we have succeeded?

Women's work here is to give men the safe emotional environment in which they can develop the ability to feel the full range of their emotions—anger, sorrow, joy, and fear—and to express those feelings in words, with tears, with the appropriate physical gestures and movements. When men can finally speak their feelings, when at last they have words for their sorrows, when men can feel their words, and not just say them, when they can finally deliver their inner truths through the common human bond of language, they will be set free to consciously experience a new depth in themselves, a new level of intimacy with women.

For all this to actually be accomplished, women will have to learn specific, unfamiliar, and perhaps even disconcerting new emotional behaviors, the practice of which in itself will result in entirely new kinds of interactions. Furthermore, we'll have to become sensitive to which men in which situations are really open to this process, and when and how to begin it with them.

In general, the process will be most effective when a man is already in a relationship with you, where he is already connected because of shared life experience, a sexual relationship, or children. You need to remember that this is a very delicate process, that you must introduce this new way of interacting very gradually, so he isn't overwhelmed, so he doesn't turn on his heels and head for the hills. As the process progresses, you'll have to exercise an ongoing sensitivity as to whether or not he's comfortable enough to proceed, to explore the next level of his vulnerability.

Be aware that you are an instrument here. The best you have to give may not be able to be received by the man to whom you offer it. Some men will not be receptive to this process and even the man who is aware of his own need for change may not be ready to go on the journey just now.

Particularly for those women who have tried in the past to encourage men into their feelings and been rebuffed, re-entering this process may be painful. But remember that you are not to blame for what didn't happen before. Just because you tried doesn't mean that that particular man was ready at that particular time, nor did you necessarily know the best way to proceed. But now you have more information and here you will learn the skills to help you on your way.

Even so, if you find that what you do, introduce, or explore doesn't fall on fertile ground, be patient and forgiving with yourself and him. And don't give up hope. Every time you open this possibility for a man, you also open new possibilities for yourself. And *whatever* you do to move a man in the direction of opening his emotional consciousness expands his opportunity and moves us all forward. Indeed, any effort, whether or not you yourself have the privilege of seeing it completed, does make a contribution to the emotional evolution of the entire male gender.

A Map for the Journey

"That's what I hope to give you—the safety to feel your fears and your fragility."

-Woman, 50, to her sweetheart

What follows are a number of very specific things you can do to immediately elevate the quality of your emotional interchange with the man you love. The object here isn't to browbeat him with your conviction that *he* needs help but to change how *you* behave; this will automatically change his behavior in response. Whether or not he thinks he has difficulty with his emotions, the magic of what you do will be that in spite of himself he will start having the kind of direct emotional experiences that will not only give him a sense of how separated he's always been from his feelings, but will also allow him to value the emotional opening he has started to experience.

1. Say Thank You for What He Already Does

Women need to start valuing all the actions, protections, and labors that men have always been doing and get off the "that's your job, honey," routine. There's no better preparation of the ground for men's own emotion disclosures than the praise, appreciation, approbation, and honor women can bestow upon them for the myriad thankless, invisible, difficult, and wonderful things they have from time immemorial done for us.

The more men are honored for what they've already done, the more willing they'll be to do even more. With encouragement, in time, they'll even be able to let go of their ego attachment to all their wonderful achievements, and start responding to your requests purely from sensitivity and love. Conversely, the more unacknowledged they feel, the more they'll stand around like starving, begging children, desperately waiting for their famished egos to be fed.

2. Stop Nagging that He's Out of Touch with His Feelings

Mere directives to "say what you feel," "communicate more," "express more," are not helpful. They just make men feel inadequate and therefore unwilling to try. Indeed, don't say anything about his "lack." Instead create the opportunities for something new to happen by following the suggestions here.

3. Bring Out the Kid Gloves

As men teeter at the feminine edge in their consciousness, it would do us well not to push them over the brink. So bring out the kid gloves, and handle men carefully. Forget the can openers and crowbars. Metaphorically (or actually) yelling "spill your guts, and do it now or else," won't win the day. In fact, demands of any kind won't work. Most men don't respond well to threats.

Patience is the tool of the day. You have to open the avenues to feelings very gently so that men taking these emotional risks won't have to be so afraid. Don't push, shove and demand. Create an environment of safety and then encourage men to enter it with you. This means saying such things as "I'd be glad to listen if you'd like to talk about it," or, "Would you be willing to tell me about it?"

If we really want the wonderful thing to happen, we'll have to make it easy for men, make it safe and inviting. We can't be five-star generals forcing men, already under enemy attack, out into the emotional mine-field. The entry into the verbal territory needs to be gentle and graceful.

4. Get Out of the Way

Let his emotional experience be his. Give him the

situation, the opportunity, and the words to say how he feels, but then get out of the way. Don't hover around waiting for him to say the things you want him to say. Don't fall all over him when he starts crying or condescendingly mop him up like a baby.

Allow him to have his own experience. Let it be whole, let it be his. Let him show you how much of it he wants to share with you. If he moves toward you, be available. If you pass him a Kleenex and he doesn't take it, don't force it on him. Be sensitive to the clues, both visual and verbal.

In addition, when you're on an emotional expedition with him, resist the temptation to rush in with your own emotional dramas—how you were mistreated at work, how you're falling apart because it's the anniversary of your mother's death—because he's slow or fumbling in getting to his own. At times this may mean allowing the silence to settle, to be the still pool in which he gradually throws the pebbles of his feelings.

Get out of the way by passing up the female predilection to fill every second with syllables, and acknowledge that the story—his—which is so slow to be told is the one that really needs telling.

5. Pay Attention to Body Messages

As we've already observed, some of the most reliable clues to men's feelings are the physical sensations they use to mask their emotions—the pain in the neck, the aching back, the headache. When you see a man generating these signals, direct his attention to the fact that there may be a connection between what he's experiencing physically and an unidentified emotion.

Once again, don't preach or assume. Your best bet is an open-ended question, such as "When did your neck start hurting?" or "What were you doing when your back went out?" This may put you on the trail of the hidden emotional component. For example, if the answer is, "Right after the board meeting when they fired Joe," this may open the way to his disclosure that he's afraid of losing his job, or, at the very least that there's conflict at work.

6. Remind Him that He Has Feelings

This may seem ridiculous, but men need to be reminded that, just like women, they experience a constant subliminal flow of feelings. You can make them aware of this ongoing undercurrent by inviting them, at any given moment, to do an emotional check-in.

Suggest that he just take a moment, be still, look inside and notice what's going on. What does he discover when he sinks down beyond the events, obligations and responsibilities of life and goes into the subterranean chamber of his subconscious?

This is an exercise in noticing the undercurrents. Don't ask him to talk about what he feels, just to notice that when he pauses, there is a continuous stream of feelings and sensations going on under the surface.

7. Bring His Attention to Emotional Events

Sharpen your own awareness to emotional events. Allow yourself to know that emotional events are occurring all the time and that you, not the man in your life, are the one most likely to be aware of them.

On a practical level, this means, for example, that when you see your husband's eyes go blank after an unexpected phone call, you don't just go back to your law brief. Bring his attention to the fact that his emotional tenor has changed. "You look upset now. Did something just happen on the phone?"

In other words, focus on the emotion-precipitating event and insist, in a gracious way, that he turn his attention to it also.

If you're given a simplistic emotion-denying answer, "No. Why?" don't let the issue drop, but graciously find another way to ask another question. Something like, "I don't want to be presumptuous, but it does seem like something is going on with you. Do you have any ideas?"

8. Translate His Actions into Words

We'll also need to translate men's actions into words so they can finally understand what they mean by their many symbolic gestures. Giving words to the feelings men have until now expressed through action requires that we start operating from the awareness that men do have a whole array of feelings which they have been unable to express except symbolically.

This means that instead of presuming he is an unfeeling beast, you search for the unconscious content of his communications and make it literal to him. Instead of harping about what he doesn't say, you'll need to start honoring what he does say with his actions: "I know you love me because you brought the porch furniture in out of the rain," or, "The roses are beautiful. Thanks for reminding me you love me."

By responding in this manner, we aren't just expressing gratitude for the actions men perform; we're also revealing the hidden emotional communication embodied in the action. By underlining his actions with the words that reveal their emotional content, we not only acquaint men with the emotional component of their actions, but also demonstrate that language is the vehicle for expressing it. To the extent that we continue to give the verbal interpretation of the action, men will begin to see that the emotional content of their actions can be expressed in language that carries meaning and creates intimacy.

Also, if you really want your desire for intimacy to be fulfilled, you'll have to stop attacking him for his emotion-avoiding behaviors and respond with a willingness to talk to him about what his actions may mean. Instead of saying accusingly, "Why aren't you looking at me?" you might try saying, "It must be really hard for you to talk about this; I notice you can hardly look at me." In this way, you make it safer for him to add the verbal component to his actions

9. Inquire, Inquire, Inquire

Men aren't just going to cough up the feelings they don't think they're having, and the only way to get them to the place where they begin to discover that indeed they're having feelings is to be curious in a very soft way, to ask politely, to graciously inquire. So if the man in question is withdrawn, don't assume he's not having a feeling. Instead, ask a foolish ("How was your day? What are you doing later?") or serious ("Are you still upset about your conversation with your mother?") question.

If you really want a window into a man's feelings, you'll have to start asking. Only after being asked a great many times will a man integrate the notion that he might start asking himself what he's feeling, and develop the new mental habit of interior inquiry, the results of which he can eventually offer back to you.

10. Invite Him to Reveal Himself

This may seem elementary or foolish, but men need to be specifically invited to participate in an emotional interchange. It just never occurs to them how important or satisfying emotional conversations might be, so women need to remind them: "Come on, lie down with me and let's have a talk." Again, this must be done lovingly, not naggingly, or it will definitely backfire.

Once in the environment where the feeling exchange can comfortably occur, in the bed, cozily on the couch, hand in hand walking on the beach, he'll have to be invited again, led into the process of emotional disclosing. You need to make him comfortable, and you need to give him a structure. Since men have such a difficult time identifying their feelings, the invitation that asks, "What are you feeling?" will be basically useless at the beginning; you'll have to take him by the heart and by the hand and start the conversation: "I'm so happy to be here with you. Tell me something you've never told me before."

11. Teach Him What Intimacy Is

Intimacy, the blending of hearts through the trading of feelings to a high degree, is created by specific behaviors—the verbal disclosure of feelings, and the responses to those feelings by another person. These behaviors in themselves—the way we speak, what we say and when we say it, the silences we keep or break, the gestures we offer or withhold, all have the capacity to significantly alter, for better or worse, the level of intimacy that is occurring. You can open the path to intimacy by revealing your own internal experience through emotion-disclosing conversations, and by inviting him to unveil his own.

Remember that emotional intimacy consists of three components: information: the facts about our lives that have implications for our emotions; feelings: the emotions we attach to these facts; and contact: the actual physical contact or physical environment which anchors the experience of intimacy. Establishing intimacy requires the disclosure of both facts and feelings and an appropriate, corresponding response by the receiver of the disclosure. It is through this process of disclosure and response that intimacy is created, and of course the more privileged and vulnerable the shared facts and emotions, the deeper the level of intimacy.

12. Teach the Language of Emotion

Unlike women, who can generally just "spit out their

feelings," i.e., find the words for their feelings without even bothering to think, men can't "just talk about" their feelings. In fact, they'll only be able to learn how to, as one man said, "put the words to the feelings" if someone shows them how. This can come from observing, or through modelling (someone else providing precisely the words with which to express feelings). Women should bear in mind that since men were specifically trained to shut down the words that expressed their feelings, in order to reconnect they may need the exact words for their feelings played out for them.

Thus, instead of wishing a man could console you about a particular loss, you may need to say to him directly: "I need you to tell me that even though Margaret got the job instead of me, I'm still a brilliant sales rep, and in time I will get the promotion." Or, in encouraging him to express his feelings you might say, "Just say to me, 'Honey, I'm scared I'm going to spend my whole life never getting to my creative work.'" The more men hear what feelings actually sound like when they're put into words, the more they'll be able to form the words and sentences themselves. In time, practice (listening) makes perfect (speaking).

13. Teach Him that Listening is Doing

As we've learned, it's not just that men have trouble telling their feelings; they have trouble listening to feelings too. As one young man complained, "I hate it when women get upset. I feel as if I have to *do* something, but I never know what to do." What he said is what most men think—that they have "to do something" in response to women's communications. It never occurs to them that simply listening *is* doing something.

Men are afraid of listening because they assume that some action is being demanded of them, and because, even if it isn't, they don't know what they should say in response. Since, to a great many of the things we're upset about, there isn't any solution, practical or otherwise, just listening is the appropriate response.

To help men get comfortable with this—to them—very foreign idea, you need to let them know that conscious listening—opening your ears and your heart and taking in somebody else's story—is an action and a gift, and often all that's required.

By conscious listening I mean that once a person has revealed a feeling, instead of attacking, discounting, or negating it, the listener needs to reflect and acknowledge it. "Thanks for telling me. I had no idea you felt that way. I'm so sorry to hear how difficult it's been." (Not, "How can you feel that way?" or, "That's ridiculous," or, "Why did you have to tell me that, now I'll be worried sick.")

In order to teach him the process of conscious listening, you may need to ask him to specifically acknowledge, in words, that he's heard what you said. "I need you to tell me you've heard how hard it is for me to go to my new job." And in order to quash the traditional instinctive male problem-solving response you may also have to say, explicitly, "I don't need you to solve the problem; I don't want you to do anything about it," or even, "I know there's nothing that can be done, I just want you to listen."

14. Teach Him the Art of Disclosure

Just as men need to learn that when we tell them our troubles, "just listening" is often enough, that we don't always need real-life, practical, mechanical or plumbing solutions, we also need to teach them that what they say is worth saying even if we don't have any solutions for them either. In other words, the medium is the message: in lots of cases, just saying how you feel is, in itself, the solution.

Therefore, you will need to let him know that conscious

disclosure creates intimacy. Conscious disclosure means that in talking, he searches for and delivers the emotional component as well as the facts. Instead of saying the classic, "I had a bad day at the office," for example, he will say something like, "I had a terrible day at work. Bob's secretary, whom I always thought I had a good relationship with, humiliated me in front of Bob." Just saying the difficult, embarrassing, painful, or delightful thing increases emotional connection; and he needs to know that he will feel better simply by sharing it.

15. Encourage Him with Your Responsiveness

Since we want to reinforce the emotion-disclosing behavior of men, we must be sure to respond very specifically when they give it. First, tell him you've heard what he said and you're glad he made the disclosure. Second, offer a specific response to the content of his remarks. For example, when a man tells you about his disappointment at ending his vacation, the compassionate response would be, "I'm glad you told me. It must be hard to face going back to the grind when you've just had such a great time fishing."

If men don't get a specific response that speaks to the feeling they've expressed, they'll feel like fools for having opened their mouths in the first place. They'll want to retreat and never risk talking about their feelings again.

When a behavior gains a response, it starts occurring more frequently and when it doesn't get a response, it occurs less frequently and is ultimately extinguished. So if you want a man to become more emotionally expressive, you will need to acknowledge even the littlest efforts you see him making, water even the teeniest seedlings of his new emotional behavior.

Encouragement creates daring. It's like the safety net under the tightrope of trying something different, so whenever you see a man tiptoeing across the highwire of his emotions, throw out a safety net of encouragement for him.

16. Don't Make Him a Fool for Talking About His Feelings

When you invite a man into the emotional territory, you have to be prepared to deal with whatever happens. When a man talks about his insecurity, for example, or his attraction to other women, you'll have to marshal not only your empathy, but also your open-mindedness in order to respond. Otherwise you might jump out with a "Don't talk to me about that," or a leaden silence that indicates your disapproval.

When a man gets this kind of response he'll say to himself on an unconscious level, "Oh, I get it; it doesn't work after all, I really can't talk about my feelings," and shut himself up even tighter. Having opened up to this level of vulnerability, only to find himself emotionally abandoned because you can't handle his disclosure, a man will resent you for having taken him into this godforsaken territory and will want to close up as quickly as possible. So, if you're going to invite a man to talk about his feelings, be prepared to receive whatever is revealed; be strong enough to listen.

17. Practice The Four Winds of Feeling

On a regular basis and, if you can arrange it, at a consistent time—for example, after dinner, or before you turn out the lights at night—ask the man in your life: "What are you happy about? What are you afraid of? What are you angry about? What are you sad about?" Through this exercise, which I call The Four Winds of Feeling, a man is very specifically invited to make disclosures from the four basic emotional quadrants: joy, fear, anger, and sorrow.

Ask all four questions each time, but don't bombard him with them; find a way to ask so they don't sound like a selection from the Scholastic Achievement Test. Don't hurry and don't

be insistent or bulldozing. Be very patient as the answer emerges—
he won't always know right off the bat what person, thing or
experience in his life is generating his sorrow, anger or delight.
Be sure he gives an answer for each quadrant, even if he thinks
he doesn't have a feeling in that particular category. And watch
for those body-oriented answers: "I feel relaxed." "I'm exhausted." "My back hurts." Just quietly repeat the question.
Stick to the emotions, because in answering specifically in these
areas a man will gradually get in touch with his feelings and get
in the practice of identifying them, no matter how primitive his
first attempts may be.

To encourage the process, be sure to acknowledge
whatever degree of feeling he does disclose, no matter how
unimportant, oddly surprising, or lacking in intensity it may
seem to you.

18. Praise Him, Praise Him, Praise Him

No man is ever going to get off his passive-aggressive
high horse and come down to meet you in Emotion-Land if you
don't give him a sense of his value, if he doesn't already know
you love him. Therefore, what you must consistently do, for,
with, and about any man you love and hope will change is to
praise, celebrate, honor, enjoy, acknowledge, and delight in—
WITH WORDS—the attributes, talents, habits, gifts, ways of
being and doing, acting and saying you recognize to be uniquely
his.

The praise you need to give isn't just the obvious praise, that
he's handsome or smart, that he always pays the bills on time. The
praise that will free a man and heal him, that will open him up to his
feelings and make him feel safe enough to open his heart in your
presence, is praise for the things he's never been acknowledged for,
the attributes that are still invisible to him, the beautiful truths in
himself he's forgotten or never quite remembered.

To praise in this way requires courage. And daring. And vision. And integrity. But allow yourself truly to see who he is, to give him freely, grandly, beautifully, unsparingly and intelligently, your recognition of who he is.

Praise creates safety. Appreciation defines the boundaries of the sanctuary. Honor opens possibility. Acknowledgement is an invitation. Therefore, if you really want to have an emotionally intimate conscious relationship with a man, praise, praise, praise him!

19. Remember to Offer Support

Along with generalized praise, men need to be specifically supported as they start moseying blindfolded down this, to them, absolutely frightening path of emotional self-disclosure. Think of the man as a newborn baby who needs to have his head supported at all times; be willing to give him the support he needs. When he takes an emotional risk, no matter how small it may seem to you, be sure to say something supportive like, "Thank you for talking to me about that, for trusting me with your feelings." Or something wonderful like, "Thank you for giving me the honor of holding your soul while you go through this sorrow. The more we follow this path, the more deeply I know you."

20. Give Him a Hook to Hang Up His Emotional Hat

Men won't get a sense of their own feelings just because you've told them about yours. In order to grasp them, they will need a reference to some experience of their own that had so much impact that there's no way that they couldn't identify with the emotion.

Generally effective referents for men have to do with power, dignity, or physical prowess—or the loss of any of these. For example, a man may only be able to identify that he's scared to death of his boss when he finds himself feeling exactly the way he felt when his father threatened to beat him with the razor strap, or that he's overjoyed about his new love when he finds himself feeling the way he did when he won the all-star trophy. A man can readily get a grasp of the emotions he felt in such situations, and so it's these experiences you should refer to in trying to get him to understand how he feels now.

Thus, in helping a man get in touch with his feelings (and eventually to understand yours), you will need to provide a male-familiar reference. So try to give him a hook from his own experience, one that refers to the male arenas of competition, physical sensation, or the outside world rather than something that has personal meaning for you. And if you're trying to get him to go directly to his emotional experience, give him a reference from his reality, not yours. Instead of saying "You must feel the way I did when I lost my job," say, "You must feel the way you did when you didn't get the promotion."

21. Ask Politely for What You Need

As we have already said, we need to start asking for what we need from men instead of complaining about what we don't get. This is because if men can give us some of what we want, they will feel safe enough to go emotionally spelunking with us.

Asking is basic human communication. It involves trust (believing the person you're asking is a man of good will who wants to make you happy) and vulnerability (showing your real, wanting self). Asking means stating very simply: "I need you to do this; I hope you will do this; I would be delighted and overjoyed if you would do this." Including the words that indicate the sense of pleasure you'd experience should your request be fulfilled, will do a lot to encourage a man to give you what you ask for.

Learning to ask is good practice for women; it's also a

good way to develop empathy for men because we need to have the experience of being as uncomfortable as we're asking men to be in opening up to their emotions. Asking—the last thing we would ever like to do—is a great way of creating this empathetic bonding.

So ask, and when you do, be specific. Ask for exactly, precisely what you need and want: "I need you to take me out to dinner on Friday night"; "I need you to kiss me goodbye before you leave for work in the morning"; "Can we go sailing on Sunday?"; "Please tell me you like my new haircut." If only daffodils or the words "You're beautiful" will please you, say it.

In failing to ask we deny men the chance to be the true heroes of intimacy we want so badly for them to become. We cut ourselves off from the possibility that they might actually respond in a way that could please us. Men deserve a chance to show that they can make us happy. For this reason we owe it to them—and to ourselves—to take the risk of asking. So ask.

P.S. It's important to note here that even when you learn to ask you won't get everything you ask for. Be careful of the expectations that put a man, once again, in the role of silently providing everything. Part of mature asking is knowing that sometimes your requests will be denied, that all your needs can never be fulfilled by another human being—even if he is the man of your dreams.

22. *Take it to a Deeper Level*

When the man in your life tells you some facts, that he saw a car accident on his way home, for example, encourage him to go to the "second round" with it. Invite him to go beyond his initial report of information by asking what the experience meant to him, or how he felt when he saw it.

I know that to women this may seem purely primitive—we'd volunteer, or even start out with the "how I felt" and "what it means"—but again, you need to remember that this is the last thing a man would think of bringing up to the level of his consciousness—let alone of communicating to you. Asking a man to dig for those feelings is asking him to do the, to you, obvious thing and to him the last thing he'd probably ever think of doing. But the more he engages in the process the more he'll discover that, beneath the level of his conscious awareness, he *is* always having feelings.

Women need to take the lead here, and even when men think it's ridiculous, or that they have nothing to say, to press on, especially when men try to convince us they're not feeling anything. So, if he stops talking but you know there's more, ask another question, "What did it mean to you?"; "How did it affect you?"; "What did it remind you of?"; "Why does it hurt?"

23. Pick Your Spot

Talking to men about their feelings works best when men are already in a soft place emotionally—before, during, or after sex (a man's feeling self is closer to the surface when his physical energies have been rearranged), when he's sick (when men are physically vulnerable, they're also emotionally open), at times of great loss (when men have been devastated, they're suddenly willing to learn). At all such times, the crust of male defenses can be more easily penetrated, and men are more likely to respond. These are the times to reach out and reach in to men. But do it with grace. Be an emotional mermaid, not an emotional piranha.

24. Honor His Sexuality

In order to open the channel for verbal communication with men, we'll have to let go of our simplistic ideas of what sex means to men—that it's only physical, that it's a conquest, that it carries no meaning—and realize that for a great many men, sex is the beginning of their emotional opening, and that for virtually all men it is an emotional communication medium.

We also need to remember that in addition to sex, men become emotionally vulnerable through the entire range of affectionate gestures, sweet kisses, healing touches, and tender holding we can give to them; that for most men, the body is probably the most powerful medium of emotional opening.

25. Repetition Wins the Day

We'd like to assume, of course, that if we're going to put forth all this effort, we'll get great—and immediate—results: "I told you once, why can't you do it?" But, in fact, we're going to have to cover the same ground over and over again. What we're trying to develop here is men's emotional functioning in two areas: first, that they start perceiving themselves as emotional beings, and second, that they're actually able to deliver their emotions verbally, interpersonally, in relationship. Like the revision of any old habit, it won't be easy; it will take many, many repetitions before men can truly integrate the new emotional behaviors. Don't be afraid of being tedious. In time, repetition will win the day.

26. Celebrate the Changes

And finally, praise men for their changes. Take note of it when they stumblingly, wonderfully do begin to tell you their feelings. Since men's efforts are often so primitive that they don't even fall within the range of what women express every day with each other, women often don't acknowledge that men are, in fact, making changes. Instead of nurturing the changes, women tend to overlook men's efforts, so men get discouraged and stop trying.

Don't be like the woman who, when her husband said, "I'm sorry I can't express my feelings very well," responded by saying, "Yeah, it's really a drag that you can't." Instead of thanking her husband, who was in fact expressing a feeling and being beautifully emotionally transparent in the process or asking how she might help him become more expressive, she confirmed him as an emotional misfit.

Men need to hear the words which will let them know that they're doing something right; this confirmation will encourage them to take the risks of further emotional exploration, of even more verbal communication. Say thank you for what is being transformed in your presence and it will be transformed even more.

If there is any advice I could give about how to improve a relationship, it would be to let not a single day go by without both of you consciously thanking each other for something. The expression of gratitude is always twice blessed, for the moment it is delivered, we become aware not only of what has been given to us by the person we are thanking, but of the miraculous gift of life itself.

In gratitude we are brought face to face with the truth that there are those who desire to love and give to us. To recognize this is at once to diminish our sense of aloneness and gather us joyfully into the bundle of life. So for all the efforts and all the big and little changes, surprises, risks, epiphanies, and transformations that are given to you or that you create, continually give thanks.

Opening to Feeling: The Transformational Questions

15

"Life for both sexes. . . is arduous, difficult, a perpetual struggle. It calls for gigantic courage and strength."
-*Virginia Woolf,* A Room of One's Own

The following is a list of questions for women to ask men to help them discover their own emotions and to encourage them to communicate with us. Although men may find them difficult to answer, it is in avoiding communication in precisely these areas that men tend to remain hidden from women and themselves.

As you ask and he answers these questions, you'll discover things you never knew, feel things you hadn't felt before with one another. From this experience of expanded transparency and vulnerability, everything in your lives can begin to change. For when you stop operating from assumptions and start using the real words for the real things, you begin to discover the depth and complexity of the person to whom you are related, and how much you hold in common. Indeed, it is a paradox of self-disclosure that the more exquisitely particular we become in talking about our own delights and sufferings, the more deeply do we partake of the common human stream, and the more inescapably clear is our sense of the similarities between us. The more we reveal, the deeper our experience of intimacy becomes.

These questions are oriented primarily toward men because women generally already have access to this kind of information about themselves, and know how to share it. But even if you know yourself well, you may make some remarkable discoveries if you, too, answer these questions; and you will certainly reveal yourself in a new light if you answer them in the presence of a man you care about. Still, the primary focus here is on men because just as men need to start talking about these things, women need to start hearing these truths about men.

Listening, being surprised by the answers, will not only draw you closer to the man you thought you already knew, but will also deepen your understanding of the similarities between men and women, show you that at heart, in terms of what we need, feel, grieve and long for, men and women are very much the same. Therefore, look at these questions as the opening of a path to his heart. For the minute you listen, really listen, to what a man has to say, you will start to see him in a completely different light. He will instantly fall out of the category of being "just a man" and become a person with whose sorrows and excitements you can readily identify.

A Couple of Rules

Ask these questions gently. Forget the can opener and crowbar. This isn't an interrogation session;there aren't any right answers. Trying to crack open his heart, to get to the bottom of it, or to get "the answer" will probably backfire; instead of wanting to open up more, he'll probably just retreat into a deeper silence. Be aware that the information and feelings that come forward may take a man into some very private emotional places, and be mindful that you need to respect the emotional state you're creating just by asking them.

Don't expect to be able to ask or get answers to more than one or two questions at a time. That would be like trying to catch a big fish every time you go fishing. Men are still unfamiliar with these depths. They'll have to roam around a while down there, in order to come up with the answer; and the roaming around is uncomfortable for them, so be patient. Try one question then let a few days pass before asking another.

Remember, too, that you're the initiator and that this implies a certain moral responsibility. You're tampering with somebody else's consciousness, with some deeply embedded patterns that have served an important protective function, so be sensitive in your approach. If a man were asking himself these questions, he'd be able to define his own limits of comfort and privacy. But when you ask, just by asking, you're invading his boundaries, so you'll need to proceed with great delicacy and care.

Finally, we can't presume that men will answer these questions in any way that's familiar or necessarily to our liking. The challenge here is to stay open, to hear what the man is really saying. The possibility for intimacy may be greater if, instead of asking him the questions at point blank range, you begin by giving him the questions and suggesting that he first write the answers by himself and talk about them with you only when he feels comfortable. Some men feel safer exploring in dialogue, others only when they have "practiced" on their own; but however you decide to proceed, ask the man in question to read the following before he begins.

Directives to Men

You have been given an invitation, an opportunity to enter into an emotional opening with someone who cares about you. Don't allow yourself to be browbeaten into it, but don't be so closed that you allow yourself to miss this chance. Going on the journey, allowing a woman to be your witness, is an act of deep trust. Perhaps you can take that step easily, perhaps in taking it you must step over years (and even generations) of conditioning. But if you have the courage to take the first step, a new gate will open before you, and when you have passed through it, you will have done as a warrior that great deed of beginning to bring down the walls that separate men and women. This, for any man, is a disarmament worth undertaking.

The memories, facts, and feelings with which you will come in contact through answering these questions will bring you closer to the person who is asking them and closer to yourself. Although some of them they may seem foolish, irrelevant or uninteresting, these questions in fact represent an opportunity to discover yourself in a very different way. They are an open window to your soul.

As you answer these questions, start noticing how you feel. What is your body saying? Do you feel relaxed or tense? Do you feel closer, that is, more intimate with the person to whom you are making these disclosures, or more emotionally distant than when you began? Overall notice how the level of intimacy has changed by the time you've answered several questions.

These questions are simple—answer them simply. In the simplicity of your answers you will stumble onto some of the elemental truths of your life. The purpose here isn't to tell an impressive tale (leave your ego at the office) or even to tell the whole truth, but rather to reach spontaneously for the answer that gives itself to you before you start thinking. If you're alone, you may prefer to write the answers. If you do, I suggest that you record them in a special notebook so you'll always have a record of this process of discovery.

What you're showing yourself through engaging with these questions may not seem very significant now, but as you move on in the journey which is being initiated through these simple first steps, you'll see that rather than being irrelevant little excursions from your real life as a man, they form the foundation of a whole new way of being. In a sense, what you say here is an emotional landmark, a commemoration of the opening of a secret province in yourself.

Make yourself comfortable and don't hurry. There's no time limit. There aren't any grades. Nobody's checking. No one is competing with you to be you or to do a better job of being you than you are. Let this be easy, graceful, an adventure. Leave time for the strangeness, the discomfort you may feel. Sit in your favorite chair, on your coziest couch, or with candles at the kitchen table.

The Questions

1. Who was the favorite child in your family? (Pick someone even if it feels as if there was no favorite.) How do you feel about him or her? If it was you, how do you feel about that? If you were the only child, did you feel favored or like a nuisance for being alive at all?

2. When you were a child, which of your parents did you love best? (Again, pick one person, even if you've always told yourself that your feelings for your parents were "equal.") Why?

3. What is the saddest memory you have of your childhood? Why did this experience hurt so much?

4. What is your greatest regret?

5. When was the last time you saw your father, and how do you feel about the encounter? Your mother?

6. What is troubling you at this moment in your life?

7. How do you feel about your body? Do you like the way it looks? Has it brought you pleasure or sorrow?

8. In general, what is it that people like about you? Dislike about you? How do you feel about their like or dislike?

9. Which of your attributes do you value the most? Name one person who honors this attribute in you. How do you feel because he or she does?

10. What is the one taboo subject in your life, the one thing you feel you absolutely cannot talk about? (And, if it's still too hard to talk about, just acknowledge it to yourself and tell the person who's doing this exercise with you that you still need to keep the subject to yourself.)

11. Which of your achievements do you value the most? Why?

12. What are you most afraid of?

13. What is your secret dream?

14. What are the words you would most like to hear about yourself? From whom?

15. What are your greatest joys and sorrows about your children? If you don't have children, how do you feel about that?

16. Who is the most important woman in your life, and why? The most important man?

17. Who loves you? Whom do *you* love?

18. What—besides sex—makes you feel loved?

19. Describe the place, circumstances and people you would like to have around you when you die.

20. How would you like the woman in your life to honor your sensitivity?

21. If someone could give you the perfect gift, the thing that would mean the most to you, what would it be?

22. You are detained in a concentration camp. You know you will never come out alive. To the one person to whom you are allowed to send a message of twenty-five words or less—their memoir of you forever, what would you write, and to whom would you want it to be sent?

* * *

The journey you've taken here is like a walk down a long dark path with a candle. You can vaguely see the direction it will take you in the future, but the distance you've come is only a small part of the journey. Asking and answering these emotion-opening questions is only the smallest beginning of the way in which we must all learn to talk to and feel and be with one another.

The old patterns of attack and retreat, oppression and outrage, tentative exploration and immediate rejection are so deeply ingrained that, as we begin, as we create the exceptional moment of intimacy, that moment will seem so extraordinary as to almost appear to be an aberration. To create an environment in which emotional consciousness is the hallmark of male experience and true emotional intimacy the birthright of every person who chooses to love, is a journey on which we have many steps to take.

But this *is* a beginning. What you have initiated here, the risks to which you have opened yourself in reading this book and asking and answering these questions, is the initial wave of transformation. Like the primal first swell when the ocean was created, it will be followed by wave upon wave of innumerable changes.

The Human Season

16

"Human beings are not born once and for all on the day their mothers give birth to them... life obliges them over and over again to give birth to themselves."

-Gabriel Garcia Marquez,
Love in the Time of Cholera

As we stand at this moment in history, we are more precariously balanced in matters of love and hate, good and evil, survival and destruction than we have ever been before. The fuse is burning. The endlessly documented rift between the sexes is no longer cute, fun or amusing, not only because we are at a crisis of faith with one another, but because our loss with one another is the measure of our estrangement from our essential selves and hence from all that is holy.

In our separation from one another we become isolated from those finest essences in which and through which we are united to all things, for when we cannot see or breathe or live the wholeness in our relationships, we risk losing our sense of wholeness altogether. In our separation from this deepest of all communions, we risk destroying nature and ourselves. Nothing we do or have done will matter in the end unless we can restore the fellowship between men and women that is embodied in the receptive feminine, for it is the feminine which is the dimension of belonging, of bonding, of union. Where male energy prevails or is out of balance with the feminine, we are subject to attack, denial, and isolation

I believe the future is the season of the feminine dimension, and that it will be heralded by women so deeply feminine, so willing to be affected that they have willingly taken on the burden of male strength to initiate men into their own emotional consciousness.

This is a holy work, for in this case, we are not bringing forth biological life but new consciousness. By nurturing the feminine in men we are completing the unfinished portion of the immense and exquisitely lovely human tapestry as, with our hearts in our hands, we stitch together its final beautiful threads

In the past, women have carried the power of the feminine consciousness as a secret in a society that has consistently denigrated it through the overemphasis of masculine values. But the time has now come for women to unwrap the powerful secret and deliver it. In having the courage to reclaim our feminine power without shame, false pride, or apology, we will finally be at ease with the full measure of ourselves. We will finally be able to give the greatest gift we have to give to men. The true service of women, loving and invoking the gifts of the feminine consciousness, will finally be revealed, and through it, we will all truly blossom.

The fruits of this initiation of men are bountiful on every level. Men will be emotionally alive, and women will at last have company with them. The essential character of intimate relationships will change from being essentially socioeconomic arrangements to true marriages of the human spirit. They will be about what can transpire in them at the most profound level, the level of emotional healing, of spiritual initiation. They will be about love, about knowing one another in the deepest of senses, and not about who pays the mortgage and takes out the trash. In short, relationships will become the environment for the evolution of individual and cultural consciousness.

To alter our consciousness in this way is to move it beyond the male aggressive-competitive paradigm, which has for years formed the fabric of our social structure and been the source of some of the greatest tragedies our civilization has ever perpetrated, and move us all toward the consciousness of union.

This is consciousness raising in the finest sense of the term, for what the individual man needs to do is what the world needs to do. To the extent that men aren't fully alive, aren't emotionally whole, can't say, live, breathe or do what they feel, to that appalling degree are we all half alive. For we hold hands on this planet. We're in this together.

The disowned feminine in men is a metaphor of the disowned feminine consciousness in the world. To the degree that society continues to conduct itself according to the values and habits of male consciousness, to that degree precisely are we as a people and the whole human community in emotional, social, and spiritual jeopardy. Conversely, to the extent that women can assist men in gaining access to the deep emotional reservoirs in themselves, men will be able to participate in the harmonious intimacy which, in the microcosm of two human beings' loving interactions, can stand as the example of what is possible anywhere between any two apparent opposites.

True immersion in the feminine consciousness moves us beyond the tit for tat, who's bigger and stronger, who's going to win out over the other guy point of view and delivers us to the place where points of view vanish altogether and we can enter into a dialogue with the consciousnesses of others, where gender is not the issue, where the essence of the person, the individual spirit, is the subject of our discovery. Instead of endlessly spending our energies making our own position clear, we will melt into the truth that when we have truly apprehended one another there is only one position, the position of union, of belonging.

This isn't mere talk. It is not only our desire but our highest destiny. We have a choice here, to continue to be separate, disgruntled and self-serving, or to melt into the union that our divine and human natures invite.

This is because at the deepest level the incorporation of the feeling, feminine dimension in men doesn't just mean that together men and women will have a nicer time of it, that they'll fight less, talk and kiss more. It also implies incredible transformations in the values of our culture itself, what is important to us, what we live and die for. It can mean, first of all, that instead of fulfilling our individual and social needs through what we can pillage, consume and deform, we can regenerate our values, elevate them to a higher level with every interaction, and that the focus of our experience can change from acquisition to transformation. Instead of turning endlessly outward to consume more goods, services, diversions, and distractions, through the healing of human emotional relationships, we will discover the experiences that bind us deeply to one another and satisfy us in a way the material world never can.

At its most expanded, this awareness will move from the concerns of individual survival to a commitment of securing the resurrection of the living suffering being that our planet is and to the awakening of consciousness itself. Through being emotionally open we nourish our spirits; through speaking to one another we heal our wounds; by loving one another we can open the way to peace, to a new spring for the earth.

It's time for us all to grow up, to realize that we're not here simply to partake of or to be indulged, but to be the architects of a future that has long been begging to be born. We need to come of age not only as men and women, but as a people, as citizens of the earth. The beginning of this healing lies in healing the rift between the sexes, for until men and women can come together in relationship, we absolutely will not be able to join one another at a higher level. So long as men and women are at odds, doggedly living by the male rules of domination, competition, and emotional repression, we will be so bogged down by the conflicts such repression requires that human consciousness will be too hobbled to proceed any further.

Thus, the task that women are undertaking here goes far beyond securing what they themselves can receive from men. Undertaken, accomplished, it moves us all toward the next step in our human evolution: the human season. This season is the emotional maturing of the human experience, the epoch in which not only our awareness but also our very experience of being alive moves us beyond all distinctions to embrace the union that is our truest purpose. If we can start to approach this grand awareness, then we shall also open the door to the ways in which, very simply and beautifully, men and women can begin to truly love one another.

Initiating the feminine consciousness in men is the next step in our psychosocial evolution, and women have been given to do this. This is the true women's work, the ultimate expression of the feminine creative power; and if we give ourselves to it, then it will surely give our best selves back to us. For in generating this initiation, we will not only be the midwives to male transformation, but will come into the full possession of our female selves. For in recreating union, we enter into creation at its highest level.

The time is now. There is much work to be done.

If you would like to receive information on the
"Opening to Feelings" Workshops for Men

Please write to:
Daphne Rose Kingma
P.O. Box 5244
Santa Barbara, CA 93150